D0423866

Swift

Delaney Traynor

Dad

You always told me to follow my dreams and write like the wind. You always encouraged me to keep writing, even when I couldn't think of anything to say. You helped brainstorm names, places, ideas, and plots. If you hadn't been there for me, well this book wouldn't be here either.

Part One

The

Destiny

Chapter 1

Torches

The torchlight cast by my followers made my shadow dance across the forest floor ahead of me; teasing me, skirting just out of reach. Our feet met together, and then were apart again as my flight through Dark Forest ensued.

My followers' armor clanked loudly, their shouts only a few yards behind me. Their wolves—fat and lazy from sleeping all day and being fed the table scraps—galloped with the men and horses. It didn't matter though, for I could outrun any wolf. I should know, for I have done so on many occasions. Always they have lost to me, because of my secret. If the men of the village begin to worry me, I have an alternative. I have an escape.

A noise from above caused me to glance upward through the tangled branches and, though my visibility was limited, I could make out the sharp shapes of falcons darting above the treetops.

I crinkled my nose angrily. *You didn't think of the falcons!* Soon, Dark Forest would end and I would arrive on Golden Plains. The falcons would dive-bomb me, attempting to distract me until the men and wolves arrived. And based on the sound of my pursuers, I knew they were close behind. Luckily, I knew what to do, for I was nimble and swift. But I had to be. I am Outcast.

The wind rustled the pine tree. I swayed a little in the breeze, attempting to blend in with the tree herself. I silently thanked the tree spirit for protecting me and the wind spirit for blowing tonight. Below me, the four wolves sniffed in circles, trying to pick up my scent.

I had chosen my tree carefully. This pine was old, and her spirit was starting to let go. The end needles had fallen off of her boughs, and covered the ground at her trunk. A dying tree smells strongly, and I had taken a flying jump at her, making sure not to touch anything but the branch I landed on.

The lead wolf, a strong male with a black pelt and white muzzle, chest and legs, growled and shook his fur in frustration.

Then he trotted over to the only man on a horse. The white stallion tossed his head as the wolf drew close. He was eager to set off on the hunt once more.

He growled something to his master. I assumed they were companions, like my wolf and I. *Such a shame,* I thought, *two people with wolf companions? We probably would have gotten along famously.*

The wolf had a rough growl, and I noticed in the torchlight his lavender satin collar. The man he addressed had a purple sword hilt, a purple cape, and purple trim on the edges of his chainmail to match. I even caught the violet edging of the stallion's saddle and bridle.

I frowned. As I looked closer, I saw that every one of the men had a lavender embellishment over his heart and on his shield. It was of a flower, and for a moment I wondered why they had chosen one for their adornment rather than a dragon or lion, until I realized what it truly was. I almost gasped out loud, but caught myself just in time. It was nightshade, the deadly poisonous flower. I knew that firsthand. My family had all died of nightshade poisoning, and I was the one to blame.

I instinctively reached for my black river stone dagger. It was always with me, in its deerskin sheath. I grasped it and rubbed my thumb against the pearl hilt. My father's family had it passed down for generations; he got it when he was only a boy, and gave it to my mother when he asked her to marry him. He was prince, and when Mother said yes, king. It was my prized possession, and the knife and my bow were the only things I ever kept around.

The tight string of my bow felt strong and sure against my chest, and my quiver felt full with the newly-stolen arrows. I let go of the dagger and attempted to understand the exchange below.

The black wolf growled something more, and slowly looked to the base of my tree. His scarlet-brown eyes travelled slowly up the trunk and finally came to rest where I sat crouched. He narrowed them and snarled a little.

The man smiled and looked directly at my pine. He said with a sure voice, "Come out, little Outcast. We want what you stole. We want our belongings *back* young child."

But I knew he was tempting me. Teasing me. He knew I was of fifteen winters, and he knew on this side of the Mountains a girl of more than fifteen winters was no longer a child. He was demeaning, and I almost took his bait.

The wolf barked a command and his she-wolves gathered around him. He growled another and all four of them started to circle the pine. I was surrounded, and there was no way I was escaping this time. The wolves hurled insults up the tree, and snarled telling me to come down. They were hungry. I ignored them, hoping that the Nightshades would eventually realize I wasn't worth it and leave.

Then I remembered the price on my head.

Dead or alive.

Five hundred-thousand coins.

I reached slowly for my quiver, and silently pulled out an arrow. If I could shoot a man down, that would distract them enough for me to jump to a different tree, and then another, and another, to make my getaway.

I pulled my bow gently over my head and notched my arrow, took aim, let loose.

The man on the horse gasped and fell off his stallion, an arrow with blue jay fletching in his heart. The arrow flew smoothly through his chainmail, through the stitched on pattern. He only was in pain for a moment.

The men all yelled commands to one another, trying to organize themselves. But the stallion was bucking madly, and without their leader they didn't know what to do. The wolves rushed to the man's side, licking his face trying to wake him, all thoughts of the hunt forgotten.

I then soared like a bird through the trees, jumping from branch to branch, as fast as a mountain cat, as nimble as a tree squirrel. I didn't hear sounds of pursuit, and not even the falcons tried to catch me. I had made a decent distraction, but deep in my soul I was upset. I didn't like killing men. But I was not to be taken dead *or* alive, and I was going to survive.

Even if I was Outcast.

❧•☙

The sound of water drew me like a magnet. I was terribly thirsty after my night of running and escaping, and I was hungry as well. But my backpack was nearby, and I was on my way to look for it.

Inside was a bounty of food; liver, stomach, eyeballs, meat, fat, skin from elk, deer, and rabbit. It had taken days to clean the elk and deer carcasses, gather the meat, the innards, and the bones for carving. The tendons or sinews from the deer and elk I liked to use on my bow's string. Every now and then when it needed new string I would replace it with some tendons in my pack and put a thin layer of fat on it. That would keep it water-resistant and nice and smooth, so the arrow flies straight.

I knelt down at the river and scooped water up with my hands. I listened before I drank, and heard nothing but the gurgle of the river. Afterwards, I shouldered my bow and quiver and set off to where I last left my sack.

I traveled upstream along the river, knowing exactly where I put it. There was an old yew with mammoth roots that all came aboveground at least once. The roots had been dug under to serve as a den for a badger or wolf, and now the den was abandoned. That's where my bag was.

The trees murmured secrets in the wind. I strained to hear them, but their language made no sense to me. They whispered their riddles without ever even knowing I was there.

Out of the corner of my eye, I saw a flash of gold running through the forest on the opposite side of the river. A dark shadow followed, pursued by a brown blur and two gray ones. I smiled. *East River wolves.* They were my good friends.

I sent out a message to the lead wolf to say I was here and to tell them who I was. But it wasn't aloud. She and I were very, very close. Closer than pack-sisters, but there is no word for that. So pack-sisters works.

The pack stayed hidden, but the leader, Goldensun, stuck her nose out of the bushes. She saw me and turned back to her pack to tell I was friend, and then waded across the stream to greet me.

Greetings, Goldensun. I thought to her with a dip of my head.

Goldensun laughed. *Kohana! You don't need to use your formal greetings with me. A simple 'hello' or 'hey!' works too. It's good to see you. All is well?*

I shook my head. *No. The Nightshades are getting even more persistent. The bounty has tripled, and everyone wants to be the one who captures me.* I sighed and pulled my knees to my chest and looked at my bare feet crossly. I narrowed my eyes and did my best to not cry, but I couldn't hold back all the tears. It had been almost three years since I was charged with the murder of my family. The public had declared I was too dangerous, and sent me to live in exile. But now…*now* they had changed their mind, realized I could kill more innocent people, and I was to be taken back. And whoever could capture me and take me back "home" would be rewarded from my family's fortune. And I would undoubtedly be killed or worse. A tear trickled down my cheek and I felt Goldensun lick it away, attempting to make me feel better.

I don't know what to tell you, Kohana. But you are always welcome to run with us if you wish. Goldensun told me gently. I shook my head and wiped another tear away, watching it run down the back of my hand and soak into the soil.

Thanks, Goldensun. But I can't. Villagers see you and your pack all the time, and I need to stay on the move. They can't—they won't—find me. I pressed my face into Goldensun's fair scruff, and breathed in her scent. Since I became Outcast, she and her pack were my only friends.

The other wolves stood on the other bank, and the black one barked to Goldensun. He didn't know what we were saying; we were communicating through our minds. That's how people and animals with special connections like us could talk. I couldn't understand him either, but I knew he was Goldensun's mate, Darkshadow, and the intention was clear. *Come on, Goldensun! We should get going!*

Goldensun looked apologetically at me. *I must go, Darkshadow is impatient.* She laughed lightly. *But we will see each other soon. Destiny calls us together, as it has so many times in the past.* She smiled and barked back to Darkshadow, licked my face, and then swam across the river.

Wait! I called. Goldensun stopped halfway across and looked back.

What?

I'm going to the Mountains, I told her. The surprise in her gaze was evident, and she paddled back over to me.

Why? She asked, and pressed her forehead to mine. I rubbed the back of her neck.

I want to be with my kind. My pack.

We are your pack.

When she said it, I realized how true it was. She and I had known each other since the day I became Outcast. She was the first thing I met on that day, and I remember how easily I had given myself up. I had, of course, thought she was there to kill me. But then she barked at me, and thought something. I understood her. I was appalled, and she explained what must have been happening.

In Desaria – all of Calleo really – everyone has a spirit animal. No exceptions, no loopholes. Everyone, when they are born really, has one. Now, that doesn't mean a living, breathing companion. No, it is just an animal that best represents them. However, some people do have a living, breathing example of that animal that they can communicate with. Just one individual, that is separate and walks, talks and thinks of their own accord, and they can communicate through thoughts with a certain individual human. She explained to me that we were a pair and had a very strong, indescribable bond.

She also informed me that if the animal dies, the human lives, but if the human dies, so does the animal, and the animal could live as long as the human. So, Goldensun, who would only live about seven years on her own, could live as long as I did, supposing she didn't fall ill or get a lethal wound.

I closed my eyes, trying to explain why I had to do this. A trip to the Mountains would tear us apart, and I could never ask her to come with me.

I must be with my kind. And the ones that live here hunt me like prey. The people in the Mountains would hunt with me, not for me.

Goldensun sighed and nodded. She looked at me with her startling green gaze. *When will you be home?*

I cringed, hoping she wouldn't have asked that. How could I return, when I could be free and have a normal life elsewhere?

I don't know pack-sister. But do not follow me. You have a family to watch, and I do not. You can't come with me. It felt as if I had wrenched my heart right out of my chest, and when I saw the hurt in her eyes, I didn't feel any better. But she understood, and nodded dejectedly. Then Goldensun trudged back to her pack.

When she reached the other side, Darkshadow nuzzled her affectionately. I watched, sad as always to see her go, even more upset to have to tell her I will not be returning. She knew I would most likely never return to Dark Forest.

Goldensun looked back at me to say goodbye, and then pelted off into the forest, her pack following her.

As I watched them go, I wished I could accept my sister's offer. I wished I could just leave everything, all my worries and bothers, behind on the riverbank. But I couldn't. I had to find a way to clear my name, and go back to rule my Kingdom.

I blinked away tears and listened to the forest. The creek gurgled in front of me. Two mockingbirds sang different songs as they flew by.

That sight brought me back to a beautiful day with the man my father had picked to be his successor if something were to happen to my brother. If I were to take the throne, he was to become my husband and the king.

I blush, and look into Tse's beautiful face. His dark blue eyes draw me, and I blush even more. But I can't pull my gaze away, and the next thing I know, his lips are on mine, and we kiss for the first time under that aspen tree in the autumn sunset.

I clenched my teeth, instantly reminded of the very next day.

I stare bewildered at my dead family. I hear the door open and my maid screams. I turn around with tears in my eyes, and she whispers, "Nukpana! Nukpana!" which means 'evil, evil!' She is warding me off! She thinks I'm evil!

Only then do I realize that she thinks I am evil, for I am sitting here staring at my dead family. Does she think that I was the one who killed them?

"No!" I say, determined to make her believe it wasn't me. "I didn't kill them! I came in and-"

But she will have nothing to do with it. "NUKPANA! NUKPANA!" She is screeching now and clutching an amulet around her neck. I can only stare as she runs away screaming "Nukpana!"

I run over to my brother. His beautiful eyes are cold and dull. My mother's skin still has the faintest warmth left, but I know she is dead. My father. He has a tiny twinkle left in his sky blue eyes, and I see the smallest rising and falling of his chest. I grasp his hand in mine and cradle it in my lap. "Father," I whisper.

He chokes and gasps. "Kohana…" I look into his face, but he is already staring at something distant.

"It was him…he put nightshade…nightshade in our wine…it was…" but then his jaw goes slack, and his arm is limp. He was going to tell me the name of the murderer. He ran out of time.

I am wrenched away from my father by strong hands. I am on a tall, brown horse. I am on a wooden platform, with people yelling insults at me. Me, just a girl of twelve winters. The head knight is taking a vote; what my punishment shall be. But the only thing I can see is the bewildered face of Tse, the perplexed look in his amazing eyes. I plead with mine; plead for him to vouch for me. But his face hardens and he looks away.

"Outcast!" the knight yells.

And about fifty hands go up.

"Hung!"

About fifty more. And among those hands is Tse's.

I cry out, "Please! You have to understand! It wasn't me!" I talk more to Tse than the crowd. I don't care what they think. He has to know I didn't kill my family. I am not a murderer.

He shakes his head, his mind made up. The only way he sees me now is as a killer, a slayer, a murderer.

The knight says, "Outcast is the deciding vote!" and he pulls out a long, sharp knife. One I recognized as the knife my father always kept around his belt. I didn't even bother to wonder how the knight got it.

The guard begins cutting my left wrist with the knife, making a symbol. It is a line that forks facing my wrist, with a dot in the center of the fork and another outside the left branch. It resembles a tiny trickle of blood as I look at it. He then cuts a single star on the side of my wrist, near the bone, to symbolize my royal heritage that I am now stripped of.

The blood dribbles down my arm. This symbol will make a scar that I will never rid myself of.

I am thrust into the streets, into the crowd. They part for me, and then I realize my hands have been bound with rope.

"Tse, please…" I whisper as they gather the few things I am allowed to own as Outcast. They put them in a small leather sack. I see the knife go in as well.

The crowd glares at me, and Tse is among them.

"No, Kohana. It could have been me in there. You killed your family, you could kill me too. I will not vouch for you. I will never see you again, and if I find you, I promise, I will kill you."

I pulled myself out of the memory, tears streaming down my face. That day. That terrible day I lost my love, my family, my friends, my home; everything. Gone, all because I was in the wrong place at the wrong time.

A hare munched on grass a few paces away, and I saw the silver darts of fish swim around in the creek. An otter lay down on top of the water, lazily drifting by.

I watched until she was almost out of sight, envying her carefree lifestyle. We were more alike than different; both of us were hunters, and hunted by people around us. Yet, the otter still had a family she could return to, whereas I did not.

The Mountains. I had been thinking about it for a long time. The prospect of being free thrilled me, but leaving Goldensun was unimaginable. Today, I had made my decision. After my latest run-in with the Nightshades, I knew that my only hope was the Mountains. I quickly dashed for my pack and set off, howling a final goodbye to East River pack.

By dusk, I was at the edge of Dark Forest. I had made good time today, and could see the Mountains in the distance.

Barely visible, jagged peaks rose to meet the sky, and for a moment I had second thoughts. The Mountains looked angry, and I knew that they could just as easily welcome me as turn me away.

I saw a tall aspen with strong branches and hung my pack, bow, and quiver on a branch high up, where no person could reach it. I grabbed my elk-pelt from the bag and covered myself with it, and was asleep in moments.

Throughout the night I woke, as I always do to make sure that I'm safe. I slept in short increments and would then lie awake for a few moments at a time, just to make sure I didn't fall out of the tree and nobody was near.

At dawn I woke for good, stuffed the pelt back in my bag, and slung it over my back. I felt my river-stone knife against my thigh, strong and dangerous. Lastly, I grabbed my bow and quiver, and set off to the Mountains.

The Mountains hardly got larger as I journeyed towards them. At midday, I paused to pull lunch from my pack. I grabbed some dried strips of deer meat and munched on them as I walked, deciding I didn't have time to stop and sit down to eat. I had to get to the Mountains as fast as possible, because I was too exposed out here in the open with no trees to hide me. I thought about what had driven me to go to the Mountains on such a short notice. I actually couldn't remember a distinct moment when I made my decision, but it was more of a gradual realization that the Mountain villages isolate themselves from the Golden Plains, Dark Forest, and Crystal Lake villages. Therefore, any town in the Mountains wouldn't know of me being Outcast, and I could live amongst people.

The thought was odd. It was exciting, but frightening at the same time. I couldn't wrap my head around life with real people…it was just so, not me. I had been on my own for three years. Settling with others of a real society was just hard to imagine.

I continued until nightfall, when I pulled my pack, bow, and quiver off my shoulders. I lay my weapons down gently against a small stone. I untied my leather bag and pulled out dried strips of rabbit meat, ate quickly, and then pulled out my elk-pelt blanket.

I lay my head down on my sack and slid the hide over me, watching the last crimson streaks disappear from the sky, replaced by the shimmering, twinkling, and sparkling spirits in the sky. The moon was full, and Golden Plains was alight with the white-blue glow.

I tried to count the spirits, but there were far too many. I saw a cluster hovering over the Mountains. Perhaps they were the spirits who wanted to stay close to home. The ones over Dark Forest and the north side of Golden Plains were clustered as well, and even though Crystal Lake was many horizons away, I knew the spirits of that region were looking down on their descendants, too.

I gazed at the ones that were alone, traveling the lands like myself. I tried to guess where my family's spirits were, if they were traveling or watching over the Kingdom. Were they mad at me? Mad at me for running away, when I should be ruling a Kingdom?

I sighed and rolled over, the questions buzzing around in my head like a swarm of angry bees. I almost howled to relieve some of the stress, but held back. Wolves weren't the only ones that could hear quite the distance on open land, and I didn't want to run the risk of being noticed.

I rolled over on my back again and looked up at the spirits. Three of them, lined in a row, continued to draw my eye. I wondered if they could be my families' spirits.

The flickering one at the top of the row had a strange pattern that reminded me of the way my father's eyes twinkled. The one in the middle was bright, like my mother's soul. The spirit at the bottom had a little blue tint to it, and I smiled. Blue was Chayton's favorite color. I remember the day my father told us the story of why we were named.

I look into Father's eyes, seeing them twinkle and shine like the whole sky.

"When you were born, Chayton, I stepped outside the castle. It was a bright, shiny day and the sky was a perfect blue. As I was standing on the stairs, a large, brown falcon landed in the tree beside me. It was no falcon of our flock, for it had no tag on its foot. It screeched at me once, and then flew away. I knew it was

a sign, so I returned in and told your mother. She agreed, and we named you Chayton, or falcon."

Chayton smiles and grabs his toes, unusually shy with all of the attention directed at him. "What about me!" I yell, impatient to hear why I was named.

Father laughs. "Patience, Kohana. I was getting to you." I laugh with him, and Mother smiles with Chayton on her lap. He still has his round, chubby cheeks; a child of no more than seven years. I am five.

"When you were born, Kohana, it was another bright spring day. Remembering how I got your brother's name, I walked outside to look for signs. The moment I opened the door, the East River wolf pack ran by. But at the time, they hadn't split East River from West River; they were still the Swift River pack." He paused, laughing. "But I knew that was a rare occasion. Swift River wolves stayed away from people. The leader looked at me with a gaze full of purpose, and then ran off. I knew that was to be your name; Kohana, meaning 'swift'".

I smile and picture the wolves running past the castle. I say, "Father, can I go play by the pond?"

Father laughs and nods. "Go ahead, Kohana. Be back before dusk!"

I wave bye and run out the front of the castle, and go to find the little fish by the pond I so love to watch swim around in their happy little water home.

I smiled faintly and closed my eyes. *Maybe my family is watching me. And Goldensun will be there when I get back. And my family, my family, is watching me.* I thought nothing more, for I was asleep the next moment, dreaming of happier times. Times with my family, my brother, and the fish I usually think nothing of. Times before I was Outcast.

Chapter 2

Travels

I woke to an overcast day.

Thunder boomed far off, but I knew I would have reached the Mountains by the time that storm hit. I was determined to get there by dusk, because spending nights out in the open bothered me. I felt too vulnerable. I longed to be back in Dark Forest, yet craved living with people again. I quickly packed up and set off for the Mountains again.

The day was long, and slow. Nothing exciting happened, but I liked it that way. I passed a small, babbling creek, and saw flashes of silver minnows that darted away when I splashed through. A hare looked up from its hiding spot, saw my bow and quiver, and was gone the next second. I shook the water off my boots and continued on.

Golden Plains' tall, waist-length grasses soon receded, giving way to a rough, hot ground. It was cracked and dusty. It was still part of the territory known as Golden Plains, but there really was no 'plains' to be seen.

The cracked, dusty ground was scarce of any life. The Mountains loomed ahead, tall and mighty, warding me off and calling me on at the same time. They were a wall of rock, so tall and frightening the sheer look of them nearly made me turn back. But I had come this far, and though my journey was unexciting and rather quick, there was no telling what would happen if I returned.

I saw a shadow at the corner of my vision, and turned to see what it was. But only scarce shrubbery was there.

Wait…

"Goldensun!" I exclaimed. She bounded out from behind a small, scraggly bush and tackled me, nearly crushing my pack, bow, quiver, and me. But I was too happy. I was lonely and needed my sister.

I sat up. *What are you doing here! I thought I told you to stay back!* I said it with a smile on my face, only slightly disappointed with her leaving her pack, but other than that completely thrilled she didn't listen to me.

I sensed how sad you were. You missed your family and village and all humans in general. And even if you aren't wolf, you still tend to live like one. And no wolf should ever travel alone. She smiled and wagged her tail. *Well? Aren't we going to the Mountains? If we want to get to safe den before the spirits come out we should go!* Goldensun thought excitedly.

I nodded, she was right. Despite the thick layer of clouds covering the entire sky, I could tell sundown was near. We had to hurry if we were to find a den in time for night.

Do you know how to get through? I asked. To my great surprise and excitement, Goldensun nodded again.

When I was a pup, my mother told me many stories of wolves that traveled to the Mountains and how they lived there. If they wanted to travel them safely, they would have to find one of the Willows that were placed by Luna, the wolf goddess. They are very old, and there is only one every sky length. But if you spend the night at a Willow, a large wolf will appear in the morning and lead you to any place in the Mountains you want to go.

So all we have to do is find a Willow? I asked.

Goldensun shuffled her paws. *Well...not exactly. Legend also says the large wolves do not like humans, and they will only lead a worthy one through.*

I frowned. *Why?*

I don't know.

I furrowed my eyebrows. *Hmmm...they could just as likely turn me away as accept me,* I said. *It depends on how they see my past, whether I'm guilty or innocent in their eyes.*

She nodded. *Worth a shot. The wolf will still appear no matter what, because they have to judge you anyways.*

Right, so what's the worst that can happen? Let's go.

We were in luck. We found a Willow and got there by midnight. I set up my elk-hide blanket on the ground with Goldensun by my side, ate a piece of cooked squirrel meat and shared some with my companion, and was asleep in minutes.

∾•↢

"Kohana..."

I stir around restlessly. I can't find where the voice is coming from! It sounds like one from the past, but altered, changed. It pulls at my memories, and I can't find the speaker behind the sound.

"Kohana..."

"What?"

"Kohana..."

The voice was starting to gain a shape. In the black, a swirl of gray smoke forms to a person. Starting as just a splotch, then gaining arms, legs, a head, hands, fingers, feet...and still all in horrific gray smoke that sparkles in the darkness.

No...no, no... I think. But that isn't helping. The person now has toes, a nose, lips, ears, hair...

No! Get away!

Eyes. They are the only color to the smoky human figure. And they are deep cobalt.

"Kohana...why did you do it? Why did you kill your family?"

I shake my head. "No! I didn't do it! Why did you turn against me?"

"You are a killer...I could never be King with a killer as my Queen."

"No! Tse...it wasn't me!"

"Always guilty. Your guilt will follow you for all of eternity. This silly Mountain journey will not save you. Guilt will follow your forever."

"No! I didn't do it!"

"Yes...you did."

And he starts to dissolve. I reach for him, needing to feel the warmth of his skin and the softness of his lips on mine. I want him to hold me tight and kiss the top of my head, and never let me go. Watch me with those beautiful blue eyes forever.

But he is gone.

"Tse...no..."

Kohana! Wake up! A cold nose in my ear started me awake and I gasped. I sat there puffing until I caught my breath again. I looked into Goldensun's eyes and she licked my nose. *You had a bad dream?* She asked, concern clouding her jade gaze. I nodded. *About your family?* I nodded again. Goldensun glanced at something to her rear. *This is the wolf in human skin, Granite,* She said behind her.

I saw what was behind Goldensun and nearly lost my breath again.

The largest wolf I had ever seen was there. He had a dark gray pelt and white underbelly. His muzzle was tinted brown at the end, and where gray and white met was a blurred sandy color. He was taller than the stallions in my village, his legs were lean. I could only imagine how fast the wolf could run. But what startled me the most were his eyes, which were dark ruby red. He noticed me watching him and said, "All of us have them. The long legs and ruby eyes. It is a trait of Tall Wolves."

I nodded, somewhat astounded at how well he spoke my language.

Granite laughed loudly. A bark that made the ground tremble slightly. "We use a unique language that, when we are speaking it, is understandable to all. However, when we are not speaking it to you, it is nothing. You can only understand this language when a Tall Wolf is near."

I nodded, and wondered why he said that. Almost as if...

"Your body language is quite clear. I don't need to read your mind to tell what you are thinking."

Goldensun smiled and wagged her tail. "So you will you take her with us?"

It was strange, to hear her talk out loud. She spoke in that language the Tall Wolf spoke in, almost as if she already knew it. Granite smiled. "You will find yourself unconsciously speaking this tongue and understanding it, as long as you're in the presence of one of us. It's strange, I will admit it, but you get used to it."

Granite frowned ever so slightly as he looked back to Goldensun, the tip of his tail twitched anxiously. "You say that she is pure, but this is the girl who has been cast out, if I am correct..." he trailed off, talking to no one in particular and seeming to look into my soul.

"You were charged with a crime you did not commit. You were taken away from your mate and pack, and sent to live alone. You wish to come to the Mountains to find a new pack, so you are no longer a lone wolf. You don't like being a lone wolf."

I nodded, slightly shaken at how he could see all that.

Granite blinked, and instantly I knew I was accepted. "Come." was all he said, and while Goldensun didn't know if that meant just her or both of us, I did.

"You will go to High Point village. They will welcome you if you do not tell them who you are." He paused, turning around and catching my eye, his legs stiff and tail straight as a stick. "But you will owe me."

I narrowed my eyes, wondering what he meant. Goldensun shrugged to me, and we continued after him.

Before we began the ascent, while standing at the foot of a narrow Mountain pass, he said, "It is critical that you remain quiet. The Mountain lions have amazing hearing, and if you are heard, by a large pack, not even all of us combined could fight them off."

"What's a Mountain lion?" I asked. Goldensun looked from me to Granite, and her eyes were asking the same question.

"They are large cats, about the size of Goldensun. They are strong and quick, and blend in well with the rocks. They have excellent ears and noses, but only normal eyesight. Long whiskers give them an amazing sense of their surroundings, even when they cannot see a thing. They are formidable enemies, and it is difficult to fight them. They can jump high and are dangerous, with long fangs and claws that can be hidden in their paws, so you will not hear them approach." Granite regarded my arrows and bow with uncertainty. "You might stand a chance with your weapons if a Tribe appears, but we will stay silent just in case. Kohana, please hop on my back. It will reduce noise levels. By tomorrow evening we should arrive at High Point village."

I didn't say anything, because I had already clambered onto his back and we were taking our first steps into the Mountains. I could instantly tell this was going to be rough, because a steep path wound high into the peaks. On one side was the slope of a Mountain, the other was a drop that I could instantly tell was deadly. It was a mouth, open wide to swallow me whole. I gulped and tried to pull my gaze away. But there was something calling me from deep down in the crevice, and I couldn't look in any other direction.

Without so much as a pause, Granite sped off up the trail, Goldensun close behind. I clung to the Tall Wolf's back like my life depended on it.

Mostly because it did.

We were speeding along the narrow pass, my leg brushing the rock face. I grew nervous quickly, and I wasn't sure of the Tall Wolf's footing. But he zoomed up the passage like he had studied every rock and pebble and tiny leaf on the trail, and that gave me some reassurance. Goldensun, however, wasn't doing so well.

She panted and stumbled. But by some miracle, she continued on. I could see the exhaustion in her eyes, and the way her tail drooped behind her.

I hadn't expected the Mountain air to be so cold, and I didn't know better to make new clothing for the journey. Granite's pelt kept me warm enough, and only my face was cold. I felt my long braided hair whipping behind me like a tail, and I wanted to pull it back and stuff it down my shirt. Just as I was about to let go of Granite's neck with one hand, a large crevice opened up in our path.

Granite leapt, spanning the gap easily, and I halfheartedly wondered if he would be able to cross the gorge that was beside us with his long, sturdy legs.

A whine from Goldensun snapped me back from my daydreams. She would never make the distance. She would fall far too short. I refused to let her make the jump.

I was about to voice my thoughts to Granite, but he turned around and stopped at the edge. A soft whine escaped his lips, and I knew what he was basically trying to say, even if I couldn't understand that whine.

Jump. I will catch you.

For another brief moment, my mind wandered. I speculated as to why he wouldn't just speak. However, I answered my own question when I remembered the threat of the Mountain lions.

Goldensun looked around anxiously, panting so hard I thought she would collapse on the spot. She backed up a few paces, gathered herself, and took a running leap at the gap.

Her front paws scrabbled at the edge, and Granite flicked his head down and grabbed her scruff. He easily hauled her back over and stood there, letting her catch her breath.

I looked around and noticed the tips of the Mountains were pink. *Sunset.* I couldn't believe my own eyes. We had been traveling all day!

I tapped Granite lightly on the head and pointed out the tips silently. He glanced up, nodded and looked around.

A small green weed grew where the Mountain slope met the trail, and he nodded again. Then, like a mother noses her pups awake, Granite nudged Goldensun up and started trotting again. Within the hour we reached a level part on the trail. It was much wider than the rest of it, and it had plenty of room for the three of us.

I jumped off Granite's back and nodded in thanks. I put my bow and quiver down against a rock gently. If something were to happen to them, I would never survive. I didn't have the stealth to catch an animal with only my knife. But I did have the aim to bring one down with my arrows.

I took a large chunk of elk meat out from my pack and tossed it to the wolves, who devoured it instantly. I then got some more cooked meat and ate that myself.

When I was done, I crawled over to where the wolves were laying and threw my hide blanket over my shivering body. Goldensun wiggled closer to me, adding extra heat. Within the minute I was warm, and I almost fell asleep counting the spirits.

The Mountains were spooky at night.

I couldn't sleep at all. The rock was too solid, too unmoving, and too dead. I was just another traveler on its slopes, and no more than a blip in its life. All it would take was the most miniscule of shifts, the tiniest of movements, and the Mountain would send a tumble of boulders down to crush all three of us.

A sudden flash on a ledge above me caught my attention, and I looked up. It was there and gone, so fast I thought I imagined it.

Pebbles clattered down the side of the Mountain. I stood up, unsheathing my knife to look at them. There was a tiny, mouse-brown hair among the rocks, and I looked up again to see what had sent them tumbling down. A small rodent, perhaps? Or something bigger? My senses were on high now, scanning the area and not missing a single detail.

There it was again; just a slight image of brown, a tiny dash of white whiskers, the whisking away of a tail. So I hadn't imagined it after all.

We were not alone.

The Mountain lions were here, and I could well assume that we were their prey.

I saw the lion above me fly off the ledge, headed for my neck. But my dagger was unsheathed, and soon buried deep in her furry stomach. She yowled in pain, and then slumped over, dead. I pushed the cat off my knife and spun around, prepared for the next attack.

The rest of them were clearly furious. They hissed at me; the sounds coming from all around, confusing me. Where should I look? Which one is going to attack next?

My bow.

My bow and arrows are only a few steps away, but I saw the shadow of a cat near there. It was tempting me to go for them, to grab a better weapon. But living as Outcast taught me that if I can't use my weapon of choice, I just work with what I've got.

A Mountain lion lunged for my throat, but I dodged it, and luckily Granite – now roused from his slumber – was right there to catch it. He bit the cat's neck, and killed it.

The others were now nervous, and I could tell they were discussing their odds. Two of them were dead now; we were obviously formidable opponents.

A large male stepped forward: his eyes were deep brown and his whiskers pitch black, his muzzle was tinged with gray and his tail swept the ground with curiosity. Finally, he blinked once and whispered something to the remainder of his group. In one swift movement, the lion was up and over the ledge, Tribe following. A female whose belly was round with kits stared at me a moment longer than the others, but then went over just as nimbly as the rest of them.

I looked back at Granite, who was staring at me as if I had just sprouted wings and flew over the Mountain peaks themselves. Goldensun was licking her shoulder, pretending not to have noticed what just happened.

Finally, Granite shook his massive head and nosed the two bodies over the edge of the cliff, deep into the chasm below. I watched them fall, twisting and turning until they disappeared in the fog. I never heard the sound of them hitting the bottom.

"Why did you throw them over?" I asked.

"To keep the Dragons away. They can get the meat down in the chasm. Only they are fast enough to catch the bodies that have fallen."

I gulped and scanned the skies, searching for the telltale shimmer of scales and the near-silent flap of a Dragon's wings. I was told that if you were to become the meal of a Dragon, the last things you would ever hear were the swish of their wings and the faintest click of their claws.

I swallowed again and Granite swished his tail in agitation. "Come. We must get there as fast as possible. The longer we're exposed, the more likely we'll be spotted."

I smelled smoke before I saw the village, and my heart raced faster than Granite's paws.

I closed my eyes and imagined life with other people; making new friends, forging new bonds with new people, a whole new *life*. I looked down at Goldensun excitedly, and she smiled back. I then noticed a minute shift in Granite's energy; something was amiss.

I patted his neck in a signal to reduce his speed, and he slowed to a trot.

"What is it, Kohana?" he asked without looking at me.

"Um…what's wrong?" I said. I felt the shift again; infinitesimal and hardly detectable, but there it was. He was nervous, or perhaps upset? Concerned? I couldn't tell.

Granite started to shake his head, and then sighed. He picked up the pace again and still said nothing. When we reached the village, he dropped down to let me off.

As I peered into his ruby eyes, he laid his ears against his head. "I am nervous for you. You are a special girl. No matter how this turns out, no matter how many friends or enemies you make here, you must promise me that one day you will return to the lower lands of Desaria. You *must* promise me this. Swear on your soul."

The look in his eyes was so urgent that I immediately nodded and said, "I swear on my soul."

He nodded, though still looking a little nervous, and turned back into the shadows. I watched him trot back down the path until he was out of sight. Only then did I realize that he blended in so well with the stone, it was a miracle I ever saw him go.

I walked into the village, head held high, Goldensun trotting nervously by my side. She glanced from house to house, head down and ears back. A big black dog lifted its head and bared its teeth, but after a short command from its owner, lay back down. It didn't take its eyes off of us.

I don't like it... she told me. I nodded my assent. *It feels far too sealed,* she finished. I looked around and realized Goldensun was right.

The village houses puffed smoke that twisted and swirled upwards until finally joining as one and billowing away in the wind. Mountain peaks towered above us, forming a near circle. I searched around and found only the path I came in as a way out. A cold breeze blew through the village and I shivered, clutching the hilt of my knife harder. This place was far too closed in for my liking.

I looked to my right and saw a boy about my age watching me. His skin was light brown, tanned by days out in the frosty sun. His sea green eyes sparkled like the rare, green sapphires that had rested in Father's crown.

The boy furrowed his thick eyebrows slightly, following me with his eyes as I made my way down the hill. Several other people sent me skeptical looks, and many whispered fiercely to the person standing next to them.

I saw a butcher shop farther down the road, and rushed to it. Goldensun's claws clicked as she trotted behind me, her mouth open and inhaling the scent of the meat.

I looked over my shoulders, and then leaned on the counter. Goldensun placed her front paws there as well, her nose barely poking over to see the inside of the shop.

A large, bald man with hairy arms was chopping up meat with a large, rectangular knife. I flinched when he brought the blade down onto the block, slicing the venison with ease.

"Hello," he said, without looking up from his work. "What can I do you for, miss?"

"Oh, um, well, I just got here, and I was wondering if there's somewhere I can stay. An inn, maybe?"

The man looked up, putting down the knife and scratching his stubble with three fingers. "Sorry ma'am, no inns around here. We don't get many travelers, you see. But, if you go talk to Chu`si, I'm sure she can work something out with you."

"Who's Chu`si?"

The butcher narrowed his eyes at Goldensun, distracted from my question. He waved his hand, trying to get her to get down. "She won't take anything," I interjected.

He gave her one last skeptical look, and shrugged. "Alright then. But if I find any of my cuts missing, I'm pointing fingers at her."

I raised my eyebrows, waiting to see if he'd answer my question.

"You're not from around here, are you?"

"Not exactly."

"See, everyone in any Mountain village knows about Chu`si." He leaned in closer, glancing around. "She's been known to do some spooky things; plays with magic and whatnot. Some people speculate that she's a witch."

"So?"

The butcher shrugged again. "I just think she's got something to hide, like everyone around here."

I tried to suppress a shiver. I had something to hide, too.

23

"Anyways," the man said, clapping his hands together, "She's the town healer, her grandson lives with her. One of the first houses; the boy sits outside all the time. He's a little odd, too, that one."

"Black hair, kind of turquoise eyes?"

"*Extremely* turquoise eyes," the man corrected. "But yes, that's the one."

I nodded, moving away from the counter. Goldensun looked at me, then back to the meat, and returned to standing on four paws.

"Thanks for your help," I said over my shoulder as I moved back up to where I saw the boy.

I only heard the knife hitting the block again as the butcher continued his work.

I headed up the hill, noticing how the boy was still staring at me. I wondered if he'd seen the whole exchange, and what he was doing out here, just sitting. It was kind of cold.

"Um, hey," I said, offering an awkward wave. "The butcher told me I should come talk to Chu`si about temporary housing...I'm new here."

He smiled at me, but only a little. Then he stood and – without saying a word – turned back to his cottage. He walked inside, and I instantly heard voices arise. I stood there uncomfortably, with Goldensun sniffing at a bug at our feet.

The boy then appeared, leaning smoothly against the wall of the cottage and crossing his arms. He flashed a smile at me and said, "Hey, I'm Niyol."

I smiled back. "I'm Kohana."

Niyol grinned wider and said, "And your friend?"

Goldensun glanced up at him and wagged her tail briefly in a friendly gesture. *I'm Goldensun. Tell him I'm Goldensun,* she said. I told him.

Niyol slightly raised an eyebrow, but he nodded and jokingly bowed to her. She dipped her head back, and then said to me, *I think I like him.*

Niyol looked from me to her, a look of confusion stamped clearly across his face. But his eyes still sparkled with good intentions. "And she said...?"

I just laughed and shook my head, waving off the question like a pesky fly. Niyol shrugged and said, "Well, we've got an extra room here, if you want it. Usually Chu`si and I take care of the sick and all the travelers, although there aren't many of the latter. Is that okay with you?"

I hesitated for a moment. For some reason, the idea of being in the same room with Niyol sent butterflies racing through my chest.

You're supposed to accept his offer, Goldensun said, reminding me of the question on the table.

Oh, right. "Yeah, I'd love to, thank you so much," I replied, doing my best to suppress the heat rising in my cheeks.

Niyol's grin broadened, stretching from ear to ear. "Would you like me to show you around?"

I smiled and nodded.

He turned around and pointed at the hut he just came from. "So, I'm sure the butcher told you that Chu`si was the town healer. Well, we pretty much run the place; if you ever get sick, I mean like, after you get your own place, then that's where you go. She's also like, the head of the town, but that's only because she's the oldest one around."

Niyol turned around to point at something else when he froze. I mean, he wasn't blinking, breathing, or moving at all. His finger indicated something behind me, still extended in his shock.

I didn't dare turn around. A part of me already knew what I'd see.

The snorting and heavy breathing, the rustle of wings and gentle click of claws told me all I needed to know. Goldensun was staring wild-eyed at the beast behind me, and I could tell she was weighing her chances. Try to protect me and for sure die in the attempt, or run and hope I could keep up.

"Turn around, Kohana."

I didn't dare. It was a trick. Dragons are tricky beasts.

"I mean you no harm. Turn around."

I swiveled my head the tiniest bit, and caught sight of the majestic animal behind me.

Dragons always seemed so much smaller when they are flying then when they stand right in front of you, or in my case, behind me. My head only reached the very underside of his stomach. His wings were tucked against a cobalt back, and claws sharper than any dagger or arrow dug into the soil. The claws led up to four powerful legs and a strong, wide chest. The Dragon's neck was long and curvy, probably making up half of his entire height, and swayed like a snake prepared to strike. Was he only curious? Or perhaps he was seizing me up; to see how exactly he should strike me down. His eyes were an electrifying yellow, and seemed to gaze deep into my soul. Small coils of smoke drifted from his nostrils and swirled high, slowly disappearing in the crystal blue sky.

"Do you not take my word for it, Kohana?"

I gulped nervously and a small twinkle appeared in the Dragon's eyes.

"I am Hinto. No need to introduce yourself; I know who you are."

"Um...can anybody else hear you?" I swallowed loudly and turned my body to face the Dragon full on, hoping against hope he would not think it a challenge.

"Yes. Don't listen to the Tall Wolves; they think they are the only ones who can alter how you speak and hear." He rolled his eyes and tossed his head a bit. "Dragons can too. I have come for a reason, though. Young one, you have a destiny to fulfill."

The playful glimmer hardened to a gaze of stone, and once more I was frightened of the beast.

"You are a child with an important future. It will change the lives of all people, animals, Dragons, and spirits. The choices that you make from this point onward will affect more than just the life of yourself."

At that, Hinto spread his massive cobalt wings and took to the sky. Never once did his stunning yellow gaze leave mine. Before I knew it, he was soaring over the peaks and the entire village was staring at me.

Great, I thought, *you've only been here for ten minutes and already something bizarre has happened to you. Way to make a first impression!*

Niyol stared blankly at me, then grabbed my arm and pulled me behind his grandmother's cottage.

"What. Just. Happened?!" The happy, peppy, excited look had left his eyes and had been replaced by a gaze that sent chills down my spine. He grabbed my shoulders in strong hands and shook me a little, repeating the question.

"I…uh…I don't…" I stammered and shook my head, not fully comprehending what just took place, either.

Niyol looked around nervously and leaned close to my face, and I was startled by just how beautiful his eyes really were. I instantly got so lost in them, that his voice startled me. "You don't know what kind of nightmare you just got yourself into, Kohana. You really have no idea."

Goldensun looked nervously from Niyol to me and back again. *Kohana?* She thought to me.

I tore my gaze away from Niyol's eyes and replied, *Yes?*

Niyol pulled away and peered around the corner while I talked to Goldensun. The villagers were ushering children inside, pulling their blankets over windows and shutting doors. In as little as one minute, this place had become a ghost town.

I don't know what just happened, she told me, *but obviously, it wasn't good. Knowing you, this might become a regular thing, so call out to me if something else happens…I am going to get my bearings.* She licked my fingers and trotted away, leaving me alone with Niyol.

"She said…?"

I grabbed Niyol's arm and pulled him out from behind his house. "Just forget it. Nothing important. So you were going to show me the village?"

I hardly fit in well, as it turned out. Most villagers tended to avoid me because of the thing that happened with Hinto, but somehow I made a few friends besides Niyol. His grandmother, Chu`si, welcomed me into her home (at least until I could buy my own) and made a lovely dinner in honor of my arrival.

Chu`si was small and somewhat plump, perhaps in her late fifties. She had sparkling blue eyes and loved to tell stories, and her gray hair was a simple braid that reached halfway down her back. She had many crow's feet spreading from her eyes; a sure sign she had spent her life smiling. Chu`si was missing a tooth in the front, and when she grinned you could easily see it. She was an excellent cook and her nimble, bony fingers spread across the sky when she told stories. She was a gifted storyteller and painted many pictures in my mind after evening meal.

Chu`si offered me a yak pelt to sleep under, and I politely refused. It was hers, and I had my own anyways.

"No. You have traveled far to come here, and you will take my pelt. I will show you courtesy as you are the guest," Chu`si insisted. Niyol looked a little embarrassed at his grandmother's assertiveness, but eventually I accepted. This poor frail lady didn't deserve to sleep on nothing but the ground though, so I offered her my own elk pelt.

"No. That's far too thin. You will not need elk pelts here; yak is far warmer. You need this one to keep you warm. Speaking of which, you will need thicker clothing than these tiny things," she said, pulling at my green shirt. She clucked her tongue. "These won't do at all, especially with winter coming. Tomorrow, we will start fixing you some new ones.

I sighed and smiled, then gave Chu`si a big thank-you hug. As I was falling asleep, I heard Goldensun whine softly at the entrance.

She walked in carefully, trying not to step on any bodies. She looked around, taking in the thatched walls of the house, the carefully hung pelts as trophies and the gentle carvings on the table. There was a ceremonial headdress that hung from the wall that was painted a variety of blues and reds, every color natural from berries and plants. The top of the house was open tonight to let the spirits come to talk to us.

She sighed contentedly and lay down by my side, snuggling close and burying her fur in my face. I chuckled a little bit, taking comfort in the warmth she brought. Within moments, I was fast asleep in my new home with my furry friend and my nice new family.

Chapter 3
New Life

Chu`si woke me at dawn. I saw Goldensun had already left, probably to go scavenge something from the other huts. I laughed inwardly; that was something my companion would do. "Come, child, time to make breakfast."

I helped Chu`si prepare the meal, and she showed me how to cook the chicken eggs over a small pan and a fire. Before it was done she asked if I would go down into the more crowded part of town to fetch some pig fat and more eggs, and she needed more horsehair for brushes and rope. I said I would, took the basket she offered and headed down.

On my way I saw little kids running around, chasing each other and playing silly games. I strolled past them down the dirt road and walked past the stables, too. The horses snorted and snuffled into their hay, and I stroked a white mare with brown spots for a moment before continuing on my way.

I started whistling a happy tune and stopped to let the black dog from yesterday come up and sniff my hand. He wagged his thin tail and licked it, then perked his ears and dashed off in pursuit of something I couldn't see.

When I got to the center of town, nearly every passerby took the time to shoot me a suspicious look. But I ignored them; handing the clerk the money and collected my things. I grabbed the basket, now full of eggs, pig fat and horse hair, then headed back towards Chu`si's hut.

As I walked back to Chu`si and Niyol, I heard a girl's voice shouting, "Wait up!" I figured it wasn't for me; I didn't recognize the voice, and nobody here knew me. But the shouting persisted, so I turned around to see who was yelling.

A tall, tanned girl was waving at me from farther down the hill. She had a pale green dress on and no shoes, and her long black hair was pulled back in two identical braids. She came up to me, panting heavily. "Phew!" she said, and stopped to catch her breath. I waited patiently, looking down at my own deep red hair, with its natural blonde highlights, which had been recently unbraided. It was beautiful and wavy, and shimmered in the early morning air. It was tinted a fiery red in the light.

"Hey," panted the girl, still a little short of breath, "I'm Tobie. You were the one that talked to the Dragon right?" Her brown eyes were so light they were almost yellow, and she was a little shorter than me. I nodded, trying not to feel offended; after all, it wasn't an insult, just a question.

"That's so cool! Do you know how many people talk to Dragons and live?"

I shook my head. "No, how many?"

Tobie's grin widened considerably. "Nobody, ever. You are...like...legendary!"

I laughed a little and shrugged. "Well, I can't exactly say it's happened to me before." I started to stare off into space, and Tobie shook her hand in front of my face to grab my attention again.

"Hello? Earth to Dragon-girl? Is anyone home?" she asked. I laughed at her tone. I could already tell we were going to be good friends. She then said, "So what are you doing now?"

"Chu`si needed some more eggs, some pig fat and we were running low on horsehair for our brushes and rope and stuff," I said.

Tobie flinched, raising an eyebrow. "What are you helping Chu`si out for?"

"I live with her and Niyol now."

"Oh, okay." Tobie's face flushed a bright red. "So, Niyol, he's pretty cute, right?" she asked, probably to ease the tension.

The question completely took me off guard. "Uh, yeah, I guess so, I mean, yeah, sort of..."

"Can I walk home with you?" she interrupted.

I nodded, thankful for the distraction, and we walked home in a newborn friendship. She told me mostly about her life, and I just edged around mine. I didn't want to ruin anything already. She was a curious little girl though.

I found out Tobie was going to be fifteen winters, just a year younger than me. She lived with her father and mother and younger sister named Suzan, but they all called her Zuzu. She was ten winters, and was in training to be a healer, because everyone knew that Chu`si was getting dangerously old.

Tobie also told me of how her mother was carrying another child in her belly, and how they hoped it was a boy so they could have a little more work done around the house in his years to come. She talked of their wolf-mix dog named Chitsa and of their horse in the stables that she liked to ride every day.

"Which one is yours?" I asked, remembering the spotted mare from only a little while before.

"He is a black stallion with a white star on his head. He is very tall and strong," she said. I nodded, remembering the horse next to the spotted mare was exactly as Tobie was describing. We talked a little more about her life, and when I was standing outside her door, saying goodbye, Tobie said, "Wait! You never told me anything about you!"

Just then, Goldensun trotted up with a slightly red muzzle and looked from me to Tobie and back again. She licked her lips and wagged her tail a little bit in greeting to my new friend, who smiled.

"Who's this?" she asked.

"Goldensun. She is…a close friend from where I came from before."

"Can I stroke her?"

I asked Goldensun, who grudgingly accepted. She was a wolf, not a dog, and usually was bothered when she was treated like the prior.

"Sure," I told Tobie.

Tobie reached down and stroked the top of Goldensun's head, and said, "Goldensun, your pelt is so soft! You must take good care of it."

Goldensun wagged her tail a little then perked her ears. She pulled her head away from Tobie's hand and barked, *Danger. Come, now.*

She grabbed the hem of my shirt and pulled, dragging me away from Tobie's house and up the hill. "Oh, and my name is Kohana! Talk to you later!"

Tobie waved goodbye and went into her little house, and I turned to Goldensun.

What danger?

Goldensun sniffed the air and closed her eyes, trying to place the scent. *Mountain lions.*

I gaped at her, not knowing what to be more surprised at. Granite had informed us that Mountain lions stay away from the villages unless they were starving. What were they doing here?

I didn't have time to finish the thought before I heard the yowls from the path. The lions streamed through the entrance and snarled at people. They cornered some against a wall and others were chased into their houses. I saw the horses startling in the stables, kicking the back wall and the door. The Mountain lions just paced in front of the meat store (where the butcher was hiding behind the counter) as if they were waiting for orders to kill the man and steal the meat.

Actually, as I looked, I saw that the cats were doing no real harm. They were only scaring the people. There was no blood to be seen, and the only screams were of terror, not true pain.

A group of cats saw me standing in the middle of the path watching the whole thing play out, and darted up to me, hissing and lashing their tails. Goldensun snarled and was about to leap at one but I told her, *Stop!*

Goldensun didn't look to me, and completely ignored my command. She hurdled herself at the cat in the middle, and they scuffled on the ground for a few moments. Goldensun bit the lion's paw and she yowled in pain, but then shoved her back paws under Goldensun's belly and threw her off.

Goldensun skidded on the ground. As I reached out to help her, another Mountain lion sprang in front of me. He hissed and warded me back while Goldensun gasped to regain her breath.

"Goldensun!" I yelled – forgetting even to send thoughts to her and make sure she was okay – and she wheezed a reply.

The third Mountain lion, an older cub, lashed his tail and snarled at me. The first female picked herself up off the ground and licked her paw, hissing at him. The older male grabbed Goldensun's scruff and hauled her away. The whole time I was thinking of how stupid I was to leave my weapons at home.

The female stood up and shook herself, then examined me closely with deep blue eyes. As if she recognized something in me, or noticed something odd, she yowled and darted away. I saw her bound up the slope and disappear over the top. Moments later she returned, leading another female with big, wide shoulders to me. The first cat was nearly jumping up and down with excitement.

The new cat regarded me as a pigeon would look upon a worm, or a wolf would see a deer. I was a lower being than her, and my life made no impact on hers whatsoever.

I heard yowling and barking coming from where the older male took Goldensun, and I watched as they fought. Goldensun was a formidable opponent with much speed, but the cat was far more nimble than her. Within moments, Goldensun was on the ground wheezing again.

"Goldensun!" I yelled again. Once more I overlooked the whole 'I can talk to her through my mind' thing, despite the fact I had done it for the past three years.

I made a move toward her when the young cat leapt to attack me. I caught him by the stomach and threw him in the other direction. The first female Mountain lion advanced, but the older one placed a paw in front of her. I could almost imagine the second one saying, "Let's just see how this plays out."

The young male hissed and bared his teeth at me, and I snarled back. I charged past him and up the hill to our little house, and didn't even see Chu'si and Niyol pinned against the wall by two large lions until they screamed my name. I notched an arrow and took down one of them, and the other spun around to see who felled his comrade. But by then there was an arrow in his chest as well, and I darted out of the room to help Goldensun. I now had my bow, arrows, and my trusty knife.

The cats on the hill were hissing at each other, trying to decide to follow or stay. I pulled another arrow out of my quiver and let loose, and the blue jay fletching caused the arrow to fly straight and true. It hit its mark; the male's heart that was guarding Goldensun.

The females spun around and both started snarling at me. Another arrow was already placed in my bow, but a deafening roar from above shook the ground and made me collapse on the ground, clutching my ears to block out the sound.

"Enough!"

The blue Dragon landed between the two cats and me, snarling furiously. Both of them shrank away in terror from him, as did the others around the village. All of the Mountain lions emerged from the houses they were guarding with lowered ears and tails and heads, trying to appear invisible. People stuck their heads out of the windows and doors to watch what was happening.

"You have given this town enough grief. Take your lions and leave now. There is nothing for you here."

I could tell Hinto was talking to the wide-shouldered female. She narrowed jet-black eyes at him. Then, to my great surprise, she hissed in broken speech, "Tatsuo has promise. It here. We no return, but we wait."

Hinto stiffened. "What did he say?"

The lioness bared her teeth in an expression that resembled a sadistic grin. "He return. We find, he make us strong. Live forever, never hungry, strongest kits." She twitched her tail in satisfaction. "Tatsuo comes back."

She then turned and bounded away, with every cat except for the three I killed following her. Even the cub that I threw to the side limped after them.

I watched curiously, waiting to see what Hinto would do. Who was the Tatsuo that the lion had mentioned, and why did it unnerve the Dragon so much? But he seemed to have brushed the thought away, for Hinto swiveled his neck to face me with a yellow fire in his eyes I hadn't seen before. His nostrils puffed more smoke than before, and his tail lashed angrily, nearly swiping my head. He then turned all the way around, neck waving like a snake poised to strike. Without moving his lips, Hinto said, "I should kill you now. You have caused much trouble. Under normal circumstances, any other human would be dead at my claws." He paused, taking the time for an unsatisfied growl to rise from his chest, like a big, dangerous sigh.

"Unfortunately, these are not normal circumstances. Regardless, this…incident would not have happened had it not been for you." He spit the last word out as if it were venom.

I gaped at him, still clutching my head when I said, "How is any of this my fault?"

He growled. "You killed three lions that were not doing any harm to you. You will not use them for food, and yet they are dead. They had not shed a single drop of blood, and you took their lives without a second thought."

I closed my eyes. Then I opened them again and said, "But we were in the heat of battle. I had to react quickly. There was no time to think…I just…"

"No!" Hinto bellowed loud enough to make the walls of the Mountains tremble. "The heat of battle is precisely when you must think the clearest!" Hinto regarded me with disdain. A deep, thoughtful silence stretched between us for what seemed like decades. Then, finally, Hinto lowered his head so he was at eye level with me. "You have a lot to learn, and time will be your teacher. You must open your eyes to see what is to be discovered. You are smart and very capable of learning, Kohana. The only thing you have to do," he paused, arching an eyebrow at me. "is think." Hinto then flapped his great wings twice, rising to the sky. He was gone in moments.

I lay there stunned. *You have a lot to learn…the only thing you have to do is think.* The words rang through my head like a never-ending echo, bouncing around and around. I numbly picked myself up off the ground and walked the few yards down the hill to where I had dropped my basket. I carefully placed the non broken eggs back inside. I found the pouch of horsehair and put that back too. Only then did I remember my companion lying in the street, panting heavily.

Goldensun? I said, well aware of the whole village watching my every move.

Goldensun whined in reply, and I rushed over to her. I stroked her fur and was surprised to not feel anything broken along her flank; the Mountain lions had shoved her pretty hard in the stomach. *You okay?* I asked, concern filling my voice.

She nodded and continued to gasp. *Just a little winded, I'll be better in a minute.*

She was right. In a few more breaths she was on her feet and limping uphill with me to the house. When we arrived, she flopped right down on my new yak-hide bed that Chu'si gave me last night, and she started breathing heavily again.

Already the scent of the dead Mountain lions was filling the two small rooms. I dragged them outside and pushed them into the chasm before returning. Chu`si was in the room that served as the kitchen and called out, "Kohana? Is that you sweetie?"

I frowned and said, "Yes, Chu`si, I what you asked for." Why wasn't she worried about the lions?

I walked in and she was tending to the eggs that had been over the fire before. "Those look a little burned, Chu`si," I told her. She just laughed and waved off my comment.

"Did you bring me any new ones?"

"I just said I did. Here they are." I handed them to her one by one, until all six were sizzling on the pan over the fire. She reached out for more and when I didn't hand her any looked curiously at me. I shook my head. "I dropped the basket when I ran up to get my weapons and they cracked on the street. Sorry."

She shrugged goodheartedly. "It happens, honey."

I looked around the kitchen-room and poked my head back in the other room, but couldn't find Niyol. "Where did Niyol go?"

Chu`si's gaze clouded over as she thought about it, and for the first time it occurred to me that she was old, and might have a short memory span. "I think he went to…to go check on the horses, dear." I nodded, knowing he didn't go that way or I would have seen him on my way up.

"Thank you, Chu`si." I turned to leave so I could find him, but the old lady put a hand on my shoulder. I turned and saw her eyes rolled completely back in her head and her mouth open wide. Her hair was standing slightly on end and looked charged with electricity.

That's when the shock hit me.

I opened my mouth to scream, but by the time I sent the breath through my throat, the sensation was gone. The burning electricity was so intense I know I felt the marrow in my bones sizzle. But just as quickly as it flamed, the current was gone.

I was standing in a field. The grass was neon green and seemed to shimmer in the daylight. There were tons of flowers too, in all colors. There were patches of blue, purple, pink, orange, yellow, red, and white flowers, and some places where they all blended together to create a rainbow-like space. I reached out and touched a pretty pink one, and it was soft and light and swayed in the breeze. The sky was a perfect blue, the clouds an untouchable white. The Mountains were a beautiful purple on my right, and the sun was nowhere to be seen, but it was clearly daytime.

All of the sudden, the beautiful field was whipped away from me. I spun for a moment and landed in a place that looked similar to the field, yet totally different. I could tell it was the same place in a different time.

Now, the setting was a dry, cracked earth where nothing grew. Dead animals littered the land, and among them were wolves, rabbits, Mountain lions, ravens, eagles, humans and even Dragons. Dead trees hinted that the terrain was a forest once between the first image and now, but everywhere I looked were dead fronds of grass and flowers and trees and animals. The Mountains were a dismal brown and gray, without the slightest hint of life, and the sky was blood red. Not red as in sunset, not in a beautiful way. It was much more ominous and threatening. Something stirred inside me and I knew the sky always looked like this in this time. The clouds were no longer a perfect white but a black that was darker than a starless night. This place frightened me, and I wanted to leave it, to go back to the beautiful field of before. I wanted to get out of here, *now.*

But the scene didn't change, or disappear, or did I get whipped away again. Instead I started walking towards a pile of bodies that was drawing me like bees are to honey, I moved to it without intending to take a step. I tried to fight it, tried to walk away, because I already knew who was in there. But as hard as I tried, I couldn't stop walking. I made it to the pile and sobbed insanely, trying to close my eyes and get away.

In the pile were the ones I loved most.

Goldensun. My mother and father. Chayton. Tse. East River pack. Chu`si, Tobie, Niyol. Even Granite and Hinto. They were all dead.

A small part of me screamed to get out, to close my eyes and walk away, but I still couldn't move. Nothing I was doing was of my own accord.

I reached out and touched Goldensun's muzzle. It was cold. Her whiskers would never twitch again; her eyes never look at the world. Not that there was much to look at now.

Then the dead world was flashed away, and I was in just blackness. Then I was whisked into many different scenes that came and went too fast for me to register.

I was running across the plains, and a snowy owl swooped over me. He held a purple staff with a glowing orb at the end. I heard laughter, coming from someone I didn't see. I didn't recognize the sound.

A black, feathery wing swept over my vision, and the scene changed again. Lightning flashed in a forest, and all I could see was a silhouette of something against the trees. I looked around me, catching a glimpse of Niyol before I was whipped away again.

I saw a mountain, its peak shrouded with clouds. It radiated darkness, so it seemed. On unseen wings, I soared to the top, where the scene went black, and then took me to the next setting.

A strange, pearly white, snakelike creature with a hawk's head was holding something in large, clawed hands. It sat on hind legs, holding the knife up to the sky, as if an offering. The ground rumbled and shook, and a wide cavern opened up, like a yawning mouth ready to eat anything. A clawed hand, larger than Hinto's head, rose from the chasm.

The setting didn't change, but I was spun around to view the sky. It was blood red, like the mountain scene of before. The moon was crimson.

Then, a scream, accompanied by a body materializing on the rocky mountaintop. The hand and the white thing slithered back into the gaping hole.

I felt my heart skip a beat as I was teleported to the body. She had a narrow nose, deep red hair and lifeless, dark blue eyes. Around her stood Niyol, a girl I didn't recognize with a blue jay on her shoulder, and a boy I didn't know with two flaming birds hovering around him. They all were fighting tears…no, the girl was sobbing now, and the boy held her. Niyol was staring angrily at the sky, as if the spirits would change things.

I choked on the last image, and it lingered even as the picture faded and I returned to the real world. I couldn't ignore what I'd seen.

I was going to die.

I gasped for air, and looked around to see I was back in the house, with Chu`si clutching my shoulder. "Darling, are you okay?"

I swallowed loudly and wrenched my shoulder away from her hand, not wanting to endure that again. Chu`si stared at me, a look of hurt in her eyes, when I said, "I…I need to get some air."

I ran outside the house, looking for a way out. A cold gust of wind hit me like a slap in the face, but I dashed out of the village before I could really feel it.

I heard Goldensun behind me, barking for me to wait up, but I kept running. Down the path, away from the village, back into the heart of the Mountains. *Kohana, slow down, where are you going?* I ignored her mental pleas, hoping she would understand that I had to be alone.

I ran until I couldn't see the billowing smoke and couldn't hear the chatter of people. I collapsed on the ground, panting heavily. I felt the wind blow through the pass angrily, trying to shove me down into the chasm below. I pulled my knees to my chest and wrapped my arms around them, and rested my head on the top. This was all too much. I couldn't take it.

I replayed the scenes in my head. I had died. I was dead. I was going to die…which meant Goldensun would fall with me. Something about my death would kill the hand and the white thing. Niyol would be there…he'd have to watch.

I was going to die.

I spent the whole day on the path just thinking. I remained quiet and listened for any straggling Mountain lions, but all had left that morning. The Mountains were silent besides the wind, providing a good time for reflection. I almost wished the lions would come back; fighting one would give the distraction I so desperately needed. I was tired of thinking about all the things I'd done and the things I'd just learned.

I throw another pebble into the pond, watching it skip four times before it sinks to the bottom. "Ha!" I say, turning to Chayton beside me. "I beat you! Four skips!"

Chayton picks up a flat little pebble in his hands of only ten years and positions himself to throw it. He lets it fly, but the little rock only skips twice before a fish jumps up out of the water and swallows it whole.

We both start laughing; that fish will eat anything. He is the only one in the pond, and he is as big as a wolf pup. I call him Goblet, because it sounds like gobble and he gobbles everything he can get his fins on.

"Goblet ate your rock...that's an extra ten points!" I squeal, delighted at having a new challenge. Chayton smiles. Just as I was about to take my turn, I hear Mother call our names from the castle.

"Race you back! Last one home has to eat a handful of mud!" I say, already knowing he will bet on it.

Chayton smiles and nods. He spits in his hand and holds it out for me, and I do the same. We shake on our usual bet. "You're on!"

I wiped away a single, silent tear. I missed my brother. My mother. My father and even the fat old fish. I frowned and thought of how Goblet was probably dead by now too. That left nobody. Unless Tse counted.

I looked up to see the clouded sky become darker than before, and I started making my way up the hill. I trudged up it with my head low, and my arms wrapped around my body for whatever warmth I could muster. It was freezing, and a piercing wind whipped my newly brushed hair behind my head and back again. I squinted against my tangled hair more than the driving wind, for it lashed my face like a leather whip. I finally made it back to the village just as the last of the light faded from the sky. I hesitantly entered the cottage where I was welcomed with warm blankets and worried hugs.

"Chu`si," I asked, "What was that? How did you...?"

"Do you know nothing, child?!" Chu`si interrupted, more with interest than genuine concern. "Going out just before a Mountain storm? Crazy! You are lucky; you could have died! The wind picks up at night and the air gets very cold. Put these on and come sit by the fire and we will talk."

She handed me the newly sewn Mountain clothing. I went to the little room in the back to change, swapped my old thin clothes for the new thicker ones, and walked back over to the fire with the blanket wrapped around my shoulders.

Chu`si told me to take a seat, and I did.

She handed me a stone bowl filled with warm, steaming broth. After the harsh conditions of outside, the hot air seemed more comforting than was actually possible. I sipped the broth gently, letting the warmth spread through my body like the roots of a tree.

"Long ago," she said, her withered hands beginning to paint the air as her words spun a story, "There was a horrible creature who ruled Calleo. The beast was only seen by one man, who claimed that it was so horrendous that description of it could call upon haunting nightmares for years on end. The only man to ever lay eyes on the beast was the very one to vanquish him.

"The creature's name was Nox."

The name sent chills down my spine. Something about the way it rolled off her tongue – the way it sounded so sinister and yet Chu`si said it with ease – was just too strange. She continued.

"Nox terrorized Calleo for many years, ruling with an iron fist. He demanded food from all the villages – capitols included – on the continent. Refusal to pay would result in extreme punishment." I didn't miss the strange way her eyes sparkled as she revealed the penalty of resistance.

"Because of this, the people began to starve. They took bigger chances, began hunting bigger animals in order to feed themselves. Even then, it wasn't enough. People were still starving. So they took a drastic measure.

"They began to hunt the Dragons."

I gasped, catching Niyol's sea-green eye next to me. His eyebrows were arched and his mouth made a small *o*, showing his emotions matched mine. Chu`si smiled.

"Back then, the Dragons and peopled lived in peace. They were allies, even. They fought together in battle, traded with one another, took care of the others' young if separated for short periods of time, etcetera. It was a symbiotic relationship; they viewed each other as one and the same. Of course, it isn't like that anymore.

"Today, we know the Dragons stay away from us. Perhaps they are frightened, or maybe arrogant, too stubborn to interact with those who are lesser than them. Nonetheless, their numbers were greatly diminished by the hunts. They withdrew to the harshest places; the locations humans couldn't follow them.

"Before they retreated, they fought. Valiantly, in fact, and no human would ever argue against it. Dragons are enormous, powerful, deadly beasts. They are also proud and refuse to turn away from battle, even if their life will not be spared.

"Many of them died, feeding the villages. The survivors watched with cold eyes, and turned away from the race they once considered friends. The common type, the ones with four legs and massive wings, fled to the Mountains of Desaria. A rarer form, the water Dragons, retreated to the depths of Crystal Lake, and many went to explore the vast unknown that is the sea. The largest Dragons, with only two hind legs and plated backs, flew to the Outlands or to the Northern Islands."

"So, why did that one-" Niyol started, but Chu`si held up a wrinkled hand. He closed his mouth and looked up at her, eagerly waiting for the remainder of the story.

"The man, whom I mentioned earlier, was tired of this bloodshed. He was born only after the bond between humans and Dragons had been severed, but his father often told of times when they were allies. The man wanted things to be the way they had been before, before the humans were driven to hunt and kill those whom they were closest to.

"He had a plan. If he could help the Dragons somehow, they would see that not all humans are bad, that there are some worth befriending. If he could help them, he would also be in a better position to ask a favor of the beasts.

"Because he was born in Enin, the man sought out the Dragons who were nearest to him; the ones hidden away in the Mountains. He knew what a difficult journey laid ahead of him, but he never backed down. He scoured the peaks for nearly a decade before luck found him.

"A mother Dragon lay at the foot of a mountain. The man found her and rushed over to her, quickly deciphering that she was deathly ill. Her breath came in short gasps, and the Dragon's very last words were telling the man where her eggs were, begging him to save them for her, and instructing him where to take them. Her eyes then glazed over, and the Dragon died.

"The man knew not why the Dragon, a now-sworn enemy of humans, entrusted him with the location of her eggs. But he did know that she was desperate enough to ask him for help, so he went to them.

"They were tiny, and he would have missed him if not for the instructions of the mother Dragon. They fit in the palm of his hand, and there were only two. When he held them up to the sunlight, he could see the faint shadow of a baby Dragon inside them. Both eggs were a pastel color, with speckles all over them. One was a gray-blue, the other soft pink.

"He carried them more guardedly than if he was carrying treasure. He followed again her directions to the lair where the Dragons he had sought for so long resided.

"When he arrived, he was greeted with flaming eyes and deafening roars. The Dragons wanted no part in him. They demanded he leave at once, and tell no one of their location or they would find and kill him.

"The man refused. He then presented the eggs to the guard-Dragons, who instantaneously shepherded him inside.

"Inside, the man found a network of tunnels and passageways. The two Dragons ushered him down the largest, and he noted how even they had an easy time passing through it. The tunnel soon opened up to a glorious sight, said to be unfit for human eyes."

I was so wrapped up in the story that I didn't notice myself leaning into Niyol until Chu`si paused for dramatic effect. I hurriedly scooted away from him, instantly feeling the heat rise to my cheeks.

Chu`si smiled and continued.

"Inside, was a cave full of gleaming treasure and massive gemstones of all shapes and colors. They lit up the room like chandeliers; the torches lining the wall cast the colorful light in all directions. Several networks of tunnels also branched out from this grand room, seemingly illuminated by the light reflected in the treasure.

"The Dragons then told him to wait, as they began to ascend to a passageway near the top of the cave. They returned quickly, with a majestic Dragon in tow.

"By now, the man had attracted many curious reptiles. Many hissed or bared fangs at him, while others – especially the young ones – just looked at him with round, curious eyes. He would smile back at them, and they would skitter behind a bigger Dragon's legs, unsure of the intentions of this strange creature before them.

"When the two Dragons from earlier returned, they brought a golden one with them. He was the only Dragon in the cave, from what the man could see, who had a golden, leather hide, one that shimmered like pixie dust in the light of the cave.

"The man then got down on one knee, offered the eggs to the obvious Dragon in charge, and bowed his head so he was looking to the ground. Cautiously, the golden Dragon sniffed the eggs, and the man often told of how the wind blew back his hair and smelled of charred wood.

"The Dragon then gently picked up both eggs, using his front claws. The man was astonished at how similar this Dragon's hands were to his own, and when he looked around, he saw that many of the Dragons resembled humans in some ways. They had hands, and necks and arms, shoulders and hips and eyes and ears. They weren't that different.

"The golden Dragon then told the man that he had done a great deed, and that he may have one request from them.

"The man didn't hesitate. He told them of his wish: to turn his ordinary dagger into one with magic abilities.

"The golden Dragon then nodded, and summoned forth the adults in the cave. The man offered his knife, and the Dragons breathed fire onto it. When the flames subsided, the ordinary iron dagger wasn't that anymore.

"Its hilt was no longer plain, but now was made of pearls and adorned with rubies. The blade had turned black as night, and the point was sharper than the slice of a shooting star through the sky. The sides of the blade were smooth, and despite the Dragonfire previously breathed onto it, it was cool to the touch.

"The Dragons then forced him to go. But before the man could take his last steps out of the cave, the golden Dragon whispered the five legendary words in his ear; 'Go forth, slay the beast.' And with that, the man left.

"He knew what had to be done. After many years of rallying an army, consisting both of humans and some faithful Dragons, he led a battle to the island where Nox made his home. They conquered the demons that guarded Nox, and the man was the one who delivered the final blow."

"Where's the island now?" Niyol asked.

Chu'si shrugged. "Some say it never existed, that it is merely a legend. Others say that once Nox was vanquished, that the island crumbled with his defeat. Some will tell you that it disappeared, simply got off and left, once the army departed from the shores."

"Creepy..." I muttered. Niyol nodded his assent beside me. Chu'si shook her head. "I believe it is just legend. Just like the prophecy."

"What prophecy?"

Niyol raised eyebrows. "What *prophecy?*" He gaped at me. "You can't be serious."

I just stared at him.

Niyol groaned in complete exasperation. "She doesn't even know-"

"Hush!" Chu'si scolded.

Niyol glared at her, and then shook his head.

"Long ago, right after Nox had been vanquished, the man received a prophecy. It was,

A girl of great injustice,
Will seek her dark revenge.
She will confront her destiny,
Resulting in her end.
The Mountains harbor safety
For the girl who may succeed,
For the blade once blessed by Dragons,

45

Will set the strongest free.
Swift death she will receive,
But if duty be done right,
Then she won't be the only one,
Laid to rest that night."

Chu`si stared at me, her gaze sliding over my body like a hunter views its prey. Suddenly, her eyes flashed. She held out her hand slowly, monotonously saying, "Your knife."

I hesitantly drew my knife from its hilt, and placed it in her hands. I wouldn't have; it was my most prized possession, the only thing left of my family. But the look in her eyes told me she needed it, she hungered for it, and I didn't know why.

She gingerly held the blade in her fingers, as if she feared it would turn to dust at her touch. Her eyes absorbed every inch of my knife, drinking in its image. Finally, without taking her gaze off of it, she murmured, "You are alone in this world, are you not?"

I looked at her, puzzled. "No…er…I don't…my family is dead, but I have Goldensun…"

"But obviously, a great wrong was done unto you, or else you would not be here…am I correct?"

"I…I suppose…" What was she getting at?

It happened faster than I thought possible. I hardly had any time to process it before it was over.

Chu`si's skin went from a sun-weathered, wrinkly tan to a deep golden, glossy hide. A tail sprouted from her hindquarters, long as my entire arm, about half as thick, ending in a tuft of long black fur. Her face widened and rose outward, giving her a flat but long muzzle. Tons of whiskers sprouted from the tips of it, all glossy white. Around her head grew long, coarse hairs that surrounded her face and were darker than the rest of her short pelt. Her arms and legs thickened with muscle, and hands and feet were now paws tipped with razor-sharp, jet-black claws.

As I stood gaping at the transformation, I realized those jet black claws still held my knife. Then the beast, or Chu`si I guess, bared its long white fangs and gave a tremendous roar, shaking the ground like an earthquake. Her shoulders sprouted long, large, muscular, golden-feathered wings, each the size of her entire beast-form. She roared again, leaving my ears ringing as she, or it, or whatever, jumped through the roof-opening for spirits and flew away.

I grabbed my bow and ran outside, barely noticing Niyol's flabbergasted expression. Chu`si wasn't that high yet. I took aim and let loose…but I hadn't counted for the wind, and the arrow that was meant for the beast's heart found itself lodged in a feathered wing.

When she roared again, it shook the air, the huts, and the mountains. I even thought I saw the clouds vibrate a bit. My ears were still ringing, and for a moment I could hear nothing at all. Niyol dashed out of the house, and his boots made no sound on the dirt path. The beast's mouth was wide open, but no sound was heard. Goldensun ran up beside me, and her barks were silent.

Then, like a rush of a waterfall, noise and sound returned to my life. The roar was still echoing, and Goldensun's growls were doing my head no good. As I looked up, the beast pulled my arrow out of its wing and flung it away, careful to keep my knife steady in its claws.

Another roar shattered my head. I sank to my knees, clutching my skull, feeling my ribcage rattle like the tip of a rattlesnake's tail.

I watched the beast fly away, desolation and anxiety welling up inside me like the hot tears behind my eyes. It was out of an arrow's range now. It was gone, taking my knife – and my only connection to my family – with it.

I finally returned to my current residence, shoulders slumped and head hanging in defeat. I walked in and glimpsed Niyol lying under his blanket, staring blankly at the roof. I couldn't recall him coming back inside, but he must have when I was hunched on the ground. The shock of his grandmother – his only family – suddenly turning into a ferocious flying cat and stealing a magic knife sure left its mark on him. I knew what he was going through. To have your family whisked away in the blink of an eye just sucked. That much I knew firsthand.

He didn't say anything as I walked in.

I tried to pick up my head and lift my shoulders a little, but if I looked as defeated as I felt, well, there was no faking hope,

I walked into the cooking room and rekindled the fire. Then I grabbed some meat kept in a crude box and drove the roasting-pole through it. I started rotating it slowly over the fire, neither of us willing to touch the soup that Chu`si had prepared before her story. Niyol wasn't going to be much help, so after it cooked and I left it to cool a little, I mixed some fresh berries from the garden out back in a small bowl. As soon as I was done I chopped up the meat with one of Chu`si's old knives.

I carried the meat on a slab of wood and the berries in the bowl out to Niyol. I gently coaxed him to sit up and eat something, but the entire time he said nothing, just stared off and chewed a little.

The sky was now dark and I crawled under my yak-hide. It felt dirty and disgusting, seeing it was once that terrible beast's. Niyol was still gazing at the ceiling, but his eyelids were beginning to droop. He would fall asleep soon enough. I rolled over and tried to do the same.

A shadow cut across the floor of the hut, showing through the open window. It was the shape of a wolf's head, so I waved Goldensun in. She jumped through the window and landed with superb balance on the ground.

She came over to me and we looked at each other for a minute, speaking in a language without words or actions. We never said a word, and yet understood perfectly.

She curled up by my side and was asleep in moments. I didn't sleep at all; I just counted the spirits through the hole in the ceiling.

Chapter 4

And So the Dragon Came

The next few weeks passed without excitement. I tended to the garden, traded for meats, and occasionally went to the Grove at the other end of the village.

The Grove was really just a small group of about one hundred trees loaded with apples, cherries, pears, peaches, apricots, and figs during the harvest season. They were all grown and harvested each year and tended to every day. But I liked to think of it as my own little piece of Dark Forest that sat up here in the Mountain with me.

Whenever I had any free time, I ventured down to the Grove. I brushed aside the weeping willow branches that belonged to the trees surrounding my haven. They were the only trees here that didn't offer some kind of harvest or benefit other than they made the Grove look rather magical.

A little bird chirped in the branches of an apple tree, her calls answered by no one. I recognized her as a sparrow. I listened to her for a little, and then tried mimicking her. She stared down at me from her perch with beady little eyes, obviously not amused or fooled by my attempt to copy her call.

She was very pretty. Usually, the females have very dull plumage, but this one was bright and beautiful. Her eyes were black, but they had a playful, friendly light to them. She regarded me with curiosity, twitching her little brown head back and forth. Her feathers were light brown with black, white and reddish-brown splashes on the wings. She had a white underbelly, chest and chin, and her tail feathers alternated between light brown and black.

"Hey, little sparrow," I said gently.

She cocked her head when I said "sparrow".

"You know you're a sparrow, little bird?"

Again, she cocked her head.

"Do you live here, Sparrow?"

The little bird chirped and fluttered down to a branch closer to me. We stared in silence at one another for a few moments.

"Kohana!"

The silence was broken. Sparrow chirped in alarm and flew off, taking her small amount of trust in me with her.

I ran up the hill as fast as I could. It was Tobie who called me, and she was right on my heels when I buzzed past her. She told me of what had happened so suddenly to Niyol, and she needed me right away.

I exploded into the room to see him staring intently at a wall. He stroked it every couple of seconds, but other than that just remained focused on the wall, as if transfixed by the slab of rock and hardened mud before him.

"Niyol?" I whispered.

He waved me off with his hand. "Shhhh. She is telling me a story."

I looked at Tobie. She bit her lip nervously.

We just stood there, looking baffled at Niyol. At intervals he would smile, or frown, or even laugh. When he turned away, his eyes held more sparkle than I had seen since Chu`si transformed and stole my knife.

"Did you enjoy the story?" he asked us. "She told it brilliantly, as always."

I glanced at Tobie, gave a tiny nod of my head to tell her to do the same, and we both nodded, fake smiles plastered on our faces. Niyol smiled back. "Kohana, come here," he said.

He stood up, grabbing my arm and leading me out of the house. Tobie tried to follow, but he stopped and said, "No. Just Kohana." The way he said it made me smile a little bit, or maybe it was just because this was the first time he had talked in weeks, let alone moved.

He led me down past the stables, the butcher shop, the pig pens, the small place dedicated to what little food would grow in this harsh climate and rocky soil. He led me past all of the houses until we were standing at the very place I had just come from.

"This is the Grove," he said. I didn't want to ruin anything, so I just nodded.

He led me in. I followed dutifully, but already having seen everything in here. What could he want to show me? Maybe just the thought of the Grove itself was supposed to make me happy, which it did anyways. There was no acting while I looked around at the trees, no longer laden with fruit now that winter was on the approach.

Niyol led me past a few rows of fig trees, the pear and apricot trees, and the peach trees. We had reached the opposite end of the willows, and he put a finger over his mouth for silence. I nodded and he pulled back the branches.

A cave stood before me. There was nothing special about it. Granted, it was one that I had never noticed before, but still, just a cave. I looked disappointedly from Niyol to the yawning hole before me, and he grabbed my wrist and literally dragged me inside.

"Niyol..." I started, but I was greeted with a hand over my mouth and another over my eyes. I scrunched my eyebrows together and followed Niyol into the dark. It was odd, the way he seemed to be quite aware of what he was doing, seeing as just minutes ago, he had been stroking a wall and listening to it tell him a story.

We wound our way through tunnel upon tunnel, and I started to fear I would never come out. I could feel the weight of the Mountain pressing down on me, and it scared me to think what would happen if I moved just one little pebble and sent the entire Mountain crumbling down on both of us.

"Okay...this is the spectacular part right here. This is the surprise."

Niyol's voice shocked me and caused me to jump a little. He removed his hands, allowing some warm light to seep in through my eyelids. This baffled me, seeing as we were still – to my knowledge – underground. "Open your eyes."

I did. When I saw what lay ahead, I forgot about my fear of being squished by the mountain, and my muscles seemed to melt inside me.

He had lit a torch, under means I don't know, and before me was a sparkling cavern of diamonds, rubies, and emeralds. More gems than you could imagine. There were towering spears

51

of rock that rose straight upwards, and most had a downward facing spike to match. They reminded me of daggers, long pointed fangs and teeth. Our shadows danced across the cavern, and a cold wind blew, causing the torchlight to flicker. It made me think of that day when I had just stolen my blue jay arrows, and I was being chased by the Nightshades.

I rubbed my arms against the breeze, and Niyol saw me shiver. "Kohana? Are you okay?"

I nodded and said, "Just a little cold." Then I turned my attention back to the scenery and tried to take in the beauty of the cave. But it was hard to do when there were two beautiful sea-green gems staring right back at me. I glanced at my friend, suddenly feeling a spark that was much more than friendship. The twinkling, friendly light had gone from his eyes and face, to be replaced by a look of seriousness. His eyes held an apprehensive, cautious, nervous, excited look to them.

I knew what was coming, even before he leaned in. But I just couldn't kiss him. I still loved Tse, I still wanted *him* back.

Didn't I?

I turned away, and ran stumbled through the twists and turns in utter blackness, running into walls countless times, until I reached the surface, hoping to leave that memory deep underground with the rock and gems already there.

Niyol and I didn't speak. As the days had passed, he began to return to normal, leaving the emotionally scarring transformation of his beloved grandmother behind him. He was doing things on his own now, too: cooking, cleaning, tending to the garden, feeding the farm animals, trading for meat. He was almost normal, but there was an awkward silence between us that wouldn't go away. It would be for one reason only; because of what happened down in the caves. We didn't speak of it, didn't mention it, but still the silence was there. Still the tension hung like a cloud, never leaving, always hovering just between us.

So I spent a lot of time down in the Grove, fingering my bow. I needed new arrows, but I hadn't made my own in a very long time. I could hardly remember where to start. Fletching first? Hunt down a bird and get the feathers before crafting the arrows?

Or do I fit them to my bow first, and then get the fletching? That sounded right. I groaned in frustration; it wasn't meant to be something so easily forgotten.

I stood up and instinctively put my hand on my hip where my knife usually lies. Even after weeks of it being gone, I still couldn't get used to the fact that it was just that: gone.

I was walking away from the tree when I heard a familiar chirping sound. I looked up to see Sparrow alighted on a branch nearby. "Hey, Sparrow," I said. By now, in the time that had passed since the day I went to the cave to now, Sparrow had completely learned her name. I talked to her almost every day, and she was almost as regular a friend to me as Goldensun was. But we just relaxed in each others' company. That was good, though. She would sing her little sparrow songs and I would sing the only song I learned as a child.

When the wind whispers
And the shadows fall
When the sun rises
And the robins call

I will be there
To hold your hand
I will be there
To help you stand.

When the wind dies
And the night returns
When the sun sets
And for songs we yearn

I will be there
To hold your hand
I will be there
To help you stand

No matter what

And through it all
I will catch you
If you fall"

When my father taught it to me, he didn't really explain what it meant. I didn't know and I didn't need to. I liked the song, so I sang it nearly every day. I still didn't know its meaning. But ever since I became Outcast, I found myself singing it in the quiet moments.

I sighed and saw Sparrow looking down at me. Her eyes practically begged me to sing more. "That's all I know, Sparrow," I told her. She sighed and flew away, off to complete some sort of sparrow mission I couldn't take part in.

I stood up, the last line of the song echoing in my head. I wiped away a small tear from my eye and marched back up to the hut, determined to tell Niyol what I decided to do.

Let's just say things didn't go quite as I had planned. Not that this was a new thing for me, but I still didn't like it when it happened.

For one, Niyol wasn't even home. Second, my dear Dragon friend decided to pay me another visit.

"I wish to speak to the leader of this township," he boomed. I and walked outside, interested in what was going to happen.

A small crowd was beginning to gather around Hinto, but everyone was at least far enough away that he couldn't bat at them with a clawed hand. As if that distance would protect them from his mighty tail or the flames he could belch.

He bellowed again, "Who runs this village?"

A man with slightly grayed hair stepped forward. "O Wise Dragon, we have no leader of this town. In times of peril, we elect one, but rarely is that the case."

Hinto narrowed his eyes, staring at the man as if he were stupid. "Who was the last person to take charge." The Dragon didn't ask; he stated, like a challenge, spitting each word as if they tasted foul upon his lips.

The man arched his eyebrows. "That would be me."

Hinto rolled his eyes and snorted. Sparks flew from his nostrils. "Humans..." he grumbled. He shook his head and stared again at the man. "Then it is imperative that you make a decision."

"Regarding what?"

"Regarding the fate of High Point. If you do not exile Kohana Silvermist, I will personally burn every last home and building to the *ground.*"

I watched slowly as all eyes turned to me. I'd seen the man with the graying hair before, yet I never knew his name. He was kind and gentle, with one son and a wife that had died long ago. In that moment, I found it strange, how easily my life depended on a decision of a man who I hardly knew.

He blinked at me, and turned back to the Dragon. "I have no reason to cast her out. She has done nothing wrong."

Hinto laughed. "How coincidental, then, that just after this girl comes to visit, strange things start happening. You're visited by a Dragon, attacked by Mountain lions with a strange message, your mage turns into a demonic beast and flies away, and her grandson starts hallucinating. How peculiar, that none of you know a thing about this girl's past, yet you welcome her so warmly into your arms."

I heard a voice start shouting, but I didn't realize it was mine. "What are you *doing?*" it cried.

Then, a soft one behind me. "Kohana, what is he talking about?"

Hinto switched his gaze from me to Niyol, who put a protective hand on my shoulder. It was the first time he'd touched me since the caves.

"This girl is already Outcast. She doesn't belong here."

The elderly man's gaze hardened. "She never told us that."

I felt Niyol's hand vanish. There it was, all out on the table, for the whole world to know. Outcast.

"If you don't believe me, look at her wrist. The mark stains her skin with its permanence."

In disbelief, Niyol marched around in front of me and yanked my sleeve to my elbow. There it was, like it had been for the last three years, the fork with the dots, and the star on the bone.

It was pink and elevated from my skin; a miniscule range of mountains.

His green eyes stared blankly at my wrist. He was dumbstruck.

"See?" Hinto bellowed. "She's lied to all of you!"

The man closed his eyes, and when he opened them again, they were apologetic. "Then it is done. Kohana, you have until nightfall to leave."

My heart cried out. The law stated that if I were caught in any town, any civilization, anyone there had every right to kill me, because I was Outcast. I knew he was kind to allow me to leave, but these people that I had begun to trust were still throwing me out.

I tried to harden my heart. What did I expect? Did I really think they were going to fight for me, slay the Dragon, and let me live happily ever after with them? *You're foolish,* I thought harshly to myself. *Stupid.*

*Kohana…*Goldensun's voice echoed in my head, and I almost forgot she was there. *You know I'll stay by your side.*

I didn't respond. I watched with tears burning the backs of my eyes as Hinto growled, "At nightfall, I will be back. I will set fire to this place if you are still here."

He began to spread his wings, but paused, looking at Niyol. When he spoke, we all knew who it was directed at. "If you choose to follow her, you too will be considered an Outcast, even if you are not branded as one."

With that, the Dragon pounded the air with three flaps of his giant wings, and was soaring over the peaks.

By dusk, I was long gone. Granite had showed up with another wolf, a female that was dark brown with a white star on her forehead to take myself, Goldensun and Niyol, who much to my delight, had decided to tag along. He said there was nothing left for him here, meaning there was no reason for him not to follow me.

Granite and the female wolf, who introduced herself as Shayde, ran tirelessly through the night, only to make sure Niyol, Goldensun and I made it out safely. I wasn't aware of Granite ever stopping to carry Goldensun in his mouth, but when I awoke he was holding her by the scruff, like a mother carries her pups.

They ran faster than Granite had on the way up, but that could have been the downhill factor adding to their speed.

As we neared the final stretch of land, I could see the faint sandy colors of the dusty area before the Mountains. I could smell the dry, warm air wafting up and I glanced behind me for my last look at what had been my home for the past few weeks.

It was then I realized that I hadn't even said goodbye to Sparrow. The poor little bird was probably looking for me, wondering why I wasn't there the rest of yesterday or any time today. The dawn sun beat down on Granite and Shayde's pelts as they slowed down on the desert-like area.

"We can go no farther," Shayde said. Her voice was deep and gave her a somewhat powerful stature, but it was filled with sorrow and affection. "May the Good run with you and the Bad stay forever away." She spun around and walked up towards the Mountains again, turning back for Granite.

He set down Goldensun and pressed his cold, wet nose to my face. "Good luck, Kohana. Your destiny has only begun." He then trotted up to where Shayde was waiting, scarlet eyes blinking, and they both traveled up the path again, practically disappearing from sight.

"Well, I guess we are on our own again..." I said, looking at Niyol. He hadn't said anything on the journey, which could have been good or bad. But my words cut through the silent afternoon like a finely sharpened blade through butter. Niyol said nothing.

"Come on. We need to get to Dark Forest soon. Goldensun's pack is there, and that is where we can hide easily. There's lots of good cover."

Niyol nodded and we set off. My pack felt heavy on my back, and soon I was sweating through my thick Mountain clothing. Niyol, too, was looking a little moist under the afternoon sun. Goldensun's tongue lolled out and her panting was the only noise to be heard.

Soon we reached the grasslands of the Plains and the heat was somewhat less intense. The grass was cool to the touch, and for a moment I stopped and chased Goldensun through the waving blades. But I soon lost sight of her, because her pelt and the grass were the same shade of perfect gold. I was walking back to Niyol when she pounced on me, flattening me to the ground. We wrestled for a little and then set off again.

The thundering of hooves is what I felt first; the beating of them is what I heard first. And shortly after, I saw the massive cloud of dust rising ahead, accompanied by a mound of brown bodies. Buffalo.

Something had to have been chasing them; they were usually docile if left alone.

"Run!" I yelled, pulling Niyol away from the herd fast approaching. Goldensun disappeared into the grass, undoubtedly allowing instinct to take over. We dashed away as fast as physically possible and only just made it.

At first, I didn't see anything out of the ordinary amongst the pounding hooves and snorts of the beasts. But a flash of purple caught my eye, and then it was gone. I stood up from where I had dove into the grass, and Niyol grabbed my shoulder. "Get down!" he hissed, but I brushed his hand away. This time, I watched with the eye of a huntress, knowing I would see more if I thought of it that way.

Another dart of purple appeared, accompanied by a face that was there and gone too quick for me to absorb. Another face, this one rounder, appeared and vanished as well.

A cry went out and the purple appeared again. Now I saw it was a girl, about sixteen, wearing a violet robe. She had a staff that was made with bark died a dark violet, clawed fingers pointed upward at the top, holding a beautiful white orb. Inside were misty swirls of light blue, teal, lavender, and pale green. It was identical to the staff from my vision, the one carried by the snowy owl.

The girl, whom I could only glimpse through a tangle of buffalo legs, was tall and had long blond hair that flowed down her back. Her eyes were scrunched up in pain, but in a flash the other girl was there. I didn't catch what her face looked like, but she wore a huntress outfit.

Without thinking, I dove into the fray. The sorceress was clutching her leg and trying to stand, but the staff had been kicked aside. I saw her yell something at the other girl, who rushed in to get it. It was a full-on stampede, and they were worried about a *staff?*

I barked, short and fast, commanding Goldensun to come and help. A blonde blur exploded from the grass, leaping onto a nearby buffalo. My pack-sister rode it for a few yards then jumped off onto the field.

Herd them! I told her. She nodded and started to push them away from the girls by snapping her jaws at their ankles. Many females with calves tried to kick back, but Goldensun was too quick and was already at the next one.

Eventually, the herd moved on. Goldensun came back, panting, but a big smile was plastered upon her face. I dashed up to the girls, and the huntress drew a sword and pointed it at me quicker than I could have imagined.

She looked to be about sixteen. Her face was rounder than the other girl's, with freckles and striking sapphire eyes. They had small green flecks in them, and were hardened with mistrust. Her sword was pointed right at my heart. I put my hands up in a submissive gesture.

"I'm here to help," I said. Slowly, the girl lowered her blade.

"I'm Tokala. This is Fae," she said, motioning to the sorceress on the ground.

"I can introduce myself, Tokala," Fae said jokingly but with a hint of pain in her voice. Tokala looked back at Fae and rolled her eyes. I could sense a strong bond between the two, even though on the outside they clearly pretended to dislike one another.

Fae stood up with the help of her staff and limped over. "Are you okay?" I asked. She shrugged.

"I'll be fine, as soon as I get back and whip up a potion. We were foolish to chase a whole herd of them down anyways." Fae ended her statement with a short chuckle. She looked around, and then added, "Where could that owl be now? He is supposed to be looking out for me." As she spoke a snowy owl perched on Fae's swirly orb. "Ah, there you are. I was starting to worry."

The owl from my vision. He had carried Fae's staff over Golden Plains, and I had heard a girl laughing. Which one of these two was it? Neither of them was the girl who appeared later, when I was...dead.

Tokala looked at Fae and giggled. "How does he do that? Right on cue, as usual Achak." The owl, Achak, I presumed, hooted and rubbed his head on Fae's cheek.

"Well, come on now. Don't want to be out after sunset. And we have a long way to go," Fae told us.

"Yeah, and at the rate she's walking, we will just make it by nightfall tomorrow," Tokala joked.

Fae ignored the comment, and looked back at me. "I presume you and your friends will be joining us?"

Niyol had gotten up and come to stand next to me. After brisk introductions, Tokala nodded skeptically. "They seem alright, don't you think?"

Fae shrugged. "I suppose. You can't always trust strangers on the Plains, but what would we be to turn them away?" she said.

"Sane?" Tokala offered.

Disregarding the statement, Fae returned her gaze to Niyol, Goldensun and I, and said with a smile, "Come on, we're burning daylight."

Fae, as it turned out, was both a sorceress and a healer. We sat and talked around a fire while Achak preened his snowy feathers and Tokala (who was also a blacksmith) honed a stunning silver sword she had made in her forge out back.

"So, where do you come from? You don't look like much of a Plains nomad to me. Besides, I haven't seen you around, or your furry friend for that matter," Fae said, her eyes twinkling with curiosity. They were a lavender color, which was strange and beautiful at the same time. I hadn't seen anyone with purple eyes before.

I glanced at Niyol, who shook his head the tiniest bit. I took a deep breath, closed my eyes, and told her what I could without directly revealing my secret. Not after what had happened only yesterday.

"I'm, Kohana...I'm from Dark Forest..." I started.

"Well? What are some details? Did you live in Enin? That's pretty much the only big place I know of. The rest are just small villages and towns."

I took a nervous gulp. "Yes...but I don't live there anymore."

Fae's eyes went wide. "Wait...Kohana? From Enin? You're the Outcast...aren't you? The one who killed the royal family with nightshade in their wine..."

I stood up angrily, cutting her off. "I didn't do that! I loved my family very much; I would have never killed them!"

As quickly as it sparked, the flame I felt inside me went out like a candle in a windstorm. I realized how pathetic I had to have sounded to someone who thought she knew more about me than I did. I sat down and stared at my palms that were open on my lap.

Goldensun sat up, placing herself between Fae and I. it was a small gesture that held much more meaning than it seemed.

Fae stood up and grabbed her staff, causing Achak to nearly lose his balance. He hooted angrily, but Fae shushed him.

Fae shoved Achak off his perch and started muttering things and waving her hand around the orb on the top.

Goldensun drew up her lip protectively; she would fight to defend me if Fae decided to try anything rash.

The orb started changing colors so now it was red, orange, yellow and white swirls. Fae closed her eyes and made a rising motion with her hand, and the orb hovered out of the violet fingers of the staff. Fae let go of the purple wood, and it fell to the ground with a hollow clatter. I watched it for a moment, fearing to look up at her.

Now, levitating between her long fingers was the orb, all swirly with the warm mist.

"Come," she whispered. I stood up without really registering I had. I walked to the orb, sidestepping around Goldensun, and placed my hand on it of my own accord.

"Did you kill your family?" hissed Fae in a voice that for sure didn't belong to her.

"No," I said, quietly.

The mist inside remained red.

Fae nodded and opened her eyes. Her pupils ate up almost all of her irises, and she said, "Staff."

I removed my hand as the staff rose to hover just below the orb, which dropped down into the open fingers of the elder bark. The branch's claws closed around the misty ball as soon as the weight was added, and the fog inside returned to its normal blues, greens and purples.

"She speaks the truth," Fae said, more to the empty air than to me. "She is innocent."

Niyol abruptly stood up. "I have to go. Hunting." And he left.

I stood in the doorway looking after him as he ran into the trees.

Fae and Tokala's forge rested at the very border, and smoke was almost always spiraling out from the crafting-fire. It was a cottage made of mostly stone; very non-flammable.

"What's up with him?" Fae asked. "Did I say something wrong?"

I shrugged. With him, it was hard to tell.

"Speaking of people going off to be alone," Fae grumbled to herself. "Where is Silver? I haven't seen her since we left to hunt."

"Who's Silver?" I asked.

"My sister. She is a huntress like Tokala. She is only a year younger than me."

I nodded. "What's she like?"

Fae laughed as Tokala strolled in from outside, wiping sweat off her brow. "Silver?" she asked. Fae nodded with a smile. Tokala's lips began to curl up in a slight grin, but she walked into the next room before I could see it get any bigger.

Fae walked over to a big cauldron and started adding things to it. She saw the look on my face and said, "It's a potion. No doubt Silver is going to need one when she comes back...most reckless huntress in all of Desaria, if you ask me."

I sat down on the floor next to Goldensun, abandoning my chair and running my fingers through her soft fur. She yawned, and lay back down, falling asleep in moments.

❧•❧

I don't remember dozing off, but the next thing I knew, a girl's face was right in front of mine.

The first thing I saw was her chocolate-brown eyes. I blinked wearily, rubbing my own, and rested my gaze back on her face, which had now retreated enough to let me breathe.

"Who is she?" the girl asked.

Fae was nodding off in a nearby chair, and I couldn't see Tokala.

"I'm Kohana," I said with a sleepy voice. My eyelids felt heavy and I just wanted to return to slumber.

The girl smiled. "I'm Silver." Just then a beautiful blue jay with silver wings flew through the doorway and perched on Silver's shoulders. "Oh, and this is Doli, she is my companion."

I started, suddenly very awake. This was the girl from my vision; the one with the blue jay.

Fae opened one eye and smiled. "Yeah, and without her you would be dead many, many times over!"

Silver shot her a look that read, *oh be quiet!* She then smiled back to me.

"Who is this?" Silver asked, pointing to Goldensun.

Goldensun looked at me. *Go ahead...* then she closed her eyes and went back to napping.

"This is *my* companion, Goldensun. She comes from Dark Forest, and we have known each other...well basically her whole life."

Silver nodded. She looked out the window where the dawn light was streaming in. Her hair was long and dark, darker than her eyes, and hung in a tangle down her back.

She smiled, and then with a voice loaded with excitement, said, "Can I go out again now, Fae?"

Fae yawned in her chair and nodded. Shortly after, I heard her snoring. Still no Tokala...or Achak for that matter.

"Want to come? We can hunt the buffalo! I was driving them back near here last night, that's what kept me out late," she added in a whisper. "So you want to come?"

I nodded, trying to hide my growing dread.

Come on, Goldensun! She groaned sleepily and got to her lead-heavy paws.

Hunting, right? She asked.

Yep.

She sighed and shook her fur, then smiled. *When does that girl sleep? She came back not four hours ago.*

I shrugged. *I know just as much as you.*

So, nothing.

Not about Silver. I tried to hide my next thought from Goldensun, putting a mental wall between the two of us. In actuality, I did know more. I knew Silver was the girl I'd seen from Chu`si's vision.

Goldensun yawned. *Well let's go then.*

We were all crouched in the golden grass, the herd only a few leaps ahead. Goldensun was right next to me, Silver hidden on the other side. We'd gotten this group of about twenty to thirty buffalo to break off from the whole herd, which had to be hundreds.

I waited for Silver's signal. She was scanning for a weak, old or sick one. No calves in this group. Doli was flying low over the herd, an invisible threat, sending little calls out to her companion. I couldn't understand her, but I knew she was giving Silver information about the buffalo we couldn't see well.

Get ready, Goldensun said. I nodded.

Silver motioned to get my attention, pointing to a cow with a broken horn and a twisted hoof. Doli was perched on her head, but the old beast didn't seem to mind. She just limped along, chewing the golden grass.

I nodded, keeping the old buffalo in sight.

She's right there. The one Doli is on, I told Goldensun. She smiled in that wolfish way of hers, and crept closer to the cow, a golden shadow in the golden grasses.

Silver gave the signal to engage the hunt. She stalked forward on the balls of her feet, bow ready. She got to the edge of the group when they smelled her and panicked. The others ushered the hurt female to the center of the group and pounded away.

A flash of gold fur flew out of the grass, landing on the back of a buffalo close to the target. She leapt from back to back until she was perched on the shoulders and neck of our prey.

Doli chirped a few times and glided off towards Silver, already in motion. I notched my bow and ran after the herd, quickly overtaking my new friend and her bird.

Goldensun was smart. The others saw their comrade carrying a wolf and dispersed. They wanted to protect the injured, but not as much as they themselves wanted to live.

Silver and I dodged hooves, horns, and heads that were almost half the size of my entire body. I had Silver's arrows in my quiver, considering I hadn't made any new ones yet.

The injured female thundered ahead of us. The rest of the group had split off from her, but she was fast, despite the twisted hoof.

I decided now would be a good time to use my speed advantage. I raced farther ahead of Silver and Doli, fast as the wind, feet barely touching the ground. I felt strong, swift, invincible. I always felt this way when I ran. I could only imagine how a faster creature would feel. I closed the distance between the cow and myself in a matter of heart beats. Soon I was dashing alongside her, and she was too scared to do anything but keep running. She didn't veer away, didn't try to trample me. Just ran.

Goldensun was trying to bite into the thick hide of her neck, but it did very little. She couldn't sink her teeth in very well, seeing as she was already struggling to stay atop the beast's back. Her claws dug into the buffalo's shoulders, drawing tiny trickles of blood from them.

I notched my arrow. I slowed down to get a better aim; I was going to shoot the arrow through her heart from behind the shoulder blade. It was a simple, effective way to end their lives without causing pain.

I let the arrow loose. It flew straight and true, piercing the cow's heart. She bellowed and fell, not to stand again. Goldensun jumped off just in time to avoid being crushed by the buffalo's mass.

Nice shot, she said.

Nice moves, I replied.

Silver came up to us, panting heavily. Sweat dripped down her forehead and neck, and her hair was beginning to plaster to her face. "How...?"

I grinned. "Lots and lots of practice."

She crouched down next to me and we began to skin the beast and collect the meat, organs, etc. By sunset, we were barely halfway done. We took the best of it and carried it back to the forge. "Hopefully a good portion will still be there tomorrow and we can finish," I said. Silver shrugged.

"Doubt it. The coyotes will most likely get there tonight. Plus, there will be ravens, vultures, and so on. The meat won't be there. The bones will be, though. I've crafted a handful of decent bows from the ribs and of bigger prey. And if you cut them up just right you can make a skeleton for a new quiver. No pun intended," she said. Silver smiled at her own silly little joke. Then her face grew serious. "So...you're the Outcast, aren't you?"

I gulped nervously. "Yeah."

"Fae told me. She told me not to think of you differently because of it, that you really didn't kill your family. But, the thing is, I can't *not* think of you like that. It is part of who you are now, the whole Outcast thing. You can run faster, think quicker, hunt smarter, all because you were Outcast. Your abilities, your strengths and weaknesses, your willingness, your determination: all of it came from that one event. One thing changed your life, and made you a better, stronger person. And while you may not have killed your family, it is still something you can't change. It's who you *are*."

I looked at my new friend, completely dumbstruck. I hadn't ever thought of being Outcast like that. It had always been negative, but she just showed me that there were some beneficial things to it. True, I was faster. Yes, I could think on the fly, and sure it made me stronger. Anything I could do that increased my time among the living was quickly learned, mastered, and became my ally. She was right. I wasn't just *an* Outcast. The Outcast...it was *me*.

"Don't get me wrong, Kohana. I think it's terrible you were framed for the murder of your family. But maybe, just maybe, being Outcast was almost a good thing?" Silver said. I nodded absentmindedly. "In fact, I kind of envy you. Truthfully, that speed you just demonstrated was faster than anything on four legs. You have to be carrying more than twice the amount of meat

I am. And you are so smart. I wouldn't have ever thought to fall behind the buffalo so I could get a clearer shot at her heart. I mean…wow."

I smiled. Somebody was jealous of me. Not that that was necessarily something to be proud of, but I was, I had, something somebody else wanted. That had never happened before.

We continued the rest of the walk in silence. It suddenly occurred to me that I *was* carrying more than her. I realized I *had* run faster than normal, just speeding along faster than a *buffalo!* I *had* thought fast on my feet, quick as a wolf's mind in the middle of a hunt with the pack.

When we returned, Niyol was standing next to Tokala, watching her craft the sword. I couldn't believe she was still making the same one, but there it was, just in front of me.

Niyol looked up as we walked in, but said nothing. Tokala never once lifted her gaze from the sword. Fae smiled from the cauldron.

"How was the hunt?" she asked, that grin still on her face.

Goldensun yawned next to me and plopped down, Doli glided up to a small perch built into the ceiling, and Silver and I both said, "Good" at the exact same time.

I looked up to see Doli almost asleep on her perch already. Next to hers was another, larger one I assumed was for Achak. Goldensun's emerald eyes were only tiny slits as she fought the sleep threatening to overcome her.

We all talked around a warm fire that night. We roasted the meat Silver and I had brought home, ate some berries from a garden out back and enjoyed some home-made wine, a treat I hadn't had in a long time. We laughed and told stories and had a good time. Goldensun lay under the table, Doli perched on Silver's shoulder, and Achak hooted a little song from his place on Fae's staff. Later in the evening we sang some common Desaria songs and drank more wine.

In all, it was a smashing night, probably the best I had enjoyed since I became Outcast two years ago.

Around midnight, we went to bed. Fae showed me where I was going to sleep; the same room as Silver. That made me happy, for she and I were already very close. Almost like sisters. Niyol went to sleep in an extra room, and Fae and Tokala took their normal room. All of the rooms were underground; it was much cooler down there on summer nights.

Silver and I gossiped most of the night. Boys we had crushes on growing up, what we wanted to do with our futures, girly stuff like that. Actually, I enjoyed it. I finally understood what it was like to be a normal, teenage girl doing normal teenage things.

I was home.

Chapter 5

From Past to Present

I woke to the sound of muffled voices. Silver was still asleep, so I crept out of my bed and peered out to watch and listen.

"We can't stay much longer, Fae," Niyol said, "We have to keep moving. Kohana has some sort of destiny, and we have to…retrieve something. We have to get it soon or else…well it won't be very pretty."

Fae nodded. "I understand you must leave. I sensed it as soon as you came. At least stay until tomorrow. Rest, eat, prepare for the journey."

"Thank you, Fae."

I pulled away to see Silver staring at me from the bed, looking extremely upset. "You're leaving, aren't you?"

I nodded sadly. But the light in her eyes shocked me.

"Can I come?" she asked excitedly. It was more of a demand than an actual question.

"Um, I, uh…" I stammered. "Ask Fae and Tokala. See what they say. I'll talk to Niyol."

She squealed happily. It made me question her actual age. Could she be really fifteen?

The day was slow. We all stayed inside, resting and eating and drinking more sweet wine. We told more stories of great and heroic adventures, and I was surprised at how good it felt for somebody to actually know me, the real me. Sure, Tokala and Fae had heard my story told by others, but Silver actually knew me, understood me, she was already almost as close to me as Goldensun.

Evening came. Silver got time alone with Fae and asked her if she could come with us, and I asked Niyol. Niyol was hesitant, but decided it would be for the better if she did tag along. Another person to help us hunt, build shelter, and scout for food. She would be a worthy ally.

Somewhat surprisingly, Fae jumped right on it. She couldn't have been more eager for her little sister to get a taste of the world. Fae was almost more excited than Silver.

I helped Silver pack her things that night. Goldensun lay down on my bed, advising me on what she should and shouldn't bring.

The nights are cold down here in winter. Have her bring thick clothing.

The prey has softer hides in Dark Forest. A knife would be advisable, and a bow and arrow would be useful, too.

Don't let her forget the feather. It will keep her connected to her family here, and if she ever misses them, she will have that.

Silver wore a necklace with three things on it; a silver blue jay feather that Doli shed a long time ago, a spotted white feather from Achak, and a little metal talisman of a fox, painted white to represent Tokala's spirit animal. Silver told me that whenever she was away from home, she touched the necklace and instantly felt connected to them again. I promised Goldensun I wouldn't let her forget it.

By early night, when all the color had finally drained from the sky, we were ready to go. We slept soundly, though excited for the adventure ahead.

The next morning was cold and foggy. A bad day to start a journey, but it marked the beginning of autumn. The warm days were leaving us, and the colder, harsher ones were arriving. Tokala and Fae offered for us to stay with them until spring, but Niyol hastily said "No! We have to get moving!"

We left with our new sacks filled with our belongings, and Tokala gave me her sword she had been working on. The handle was designed with small swirls, stars, and at the very base was a small engraving of a fox. "You take it," she had said, "You can't live off of arrows all the time."

We traveled through the day, the clouds never lifting. A light drizzle fell, and Doli proceeded to take this as a wonderful opportunity to sleep inside Silver's sack. Goldensun walked faithfully beside me, fur dripping and ears down. Her wet fur made her look skinnier, almost unhealthy. It scared me a little.

Niyol led us, although I'm sure he wasn't the best choice of guide. He had never set foot in Dark Forest before, while I used to live here and even Silver hunted these woods occasionally.

"Niyol, why the rush? Do you even know where you're going?" I asked.

He glared at me over the shoulder. "Yes. I know where I'm going." Then, his eyes sparked, his brow furrowed, and he stopped, turning around completely so he could stare at me better. "How long has that knife been in your family?"

I squinted even more. "What?"

"How long?"

I thought back to all the times my father talked about that knife. Only once did he mention its importance, and that was when he gave it to me.

A thought burrowed itself deep into my brain as realization dawned on me. "I don't know…for generations, as long as anyone can remember."

Niyol slapped his hand to his forehead. "Stupid!" he said to himself. "Why didn't I understand sooner?" He then fixed his sea-green eyes onto mine, so intensely that it took all my willpower not to look away. "Kohana, what if that knife from the story is *your knife*. Your knife is magical, therefore it had to have been that one to use to raise Tatsuo!"

I raised my eyebrows. The puzzlement had to have been plain on my face, for Niyol went on to explain. "Do you remember when Chu`si stole your knife?"

"Of course. What does that have anything to do with this?"

"Well then allow me to enlighten you. I pieced it all together while you were out talking to birds, back in High Point. There's a certain event that can do certain, horrible things. It's called the Red Moon. Next moon is the Red Moon, which only comes once every couple hundred years. I'm going to guess you have no idea what your knife can do on the Red Moon?"

I shook my head. "Of course I don't." I narrowed my eyes, snapping, "But I bet you're going to enlighten me."

He ignored my rude, uncalled for comment. "On the night of the Red Moon, the possessor of a certain, magic knife – the one

that Chu`si told us about – has the ability to summon a being –
named Tatsuo – up from the underworld. He *created* all Dragons,
and by summoning him, he *will* avenge his banishment, and
recapture all his Dragons. But they can't just have the knife. No,
they must be in the place called 'Galdur Fjall' or 'Magic
Mountain'. There is a whole ritual that, if done correctly at Galdur
Fjall, Tatsuo will rise, and he can possess the Dragons' powers.
And the only way to fix it is to wait until the next Red Moon
arrives, which would, by then, possibly become the downfall of
the entire world. This cannot happen. If your knife is the one from
the story, and Chu`si has it now, I think she plans to use it to raise
Tatsuo."

Silver looked bewildered. She just stared between the two
of us, dripping in the rain, like we had both just sprouted purple
wings and ate the branches off the nearest trees.

"What in the name of all good wine are you two *talking*
about?!" she yelled. Her hair swung when she stomped about,
plastering itself to her face.

I put my hand on her shoulder to comfort her.

"Chu`si is a demon, who disguised herself as my
grandmother for…well for my entire life. She probably serves a
master, which we all should know is bad news," Niyol said
calmly, like he would say "it's raining" or "that's a tree".

"How do you know she's a demon?" I asked.

"Ancient stories have been passed down in my old village,
stories of a demon with wings of a golden eagle and body of a
lion. You were there when she stole your knife. You saw her.
Definitely the demon, if you ask me."

I nodded. Silver still looked totally lost. "What does this
have to do with us?" she asked.

Quickly, I told her my story. Starting when I arrived at
High Point and ending when Chu`si stole my knife.

Silver nodded like she was starting to get it. Niyol turned
back around and led us through the rain. We had to get to Galdur
Fjall soon, unless we wanted Chu`si's master controlling all of
Dragon-kind.

"Wait!" I said. Niyol turned so half of his face was
towards me. He glared at me from those aquamarine eyes, which

were as hard as stone. It took all my willpower not to just close my mouth or mumble 'never mind'.

"Where is Galdur Fjall? I haven't ever even heard of it. And it doesn't exactly sound like a name of a place in Desaria, and I would know. Or even Idess, for that matter!" I stopped talking, his eyes freezing the words as they formed in my throat.

He nodded. "You're right. It is not in Desaria. Nor is it in Idess. It is in the Outlands beyond Aliyr."

"But that's on the complete *other* side of Calleo! We are only a two and a half week journey from the Idess border if we turned around and went back…it will take forever to get to the other side!" I realized I sounded like a whining child, but I had a valid point. How were we supposed to get to the other side of Desaria, let alone Aliyr, in a month? There was month until the Red Moon. That was *not* enough time to cross three-fourths of Calleo.

The kingdoms were somewhat easy to learn. Calleo is the combined three kingdoms, plus the Outlands. Idess was west of Desaria, and was a rather small kingdom. Desaria was by far the largest, and we were smack dab in the middle of Calleo. To the east was Aliyr, which was slightly larger than Idess. The very eastern part of Calleo was called 'the Outlands'. A dry, desolate area, they were where people were sent long ago if they broke laws.

When I was just a little girl, Father always told me stories of the people that lived in the Outlands. He said they were wild savages that killed each other and ate the meat of their fallen comrades. They were people who didn't know how to farm and were never in groups for very long. The animals were either too stringy to eat, or they were big enough to eat you. He told me of great cats – larger than the Tall Wolves – that screeched at night, and were said to have golden pelts dappled with black spots, or orange hides with black lightning strikes. The top predator was the Night Cat; larger than any of the other felines, and jet black. It would kill silently, in the pure darkness of the new moon, and was said to have piercing red eyes.

At first, I didn't understand what was so bad about the Outlands. Father had started with what they looked like; long, rolling green grasses and tall, towering trees with boughs spread wide like open arms. But then he told me of the poor soil beyond the tree line, where only the scraggly, tiny bushes could grow. No crops would feed the Outlanders, so there was nothing but meat in their diet. The fruit on the trees were poisonous, and if you touched the bark of one, you would be stabbed by a thousand tiny barbs embedded as self-defense for the tree. The Outlands was no place I wanted to visit anytime soon.

I snapped back into the present when Silver started talking.

"Guys, calm down. We can do this. A whole moon is a long time. We have roughly thirty days until the Red Moon, give or take, and all we have to do is find a decent map to Galdur Fjall, get there, and not die in the Outlands. Not too bad, right? Surely Kohana, you've been in far more grim situations? We can do this! Come on!"

Her words made a good point. I had outrun, out-climbed, outsmarted and outshot anyone who ever tried to pursue me. I had been in far worse circumstances. This was cakewalk. Right?

But the Outlands still sent shivers down my spine. I had a feeling it wasn't just from Father's stories, either. Something deep in my gut told me this was a bad idea, that we should *not* be going to Galdur Fjall. That maybe Chu`si's master taking over all of the Dragons was actually alright, if we could avoid that place.

An image of the mountaintop from my vision flashed through my mind. *"She will confront her destiny, resulting in her end"* No. Galdur Fjall. It had to be the mountaintop I saw in my dream. That was where I was going to die. I couldn't...

No, I chided myself, *Fear shouldn't stop you; you don't even know if that's right. But no matter what, this must be done. For someone other than yourself; do it for the world that will become better without Tatsuo to ruin it.*

Niyol nodded, his face grim, and turned back to the path ahead. He didn't wait to see if we were going to follow, but we did.

We trudged on through the drizzle, which soon turned to rain. Mud sucked at our boots, dripped down my bow and filled my empty quiver, and soaked the hilt to my new sword.

Goldensun's pelt was now soaking wet and covered in mud, making for a very interesting fashion statement of spiky wolf fur. I couldn't tell if her jade eyes were sparkling with excitement, or fear, or both.

How are you? I asked her.

She shrugged and plodded on. *Alright, but if I fall in one more puddle, or trip over one more root, I'm going back to rest by the fire with Fae and Tokala.* She smiled, but seeing the look on my face added, *kidding.*

She heard it first.

My ears were great, but they were no match for a wolf's. Goldensun turned to me with a wide wolf smile, and now I knew her eyes twinkled in excitement. *Darkshadow and the pack!* She was so happy she wasn't just thinking, she was barking her exhilaration to the others, too. She ran ahead a few steps, turned back to me, barked again for good measure, and dashed back into the forest.

"Where is she going?" Silver and Niyol said at the same time. I had already begun to chase after her.

"She heard the pack howling! Follow me!"

I turned to where Goldensun had gone and followed her. In no time at all I had caught up to my mud-covered pack-sister, and we ran side-by-side, not wanting the other to see our pack mates before ourselves, but also not wanting to steal the show. We moved in unison: dodging branches, swerving around trees, clearing bushes, leaping over roots. We climbed the place called Tall Rocks together, jumping from boulder to boulder in a synchronized dance, each countering the other's move as they made it. As soon as we reached the summit, we both howled at the same time, our voices mixing and harmonizing, making a beautiful sound. Niyol and Silver climbed the rocks, panting hard.

We stopped our howl and listened. Our eyes looked onto the silent forest, the mist swirling around the treetops below us. Tall Rocks provided the perfect meeting location, especially because we could usually see far and our howls would travel a long distance. We were all silent as we waited.

The raindrops that bounced off the gray stones became fewer and fewer as the small storm passed, and finally, subsided.

No one breathed. It seemed Dark Forest itself was holding its breath to see what happened next.

At first, it appeared to be just the wind. But it was the trees, carrying a small sound, framed by the breeze. And even though it was almost impossible to detect, it was still there.

The pack was howling back! Goldensun and I lifted our voices to the wind, and the happiness coursing through us made the others chime in with their own imitation of our beautiful song.

They appeared over the ridge a few minutes later, panting hard. But a light shone in their eyes; a clear example of how much they had missed us. However, the greeting was short. I could feel that the pack was stressed over something. It then occurred to me that one wolf, the dark, reddish brown one, was not here.

What's wrong? I asked Goldensun. She was picking up on the mood of her pack, too.

I don't know. I'll ask.

She barked and yipped and wagged her tail, and the other three shuffled from paw to paw and nervously looked at each other.

Darkshadow growled something in response, and Goldensun's ears twitched backwards, and the sparkles in her eyes darkened. In anger, fear, or both, I couldn't tell.

She turned back to me. *It's Fallenoak,* she explained, *He's gone missing. They have searched the entire territory, and claim not a drop of his scent anywhere. He just disappeared.*

I scrunched my eyebrows together, an idea already forming in my head. *Ask them if there were any other clues.*

Goldensun nodded and turned to ask her pack. She looked back to me. *Stormchaser says he remembers a paw print, a very large one, that didn't belong to any creature he had ever seen before. The print held no scent, besides just a whiff of Fallenoak's.*

I saw Darkshadow look at Stormchaser with fire in his eyes, but he didn't appear to say anything. The dark gray wolf stood with his head bowed, tail slightly tucked, and ears laid back.

I nodded. *Take me there. I have a hunch,* I said. Goldensun's eyes reflected my emotions, and she nodded. She told the pack what to do, and they bounded back down the rocks. Goldensun stopped at the bottom, waiting for me to catch up.

"Niyol, Silver, stay here. There's a cave lower down on the Rocks to rest for the night. Find it. I will be back soon," I told them.

Niyol nodded.

"But what's happening?" Silver asked.

"One of the pack members, Fallenoak, has gone missing. I have a theory on where he went, and we are just going to check it out. We should be back by dusk."

"Okay."

I nodded and followed East River pack, leaving my friends behind so I could find Fallenoak.

Chapter 6

Tear Tracks

Just as I had thought, this was no wolf print. It was as wide as my hand when I spread it as far as it would go, and there were no claw marks that would suggest a bear, or some other normal large predator had made these tracks. The thing was walking on silent paws. Some marks so small I almost missed them outlined the paw, suggesting the animal had furry feet.

Chu`si, I growled in my head. Goldensun snarled and raised her hackles, still sniffing around for any scent of her.

Why would she leave this? She knew we would find it. What was her incentive? Goldensun asked.

I don't know. She is too careful to do this by accident. Maybe she wants us to be mad, and follow her. She wants us angry and motivated enough to go after her to save Fallenoak, and that would play us right into the trap I have no doubt she and her master are laying, I said. Goldensun nodded.

She relayed our conversation to the remainder of East River. Her sister, the lighter gray wolf with a white muzzle and stomach, and a sandy brown back, stepped forward. She and Goldensun had a heated discussion, or so it looked like, then the gold wolf looked back at me.

Echosong wants to come with us on our journey. She and Fallenoak were close friends; closer than any of us were to him. She wants to help us find him. Plus, she is my sister, Goldensun said.

And Darkshadow is your mate, and Stormchaser is your mate's brother. So why don't we just take all of them? I didn't like to admit it, but I was sometimes jealous of Goldensun and how close she was to her real sister. I realized they were kin, but sometimes I couldn't help it. I felt like I should be closer to her, and receive all of Goldensun's attention, because that's how I felt about her. She was all that I had after my family was taken from me.

Goldensun looked at me with what I took to be hurt, hidden by resolve.

Echosong is my sister. I understand how you feel towards her, but you have to understand that even our relationship can sometimes be matched by that of true blood-sisters. Please, Kohana. Let her help us. She is the best tracker in East River, and she could benefit the group immensely.

I sighed, a long, drawn out sigh, and finally nodded. *I'm sorry. I don't like feeling this way, and I realize I can't always be the center of your attention. I'm sorry.*

I wasn't. I hoped she didn't see through my lie.

She trotted up to me and placed a paw on my leg. I patted it and pulled her into a big, loving hug. I realized how much she meant to me, and I didn't know what I would do if I lost her. This journey we were taking was dangerous. She shouldn't come at all. But I also knew she wouldn't let me face this alone. A pack-sister wouldn't leave another.

The whole pack followed us back to Tall Rocks, where Silver was waiting for us. She led us all down the slope to a cave where Niyol was starting a small campfire. That night, we roasted meat (much of it was left over from Silver's and my hunt yesterday) and sang songs. I sat at the cave entrance, a little ways away from the group, thinking about the trip that lay ahead.

A line from the Prophecy kept running through my head. *She will confront her destiny, resulting in her end.*

A hand on my shoulder startled me. I looked up and saw Niyol looking down with warm green eyes. "Mind if I sit?" he asked.

I shook my head and gestured to the spot next to me. We sat in silence that was filled with tension, but I didn't want it to end. Just having him here next to me made me feel better. It made me realize that maybe he would take an arrow for me, that maybe I had just one more person that loved me enough to die for me. Although, that didn't help with the thought of having one less person who would care about me in the end.

"What's up?" he said, shattering the silence like an arrow through a glass vase.

I sighed. "Just…thinking."

"About?"

I cringed. "About…the journey that lies ahead. I mean, I thought for sure my destiny was to clear my name and take back the throne…but now I don't think so any more. Maybe that was just something I wanted to do?"

Niyol looked outside, staring at the early fall forest, bathed white in the full moon's light. One month from now, according to him, the moon would shine red.

Finally, he responded, "I don't know. Before you came along, I don't think I believed in destinies at all. I just thought we are faced with challenges, and we have to choose how or even if we want to take them on. But, if destines are real, I don't think they are supposed to be easy, or fun, or something you look forward to. I think they are supposed to be something that is challenging, or perhaps something you don't want to do at all, but you have to overcome them. And, in your case, for the sake of the world.

"I don't doubt that you should clear your name and take back Desaria. If you're innocent, like you say, then I'm sitting here with the girl who rightfully should rule it." He smiled to himself. "But I think that…I don't know…maybe *this* is your destiny. I think *this,* right here, right now, is what you were born to do; save the world from the power Chu`si holds in her hands now."

"So, once we complete our destinies, do we die?" I didn't mean to ask, but the words just spilled out of my mouth before I could stop them.

He shrugged. "Maybe we get new destinies."

"If we don't?"

Niyol smiled absentmindedly. "If we don't, then we go to the beach."

I laughed. I had heard about beaches in storybooks, but never actually been to one. I imagined Niyol chasing after me, kicking sand up behind his feet. I saw Silver diving out in the waves, and Goldensun trying to catch fish in her mouth.

"Okay, you have a deal."

"Pardon?"

I grinned. "When this is all over, we're going to the beach."

I pretended to be drawing on the ground with a twig, but really I was trying to look through my curtain of red-blonde hair, to look right to his face. I wanted a good look at his gorgeous eyes.

I put the twig down. I still wanted to believe this was a bad dream; that I would soon be in my cozy little home in the cottage at High Point, that Chu`si would wake me up with a bowl of nice, warm eggs in a bowl, and I would go down to the Grove and talk to Sparrow. Goldensun would come get me for lunch, and then afterwards I would tend to the garden with Chu`si and we would take care of the animals. However, my life was far from normal. I don't think it ever will be again.

I stood up and walked outside, not saying anything to Niyol. I climbed the rocks and stood at the top, looking up at the sky. I heard boots crunch behind me, and I knew Niyol had followed.

"Kohana, something is bothering you. Please tell me; I might be able to help," he said quietly. Instantly, I knew he was right. But I couldn't tell him about my vision. "Please?"

I turned to him, faster than I intended. It came off as aggression. He took a nervous step back, but his eyes were still calm. My voice was steady, monotonous, as I spoke. I'm sure it would have been less threatening if I had screamed instead.

"Listen. I don't know what's going on. Frankly, I am still trying to grasp how I just lost *another* good life, to the fact that I am an Outcast. I lost friends and a home, because I was accused of killing my family. I lost *everything* because I couldn't speak up for myself when I needed to. I lost everything that was ever close to me, everything that ever meant anything to me, simply because I was at the wrong place at the wrong time."

I felt tears stinging the backs of my eyes, resisting the urge to fall onto my knees, and cry into my hands. I don't think I had cried, really, really cried, since I was a small girl. I don't think since the day I became Outcast I had cried like this. Before I knew what I was doing, I was on the ground, I was crying, and my hands were shielding my face from Niyol's gaze. "It just isn't fair," I sobbed into my hands, now soaked with salty tears.

Niyol walked over and hesitantly put his arm around my shoulders. "Kohana. It will be okay. We are going to get your knife away from Chu`si, and we are going to get you back where you belong. You won't be Outcast forever."

I will always be Outcast, I thought. *No matter where I live or who is with me, I will always be Outcast. And if I die on that mountaintop, I will die an Outcast.*

"If it means anything, I don't think of you as an Outcast girl. You aren't an Outcast, you are Kohana. And those are two *very* different people," he said.

He stood up, kissed the top of my head gently, and walked back down the rocks and into the cave.

And I just stayed there, thinking about whether or not I was ready for what was to come.

It was late that night when I went back to the cave. Goldensun lifted her head as I crawled in, but I said, *I'm fine. Go back to sleep.* So she did.

I crawled under my elk-hide and fell asleep quickly, completely exhausted from the three years worth of tears that had flowed out tonight.

That morning, I woke late. I was the last to rise, and the others were all already outside cooking breakfast. Niyol stood over the fire, trying to snuff it out. East River pack, including Goldensun, was nowhere to be seen, and I had guessed they were out hunting already. Silver was sharpening some arrow-tips over the fire, sending sparks into the embers Niyol was trying to put out. He pointedly glared at her a few times, but she didn't really seem to notice.

"Hello, sleepy head!" Silver said, glancing in my direction. "How are you?"

I sighed. The journey and my destiny weighed heavy on my shoulders, and I felt myself slump over with the enormity of it all.

"Fine. I'm fine. Where is the pack?"

Niyol spoke without looking at me. "They went out hunting. Why?"

I shrugged. "Just wondering," I said.

The rest of the morning consisted of us all packing our things and tending to the deer carcass the pack brought down. By dusk, half of the deer was done being tended to, and the wolves had the rest. By daybreak the next day, we were on the move.

After quick goodbyes to Darkshadow and Stormchaser, Echosong came along with us, and the journey began.

It took no time at all for me to recognize the forest around me. Goldensun and Echosong frolicked in the leaves that were just beginning to fall, and they marveled in the mass amounts of butterflies that were zooming past us in their yearly fall journey.

I saw the leaves on one of the trees already a bright scarlet. Without realizing it, I was thinking about my very first memory of fall.

"Mother, why are the trees orange?" I ask, curious about the world around me. Mother has me balanced on her hip and she laughs at my question. I don't think anything is funny, but wait for her answer.

"Kohana, dear, the trees turn orange in the fall. It is before the winter comes, and the trees give us one last burst of color before the many months we spend in the gray of winter."

"But why do they lose their leaves, then? Can't they just keep them in the winter, too?" I ask. At this age, I am so full of questions. So full of curiosity, and the whole world is a wondrous place that I marvel at constantly.

"I don't know, Kohana. Ask your father. He knows more about the trees than I," Mother says, but I know that isn't true. She sets me down on the ground and I stumble on little girl legs.

"Father knows a lot about things you don't, Mother!" I giggle. She laughs with me.

"Well, that way I can send you off when I don't know the answers. Run along, dear!"

I run off to find Father, but by now I have already forgotten what I wanted to ask him. I turn around and feel my little braid fling around, and I see Mother staring at the beautiful red trees. She puts her hand on one trunk, a white one, and says something, but I am too far away to hear.

When I think back on my childhood, Mother was far more spiritual that I recognized. She had dozens of dream catchers hanging in her and Father's room (although I don't think he minded), and she loved the trees and the animals. She constantly kept a journal with her, and I always saw her writing in it with her back to the trunk of a tree. I never knew what was inside it. When I'd ask, she would always say, "Why, me, of course. What else does one put in a journal?"

Sometimes I wondered if she was spiritual, or just crazy. The answer didn't matter; I loved her all the same.

"Kohana?"

I looked around. Niyol was looking at me weird, and I realized I was tracing my thumb along my cheek, as if I expected to feel Mother's soft caress there in the memory.

"Oh. Sorry." I pulled my hand away and kept walking.

Goldensun raised her nose to the sky, and barely had time to think, *hide,* before I heard a horse crashing through the bushes. I leapt into the nearest tree, and I crouched down to see what would happen.

A man on a black mare with white markings leapt through the undergrowth. He pulled up short to avoid running over the group, and his horse whinnied in distress. "Kitchi! Come here!" he shouted. A second man on a red stallion followed, making less noise. The first man held an air of regality to him that made me instantly respect – and fear – him.

"What, Ahote?" Kitchi said. He took in Niyol, Silver and the wolves without much interest. "So? Travelers. Nothing the King will be interested in."

A wolf the same color as the stallion emerged from the forest, too. She stood beside the horse, carrying the same air of nobility as the rider, whom I assumed was her master. However, as soon as she caught sight of Echosong and Goldensun, she snarled, bared her teeth, and raised her hackles. Goldensun and her sister matched the she-wolf's ferocity.

"Haunt! Stand down!" commanded Kitchi. She reluctantly stepped back, but her tail was still held stiff, a sign of hostility.

"State your business," Ahote, the first man, said.

Niyol stepped forward. "We are simple travelers. We are on our way to Aliyr to visit one of my sisters. She is very ill and requested to see me before…she passed on."

Kitchi nodded, but Ahote didn't look like he was buying it. "And the wolves?"

"One is my companion. The other is her sister."

Ahote glared down at them from his seat atop his horse. "Very well. Kitchi, are you sure the King wouldn't like to hear about them?"

Kitchi looked down with a raised eyebrow and a skeptical look across his face. "No. He would. We should take them in, just to be sure. We are only a few days away from Enin anyways." He drew his sword, which gleamed bright silver in the daylight.

"No!" I yelled, and jumped from behind the tree. In one brief, fluid motion that I've done a thousand times, I whipped out my bow, and in that same movement, I reached behind me to draw an arrow. Then, I remembered I didn't have any. And now I had a shining sword at my throat and a man staring down at me. His gaze flicked over me, pausing at my left wrist. A knowing flash went through his eyes, and he grinned.

"Ahote...I'll go tell him now. We've found the Outcast. Oh, King Tse will be most delighted." Kitchi smiled wickedly, but I barely even registered it.

King Tse. *King* Tse.

No, no, no.

It couldn't be.

No...

I felt myself falling, and an excruciating pain in my head caused my vision to go black.

I woke up. It was dark, and my heat hurt. I groaned and tried to sit up, but my head swam and stars danced in front of my eyes. It was night, and the world smelled like forest. Crickets chirped all around me; their chorus hurting my already throbbing head. As far as I could tell in this state, I was alone.

I tried to stand again, but as soon as I was up, I swayed dangerously. I stumbled to a tree nearby and wrapped my arms around it. I scrunched my eyes tight, trying to make the throbbing, pumping pain in my head go away, but it didn't, and I collapsed on the ground.

The next thing I knew, I was waking up again. The sky was bright red, but I couldn't tell if it was sunset or sunrise. *Go back to sleep. You need it.*

Goldensun's message caused my head to pulsate again. I saw her lying next to me, head up and ears alert.

I gulped and looked up. I didn't know which way was west, or east, or north or south. I didn't recognize any of the treetops here, or the clouds puffing along above me. Nothing was familiar at all, until I brought my gaze back down to the ground.

A tree with a long, gnarled root was right next to us, and it had a long zigzag down the trunk. The first summer of my days as Outcast, I came along this tree. Its wound was fresh from a storm the previous evening. It had been hit by lightning, and I cared for it. I tied the two parts of the tree together with long, leather strips that held all summer long. It was something my mother had taught me.

She always said that, given time, everything healed.

Eventually, the trunk and leaves looked healthy again, so I took my leather and left it to be. I still think of it as the Lightning Tree. This was my favorite tree in the whole forest, because it seemed to be the only one that had an injury that showed both on the outside and the inside, just like mine. And just like Mother said, with time, everything heals. My mark on my wrist was just a scar, and the ache in my heart was less so than it used to be, even if it was still there.

Why are we at the Lightning Tree? I asked Goldensun, fighting the pain it caused me.

It was the only place I could remember from around here. If you recall, a wolf's memory isn't as good as a person's, because we don't live too long and don't need to remember as much. Goldensun replied.

Oh. That made sense to me. *Where is everyone else?*

Goodness knows where Niyol went. He left without a word. Silver went to look for new supplies for arrows, and Echosong and Haunt went hunting.

Haunt?! I sat up so fast that my vision clouded at the edges and thoughts became blurry for a moment. I waited for my head to clear.

Yes. She told us – after Niyol took care of the men – that she was tired of living like a pet, and wanted to live like us. There is always somebody keeping a guard on her, so she can't betray us or give away our whereabouts; she isn't even allowed to relieve herself alone. She will not be denied something she wants, considering we are supposed to be the good guys, but she will not have total freedom until we know we can trust her.

I slowly nodded. *When will they be back? Any of them?*

Soon, I would think, considering it is sunset now. Echosong and Haunt probably will not be back before the spirits come out, but I don't think the others went too far.

As if on cue, I saw a flash of blue through the undergrowth, and Silver and Doli emerged into the small clearing. Silver held many small but thick stones in one hand, and some long sticks in the other. Doli perched on Silver's shoulder, and she had a variety of colorful feathers in her beak. They appeared to be deep in conversation, but through their minds like I and Goldensun communicated.

Silver put her arrow supplies down, and Doli deposited the feathers right next to them. Silver then dug around in her bag and brought out two sharp pieces of metal, and began sharpening the rocks into points.

Goldensun stood up and barked. The sound made me reach for my head, because frankly that didn't feel too good, but Silver was already rushing over and talking to me.

"Oh Kohana! You had us all so worried; we didn't know what to do! I mean, Kitchi hit you with the flat side of his blade on your head, and then Niyol got really mad and he nearly killed the men, and then I told him to calm down and he just tied them to a tree…oh and then we cleaned out your head wound and only made it here until the horse started getting really mad–"

"Horse?" I asked. Silver nodded.

"Yeah. We took Kitchi's horse; he didn't need it. Ahote's was strong enough to carry both of them back…if they ever get off that tree. Niyol took her to go do who-knows-what out in the forest. He had been awfully quiet for awhile, but I mean I guess I haven't known him long enough to know if this is quiet for him or what…" Silver was just rambling on and on. This wasn't saving us on time at all.

"Silver, how long have I been out?" I asked. I had to know how much time we'd lost; how long until the Red Moon.

Her face went grim. "One and a half days. We found you wrapped around a tree yesterday night, and it's a good sign that you can move. 'Healer' Niyol thought you might have serious trouble with mobility from now on, but seeing as you could get up and move and go hug a tree was a good thing. But don't rush yourself. Niyol told us yesterday, 'Even if she has full mobility when she starts to wake, don't rush her. She will want to leave as soon as possible, but she needs to rest before we can set off again.'" Her Niyol imitation voice was deep and full of a mocking tone. She rolled her eyes playfully. "He told us it would be about a week more before we could start making serious progress again."

"What if I just rode on the horse? We have to go; we have to get to Galdur Fjall!"

Silver shook her head. "Jaci needs rest too. We found a lot of scars on her; she was clearly abused when she was with Kitchi. She needs time to get used to her new family."

"You guys named her?" I asked, "What about her real name? I'll bet Kitchi had a name for her before."

Silver laughed. "Yeah, but do you plan on walking over to him and his buddy all tied up and asking him what his horse's name is? After all…we did steal her. He probably wouldn't appreciate that too much." I had to admit, that was pretty funny. I laughed.

I tried talking to Silver for awhile, but my head pain only got worse. Niyol came back riding on Jaci, but she didn't seem too happy about it. When she saw Goldensun, she almost turned tail and ran, but Niyol kept a firm grip on the reins.

"She let you ride her!" Silver exclaimed. Niyol nodded.

"Took awhile, and a good bit of apples, but she finally let me. She's warming up to us already, which is excellent. The sooner she gets used to us, the better."

I scowled. "We only have one horse. If we took a few more from a village, we would be able to get around quicker. We could make it to Galdur Fjall with time to spare. It would be much quicker than going on foot."

Niyol shook his head. "But three horses, three people, a bluebird, and three wolves seem awfully suspicious walking around, don't you think? Plus, you can't exactly go strolling in anywhere, and people would notice if two horses just disappeared."

I felt angry at how easily he had shot down my idea. I had thought it was a fairly good one. "So we get the horses from two different villages. We need to get there fast, and my head injury isn't helping the cause. If you won't let us leave tomorrow, we are taking horses and riding there. We still have get through Dark Forest *and* Aliyr before we even make it to the Outlands. We'll never make it in time if we go on foot; we barely would have made it before I got hit. We need to make up for the time we are losing by using a faster mean of travel, so unless you have a better idea, that's what we are going to do."

The clearing was silent. Goldensun pawed the earth nervously, while Doli pretended to preen her feathers. Silver bit her lip anxiously and went back to making arrowheads. Niyol glared at me with a burning fire in his eyes that made me want to look away, but I knew that would be backing down. So I waited. He crinkled his nose and set his lips in a firm line, and I knew I had won the argument.

I nodded. *Kohana, you need to rest. Go back to bed,* said Goldensun. I looked over to her and sighed in agreement.

"I'm going to bed," I said with a hint of a challenge in my voice. I don't know what or who I was challenging, but that's how it came out. "Goodnight."

I woke up later the next day. Silver was crouched by the fire, studying the dying embers. Jaci was tethered to the Lightning Tree, grazing the soft grasses below. I thought how this season was the worst time for horses, because when winter comes, their food goes away. Well, Jaci's probably didn't; she was a tame horse and probably ate hay all the day and stood under a warm blanket and light in her stable with her horse friends. This would prove to be a rough time for her, and whomever we took with us.

I sat up, and the black mare turned her head in my direction, ears peaked high above her head. The white streak down her forehead glistened in the afternoon sun, and her hoof pawed the ground anxiously. She still wasn't used to me.

My head throbbed, but not as badly as last night. Granted, I hadn't done anything yet, but it was a start.

Silver turned away from the embers to smile 'good morning' to me, then stood and walked off into the forest. Nobody was left here at camp besides me and the horse.

I stood on shaky legs, thanking who ever put me down here that I was near a tree. I stumbled from tree to tree to get to Jaci, and she snorted in warning. *Back off,* I could imagine her saying, *you are a stranger. Back off.*

I walked even closer, ignoring her threats. Jaci snorted and pulled away from me, but she was still tethered to the tree and she couldn't back up any further.

"Shhhh... it's okay Jaci.... I'm not going to hurt you..." I talked in a soothing and calm voice. At the sound of her new name, Jaci perked her ears. She held still, I inched closer, still talking to her in the same voice. I held my hand out to touch her nose, and I turned away and closed my eyes. I waited.

I felt pressure on my hand, and looked over to see her resting her nose in my open palm. She was staring at me with deep chocolate eyes, completely trusting me and daring me to come closer. Daring me to trust her, too. I knew something had just passed between us, something untouchable. Not the bond that Goldensun and I have, but something different. Jaci realized that I was her new rider, no longer a stranger. I would not treat her as her previous master did. I realized she was not my pet, or something I could control. She was a creature of free will, and we both knew it now.

The moment was over. She snorted and pulled her head away, returning to grazing. I smiled and leaned against the tree.

"Looks like somebody just gained Jaci's trust!"

I turned around and saw Niyol walking into the clearing, Tokala's sword in hand. Scarlet blood dripped down the blade, and the smile vanished from my face.

"What's with the...?" I motioned toward the bloody sword.

He shrugged. "Ran into a nasty-tempered boar in the forest. Don't worry, I didn't kill it," he said when he saw the look on my face, "I hit it once across the flank with this thing and it was off like a rocket, running away like I was possessed."

I shrugged and put my hand to my head. After the thing with Jaci, I had started to feel lightheaded again. "Niyol...where are the wolves?" I asked.

He scrunched his brow as he thought. "Goldensun went off awhile ago, and the other two have been gone since we made camp here. I thought they were going hunting, but the fact that they haven't returned is kind of troubling," he said. "Maybe Goldensun sensed something was wrong and went to go check on them?"

"No, she would have told me she was leaving. She would have waited for me to wake up before she left if she was going on a long journey. I'll bet she just went looking for small prey."

He shrugged. "And Silver?"

"She went off just a few minutes ago. That direction," I said, pointing with my finger to where she disappeared last. Niyol looked as if he was debating going to look for her, but he didn't.

He sat down by the dying fire and we talked for awhile. Silver came back and joined our conversation, and neither of us asked where she went, and she didn't tell us. The wolves came back a little bit before sunset, and Goldensun told me how they had followed a small herd of deer all of yesterday before bringing one down.

We went to bed right after dusk, and I fell asleep counting the spirits.

Days passed. Two days later, I could stand for longer than five minutes without fainting, and I no longer needed the support of a shoulder to walk. My ability to run was still lacking, but two days later, I could jog short distances. We were ready to set off.

We hadn't tested how long I could walk for, so the others told me to ride Jaci. I hopped on the horse's back and we walked through the forest. We traveled for a long time, all day actually, before we stopped near one of my old favorites.

A willow tree with long, wispy branches hung beside a gurgling creek. I had spent many nights under this tree. It had long, gnarled roots that wound up from the ground like twisted arms, begging to reach above the surface but being coaxed back into the soil. I tied Jaci to the tallest root, which reached up to her chest. She snorted and leaned down to munch on more grass.

Haunt, Echosong and Goldensun took one of the deeper crevices in the roots, preferring to spend the night in what felt like a den. Silver, Doli and I slept up high in the branches, and Niyol took the first watch.

I was woken by a gentle hand on my shoulder. I started awake to see Niyol crouched in the branches just below me, only a silhouette in the dark. I was about to say something, but he placed his finger gently over my lips. *Stay quiet,* I could imagine him saying.

He removed his finger and motioned down below the tree. I finally understood what he meant.

Below, a series of guttural noises, growls and barks sounded out of the dark, like a chorus of wolves arguing. In fact, that's what it was.

Goldensun, what's going on? I asked her. The only answer provided was more growling.

The clouds parted and I caught my real first glimpse of what was going on down below. The quarter-moon provided little light, and the canopy filtered out most of it. However, it was just enough.

Two blackish shadows stood, and the white light lined their pelts. Both wolves had piercing amber eyes that sparked and gleamed, like little ocher fires within a sea of blackness. Goldensun, Haunt and Echosong had their backs to the tree, and the moonlight never even reached them, for they were standing underneath the thick layer of willow fronds.

There was more snarling. "Can you understand them?" Niyol breathed. I hardly could make out what he said, but apparently it was still too loud. One of the black wolf's ears perked high, and it looked pointedly right at us. It snorted something to its companion, who followed the other's gaze. The second one, a darker, more feminine looking wolf, twitched her whiskers and her tail was stiff. The first didn't even move, it hardly even dared breathe. Its face was broader, and its eyes had a certain glow to them that said it was a male.

The male looked back down to the three she-wolves in front of him. He growled something and touched the female's cheek with his nose, and they both ran off into the night. They disappeared within a few pawsteps.

They thought we were trespassing on their territory. Those were two West River wolves, Goldensun informed me. *Keep an eye out. They haven't seen us in a long time; the border disputes have been few and far between, so they don't recognize us. And none of us even smell like East River anymore, so they were right to mistake us. Still, this is not their territory. It's near the border of East River. We should just be more careful, Kohana. West Rivers are untrustworthy.*

Okay. I will. And I will tell the others to do the same, I thought back. After relaying the message Niyol, we both went back to bed and slept soundly, and without further disruptions. The wolves sat tall at the base of the tree, guarding us until dawn light broke through the leaves.

The sun was warm on my stomach, and my eyes were closed. The golden light of probably the last warm day of the year filtered through my eyelids, and the autumn breeze stirred the dying trees. I was laying on a warm boulder, with a gap in the treetops above me. The sun streamed through, warming my skin and the whole clearing.

The wolves were grooming each other, undoubtedly sharing stories and enjoying one another throughout the whole time. Niyol, Silver and Doli had gone to the town to 'appropriate' the other two horses, figuring that the sooner we could get them, the sooner we could leave, and the more likely it would be that we could stop Chu`si and her master.

Jaci nibbled grass and kept a wary eye on the wolves, even though she probably knew they wouldn't harm her in any way.

The sunlight shining down on my eyelids was interrupted for a quick moment, and I opened them, shielding my eyes with my hand. Doli was chirping madly and was perched on a nearby branch, and she wouldn't stop. Her little black eyes wide with alarm and her feathers ruffed up in distress; Niyol and Silver were obviously in trouble.

I silently cursed for not utilizing this quiet time to craft more arrows, reprimanding myself for *still* not making new ones, when clearly they were my greatest ally.

I ran over to Jaci and hurdled onto her back. The wolves – instantly sensing my swift mood change – stood and paced, awaiting further instructions. *Goldensun, come with me. Make sure Haunt and Echosong follow.* After relaying the message, I led Jaci at a swift gallop, following the blue blur of Doli, and Goldensun ran beside me, and shining, golden star streaking among the wood. Echosong and Haunt followed farther back, ducking and dodging to avoid the clumps of dirt that were flipped out from Jaci's angry hooves.

I yanked backwards on the reins as I saw the trees thinning, and Jaci snorted angrily. Small mounds of dirt and soil piled up in front of the horse's hooves; little brown mountains that had sprung from hasty realizations. She looked back at me, her eye glimmering with irritation. She stopped and I got off. I quickly lashed Jaci to a tree, then asked Goldensun to tell Echosong and Haunt to watch her. Goldensun relayed the message and followed me.

We were at the edge of a small town, one of several on the outskirts of Enin. I crept up close to one of the houses to see what was going on, and in fact there was a small crowd gathering around the house across the road. I caught a glimpse of sea-green eyes covered mostly by choppy black hair. It was Niyol. A quick snatch of dark brown hair that shone in the weak autumn sunlight. That had to be Silver.

Is there a plan? Goldensun's words fell heavy in my ears, and felt as if they had been tossed across the street in attempt for the villagers to here. Nobody did.

Yes. I'm going to grab their attention, and I want you to make sure Niyol and Silver don't come after me. We need those horses, or else we'll never make it to Galdur Fjall in time. Once they've gotten the horses, lead them back to where the wolves and Jaci are; I'll meet you there.

She nodded apprehensively. *Just be careful. We don't know how far you can run yet.*

I grinned. *I don't need to be able to hold out long, I just need to be able to get out of there fast.*

I paraded out into the open, still trying to decide how to get their attention. I didn't have to decide; somebody saw me. Their mouth opened wide, they pointed a finger at me, and shouted, "It's the Outcast!"

Several heads turned to me; everyone in the little mob, plus Niyol and Silver. Niyol's eyes filled with dread, and Silver was mouthing something to me. I didn't catch her words before one of the men said, "That fortune would make me rich!" and he moved towards me. Everyone else followed him, my friends forgotten in their quest for gold.

I had less time than I thought would be allotted before the people caught up with me. I dashed through the town; fast enough to keep away but slow enough to keep them interested. Insults whistled past my ears, along with people shouting, "Get her!" and "Don't let her get away!" I laughed as the wind whipped my hair around me.

I led them out of the town and into the forest, where I was far more at home. I pretended to be in trouble; stumbling over imaginary rocks and swerving around trees. The people were getting tired, but their lust for riches kept them going.

As I ran through the trees, a splash of beige caught my eye. It had black marks on it. For a second, I thought it was an aspen tree, but I looked harder and saw otherwise.

There was just enough space between me and the mob for me to rip the paper off the tree. I'd look at it later.

A short howl echoed through the trees, distracting me from the task at hand. They were waiting.

I sped up, lengthening my strides and becoming surefooted. I dodged branches and leapt over bushes and snaked through the trees like I owned the place. The forest, as far as I was concerned, *was* mine. I ruled the trees, I called the shots, and I *certainly* didn't get caught by a group of mangy, gold-craving villagers.

I was long gone, and the people were too far behind me, by the time I returned to our arranged meeting place.

When I arrived, Goldensun was pacing anxiously. She saw me and leapt at me, licking my sweaty face and wagging her tail. *What took you so long?* She asked.

I smiled. *I had to make sure they wouldn't follow me.*

I turned to everyone else. Silver was sitting on the rocks, feeding a pile of grass to her new friend; a grayish blue mare with dark chocolate eyes and a black mane. Her body was lighter than her head and legs.

"We need to set off first thing tomorrow," I announced to the group. The wolves glanced up at me, but kept their heads on the ground, seeing as they didn't understand a word I was saying. Doli didn't even look up from the nut she was cracking. The horses were all grazing happily, but at the sound of my voice, Jaci lifted her big black head. Niyol and Silver both nodded absentmindedly.

"I'm serious. We can't stay here, or the villagers will find us. Kitchi wasn't all too happy you stole his horse, and we only got away with her because you tied them to a tree. We can't tie up a whole village of people single-handedly. So I say we leave at dawn."

Silver sighed. "I know you want to get going. I really do. I understand why we need to go. But now we have three horses, and the wolves can run just as fast. Doli doesn't need to worry about her travelling arrangements; she can fly or hitch a ride when she gets tired. So what are you so concerned about? If the villagers come anywhere near, the wolves will hear them first. We are totally safe here for a few days," she said. The words flew across the clearing and echoed in the still forest evening. My feet itched to move, my eyes craved the sights of the land that was yet to be seen in the journey.

Niyol broke the awkward silence, "Silver, have you forgotten that we need to cross a whole Kingdom still? We aren't very close to the border, and we are *too* close to Enin for my liking. I agree with Kohana. We should leave at dawn and get out of Desaria as soon as possible. Besides, if we can get to Galdur Fjall well before the Red Moon, that would be even better. We could stop Chu`si before she even has time to prepare for the ceremony. And Fallenoak will more likely be alive if we get there early," explained Niyol.

Silver scrunched her brow in that way she does when she agrees but doesn't want to, and sighed again.

"Okay. First light. Don't you two be late, or I'm leaving without you."

I laughed, and then left the clearing, claiming I had to relieve myself. I walked out of sight, and stole behind a tree, just in case Silver or Niyol decided to follow me. I glanced quickly over my shoulder, and then opened my palm to reveal the paper I had seen on the tree. It was crumpled up. I smoothed it out, reading what it said.

WANTED

KOHANA SILVERMIST

NIYOL STORMBLADE

SILVER SHININGOAK

FOR CRIMES AGAINST DESARIA, THE KING, AND HIS

PEOPLE.

REWARD: 10,000 GOLD PER FELON.

DEAD OR ALIVE

I furiously shredded the paper, throwing the pieces into the breeze. My friends were in danger. They were wanted criminals now, all because of me.

What had I done?

I slept fitfully that night. I couldn't remember any of my dreams, only snatches and wisps of them. I recalled running through a world of colors, dresses, masks. The one I wanted wasn't there. There was a half moon, but with edges the color of fresh blood. And I saw a golden star, falling from the sky. Somehow I knew everything I had dreamt about that night was important.

I couldn't have been more right.

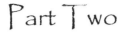
Part Two

The
Killer

Chapter 7
Predator and Prey

Dawn came and I was the first one awake. I sat up under my little yak-hide pelt, which was proving to keep me quite warm at night. I had just woken from a nightmare and was panting heavily; that much I knew. But try as I might, the actual nightmare itself eluded my mind. Like an itch I just couldn't reach, it sat in the back of my head annoyingly.

I stood up and walked up to the rocks I had sunbathed on just the previous afternoon. The rock was cool to the touch. I clambered up to the top, looking up into the gray dawn sky. I felt the presence of someone behind me, and expected to see Goldensun walking up the boulders, but I was shocked to see not a wolf, but a cat.

The cat was black. With neon-yellow eyes and pupils only slits, despite the darkness in the forest. It was roughly the same size as Granite.

I knew instantly that I stood no chance. *Please,* I prayed, *kill me quickly...*

"I do not intend to kill you, Kohana."

The cat had a deep voice that sounded like purr. It was clearly a male. His mouth didn't move as he spoke, almost as if he was projecting his thoughts into the open air. He sat down beside me and looked up into the dawn sky, as I had moments before.

"Kohana, I know you have heard this before. I know you have talked to the Dragon with the shining blue hide, and the Tall Wolf that took you to High Point. Now, it is my turn to speak with you. Your destiny is unmatched by that of any other human to walk Calleo, since your ancestor who possessed that knife." He paused. "I assume you are familiar with that tale, correct?"

I nodded. "I am aware that my ancestor vanquished Nox with the knife that was created with Dragonfire."

The cat twitched his whiskers grimly. "Yes, indeed. However, it brings me dread to inform you that the evil of Nox pales in comparison to that of Tatsuo. But, it is imperative that you know of what he is capable of."

I swallowed nervously.

He continued on, seemingly without registering my anxiety. "Chu`si's master is powerful enough to do the unthinkable." He fixed his yellow gaze on me without blinking. "He will not stop with the Dragons. He will not stop with Calleo. He will seek to control the entire world. Everything will be ruined if Chu`si can wake him." His voice rumbled across the trees, and I looked at my friends sleeping soundly below me. Why couldn't they hear him?

"I do not wish them to hear, so they do not," he said in that voice of silk. His whiskers twitched and he returned to looking at the sky.

"Do they hear me?"

"Do you wish them to?"

I glanced back at Niyol's chest, gently rising and falling. "No."

The cat nodded. "Then they do not."

We shared a comfortable silence. A hundred questions buzzed in my head, but I would have hated to break the stillness of the air.

Finally, my curiosity got the better of me.

"What do you think of destiny?"

He was silent for a moment, sweeping his tail across the rock thoughtfully. "Well," the cat purred, "I know destiny is something that belongs to you and you alone." He paused. "But I do not think that, just because you have a destiny, you must accept it, or let it rule you."

He stood up, looking me dead in the eye. "Remember, Kohana, the night is always darkest just before the dawn."

He started walking down the rocks, tail waving in an effort to keep his balance. "Wait!" I shouted, "What does that mean?"

He looked back. "If you do not succeed, the ensuing battle will be long and bloody. Hundreds upon thousands of *human* lives alone will be lost, and many more will be enslaved. This is no game. I wish you the best of luck, and I am on your side."

He glanced over at my sleeping friends. "Speak not of this. They may not have heard us, but they still may not know." He leapt straight into the dying fire and vanished. A flurry of embers shot up behind him, but disappeared in the sky within a few moments.

Silver sat up and yawned. She looked around, and then saw me atop the rocks. I wondered how she didn't catch the look of puzzlement upon my face.

"Good morning, Kohana! Glad to see you up and about; as I recall, we leave at dawn." She winked and grinned, but I was in no mood to smile back.

We woke Niyol and the wolves, roused the horses and got them ready. We started at a brisk trot, and the only thing on Silver's mind was naming the new horses. "Come on! We named Jaci; it should be only fair that we name the other two! They are part of the family now! Come on, please? Please, please, please, please, please, please, please?"

I sighed and laughed. Jaci trotted along, occasionally snorting and shaking her head. "How about, for your horse, Sky?" I suggested. Silver's eyes went wide in that way they do when she gets excited. She looked back to her horse and started calling her by her new name. Sky glanced back to her new rider, but didn't react in any special way.

"What about Niyol's horse? He is so beautiful; he should have a name too!"

Niyol chuckled from atop his stallion. "Blaze. He has the hide like fire, so the name fits."

We all nodded our agreement. "Blaze and Sky, welcome to the family," I whispered to only myself.

We moved through the woods all day, and into the night, which shielded us from prying eyes. We rode well past midnight. Dawn was breaking when we stopped.

"Is this a good idea? Traveling by night and sleeping by day?" Niyol asked as we tied the exhausted horses up. "I mean, sure it provides us cover when we travel, but when we sleep we will be completely vulnerable."

I shrugged. "We should head out at sunset. Everyone needs some sleep, but we really need to move."

My friends nodded and we all got ready for the coming resting time. I volunteered to take first watch.

Goldensun sat with me and we surveyed the area. After Niyol and Silver's carelessness in the last village, we really didn't want to risk another run-in with people.

Before I knew it, it was around noon; I wasn't tired yet and it was nearly time for Silver's shift. I decided to let her sleep some more. *What's on your mind, Kohana?* Goldensun asked me.

Nothing. Why? I hoped Goldensun couldn't hear the lie in my thoughts.

But wolves can sense lies better than food nearby, smell them like a scent marking. It's especially hard to fool one who shares your thoughts. Goldensun looked at me with a jade gaze and it took all my will to force out, *I'm serious. Nothing is wrong!* She knew I was lying. She tried to hide the hurt look in her eyes and turned back to the forest.

We kept watch in silence. I could sense her need to get going, to run and frolic, jump and play with her pack like the old days. Like it was back before this insane mission started. I reached down, wanting to stroke the hilt of my knife. Once again, I had to be reminded by the empty air that what my hands sought was way far away, probably in the Outlands by now. Three years of habits die pretty hard.

About an hour later, I woke Silver so I could get some rest. I was asleep in moments, and the next thing I could remember was Niyol waking me. Behind him, the sky was fiery in the dawn. So much for heading out at dusk.

"Where are we going now?" I asked. Silver and Niyol seemed surprised, I guess they thought I was the leader of the group. "I know we are near Zomer river. That's the border. We can't go anywhere unless we have map, because as soon as we cross into Aliyr, we are going to be lost."

Silver smiled. Her bright teeth shone under the morning sunlight that was now bursting through the branches. She untied Sky and said, "Follow me. I have a plan."

We rode the horses into a nearby town. I knew there were many towns Enin, but I didn't realize just how many. After all, we were a good three days ride away from my home, and yet there were plenty of villages just waiting to snatch us up and turn us into the King's Court. And what a prize I would be if caught.

I pulled out of my pack – which I couldn't believe I still had after all that had happened – a hooded cloak. It was a little small, but it would work for my purposes today. Silver too had a cloak which she threw over her shoulders. Niyol had nothing, so we told him to wait with the horses and wolves.

We snuck into town, trying to play as travelers in need of a map, some food and then we will be on our way. Some children skipped through the streets in bright clothing, but stopped dead when they saw us, undoubtedly looking like horrifyingly dangerous hooded figures. They looked nervously from one to another and ran off.

"Hmm…this isn't going quite as I expected, Kohana," Silver whispered. "We are drawing too much attention."

I pointed to a hanging sign farther down the road. *Maps, atlases and antique items from all across Calleo*, it read. We headed for it.

As soon as we opened the door, we were welcomed with the sounds of a good time. Laughter, haggling, and surprisingly, the smell of alcohol. *What kind of store is this?* I thought.

A plump, short man came over to us. He had blue sparkling eyes, and all his teeth were yellow and rotting. He had a few days worth of stubble on his chin, cheeks and upper lip, but he was happy all the same. His short, dark brown hair was tousled and he smelled as if he needed bathing. "Hello!" he said in a surprisingly cheery voice. "Name's Matt. Short for Matthew. Come from across the seas, I do. Nice to meet two fine lasses as yourselves!" Matt grabbed my hand and shook it vigorously, and did the same to Silver. We introduced ourselves cautiously, using fake names. Matt scratched his stubble curiously.

"I do fancy the names o' all the lasses and lads on this side o' the world," he said, "Quite the change for someone such as myself!" He stopped scratching and smiled broader than before, if that was possible. "And what can I do you fine lasses for, then?

We got ourselves all sort o' maps, atlases, an' curios! I got me some items mighty fine o'er her if you want to be looking at them—"

"We need a map of all of Calleo," Silver interrupted. "Thank you for your hospitality, but we really need to be on our way. Just a map, is all."

Matt nodded. "Right you are, then." He walked past a heavily drunken man who asked him for horse hooves, where Matt just shrugged him away and pointed him back to his mead.

The plump man rummaged around in a shelf or two, then came back holding a rolled-up piece of paper. "That'll cost you, lasses. I need payment. Finest map o' Calleo, this is. Not gonna be cheap…" Matt rubbed his pudgy little fingers together. I was about to just take the map and run when Silver reached inside her pocket and pulled out three gold pieces.

"Will this do?"

Matt nearly dropped the map, along with his jaw. He snatched up the coins and said, "Take it! If you fine lasses ever need anything ever again, feel free to drop by!" Matt said. We smiled beneath our cloaks and left the little store.

Outside, the weather had changed drastically. We had only been in the store for less than five minutes, and now the sky was heavily overcast. The air felt wet and heavy. *I'll bet rain is coming,* I thought to myself. "Silver, how did you get that kind of money?" I asked.

Silver grinned. "I have my ways." But that wasn't good enough for me. She rolled her eyes good-naturedly and said, "Before I left, Fae gave me some fake coins that she made. They look just like real ones, feel just like the real ones, but if you actually study them closely, they aren't real at all. Fool's Gold, she calls it." Silver laughed. "Hey, it's not stealing. Did you see how happy he was? Besides, he was a pirate. Don't listen to a word he says. I doubt this is the best map of Calleo anyhow."

We unrolled it. The map certainly wasn't anything to scoff at; it was extremely detailed and labeled with all sorts of towns, villages, borders, rivers, lakes, streams, mountains. You name it, it was on this map. However, it was brittle and hard, and torn at the edges. Clearly it had been used by many travelers.

Silver let out a low whistle. "Impressive! Come on, we should get out of here before Matt realizes those are fake coins."

Back at camp, we studied the map further. We were right in between Enin and Aliyr. The closest border to us was the one that was of the 'Zomer river', or 'Summer river'. It was a river famous for its length and the spectacular falls at its end. The Falls sat just a few miles southwest of the capital, Orazin, and proved to be the only waterfall worth seeing in all of Calleo.

I held the map in my hands, and butted my head in front of Silver's as we both tried to memorize every stain and scratch and scrawl on the parchment.

"Aliyr is a Kingdom well known for their falconers," Silver pointed out. "Should we see if we could buy a falcon before we cross over? It'd certainly help us blend in."

I shrugged. "I don't think getting one would be smart. Three people, three wolves, three horses, and a blue-jay? We're pretty much pushing our luck as is," I said with a slight chuckle.

Niyol looked upset; I knew he wanted his own falcon. But another member to our family and we'd practically have a village. Silver nodded, understanding completely, and Niyol agreed too, but not without some grumbles.

"So it's settled then. We'll see what we can do once we arrive in Aliyr, but for now, we just need to cross over. If we cross the river before it freezes, I doubt we will run into any border patrol," I said.

Silver looked unconvinced. "But we can't exactly *swim* across the river; we'd freeze! Or worse, drown!"

"And *that's* what makes this a good idea. Any border patrol will think the same thing, so they've probably gotten pretty lazy. They won't expect us to be there. We could cross with so little chance of getting caught that it practically is foolproof."

"Unless it doesn't work..." mumbled Niyol. I pretended he hadn't said anything; I figured he was still cross about the falcon.

The plan was set. It was simple. After relaying it to Goldensun, she pointed out one flaw. *What are you going to do when you get there?*

I squinted at her. What *were* we going to do after we had crossed over? *I don't know. We'll improvise.*

She rolled her jade eyes, and her message back wasn't lacking in disapproval. *Because your 'improvised plans' always work perfectly...* and she stalked off.

The rescue plan I used just the other day to get Niyol and Silver back was improvisation! I called after her. She twitched her ear to tell me she heard, but flopped down with Haunt and Echosong.

We studied the map a little better, making sure we knew exactly where we were going, and almost got ready to leave.

"Wait," I said just as the others were mounting their horses. "We don't have any food! My pack is empty," I said.

Niyol cursed under his breath, and Silver glared at the space next to me, undoubtedly thinking about what we were going to do. "We could always go back into town," she stated, "I still have a few fake gold coins."

I nodded. But before I could say anything else, Niyol said, "But I want to go this time. Kohana, you should watch the animals." He smiled at me in a kind of childish, almost playful, 'this is what you deserve' way, and the two of them left.

They were gone a long time. I sat around and talked to Goldensun and oiled my bow. I found some sticks and rocks and started making new arrows. The only thing I needed was some feathers. I looked around, but Doli was nowhere to be seen. She probably wouldn't let me use her feathers anyways. But that would have looked beautiful: she had what had to be the most striking fletching of all the blue-jays this side of the river.

I sighed. *Goldensun, why do they always get themselves in trouble when they go out on their own? Angry mobs can't be our main concern on this journey!*

She wagged her tail in a wolf-laugh. *They might not be in any sort of predicament. Maybe they just got a lot of food, it's heavy, and they are having a hard time carrying it all back. They can't* always *be in trouble!*

I rolled my eyes good-naturedly. *Oh yes they can.*

Just then, they walked through the trees, arms laden with all sorts of meat, vegetables, fruit and bread. They deposited the goods gently on the ground, and Niyol said, "Want to come help us get the saddles?"

I laughed. "Good one. But how are we going to carry all of this food?" It looked like more food than I had eaten my whole life as Outcast.

"I'm not kidding! We got three saddles and saddlebags too!" he said. Silver nodded behind him enthusiastically.

I laughed again and stood up. Turns out that I was wrong; they really did get new saddles and saddlebags for the horses. They were very heavy and the walk back seemed to stretch for many more miles than it really was, but as soon as we returned, I was delighted on how wonderful the saddle looked on Jaci. She looked like a very important horse, one whose master would be the general of an army or a guard to the palace.

"You look good, Jaci," I said, stroking her nose. I looked around and smiled, because Sky and Blaze looked just as dashing as my horse.

We took about half an hour to load up the saddlebags with food, and soon we were galloping off to the northeast, looking for the infamous Zomer river. The wolves ran beside the horses, relishing in the feel of the wind through their fur and no doubt loving the closeness we all shared. Almost like a pack, running for the hunt.

We were closing in on our prey without even knowing it.

We heard the river long before we saw it.

The clouds from earlier today had begun to dump their long-held rain onto the land, and the Zomer river was nearly overflowing. Its banks flooded and the water was rushing almost up to the grass. Bits of debris – everything from small branches and leaves to decent sized rocks – tumbled through the crashing waters. We were all drenched through our clothes and the wolves looked as if they had just taken a swim. The horses were dripping from both rain and sweat and were shaking heads worriedly. They out of all of us knew best that this rain would be a problem.

It was strange to be getting rain this time of year. It was mid-autumn, and usually here the rains stopped around the beginning of the season. Considering how dry of a summer it was, we all were pretty shocked to see a rain so late in the season, and so heavy.

It was pouring buckets. We took shelter under a large oak tree, but it was missing many leaves, making for poor protection from the storm. The wind picked up and we had to shout loudly to even be heard amongst each other.

Goldensun, I need you to take and Echosong. Find shelter. We will wait out the storm here. Okay? I said. Goldensun rolled her eyes and twitched her nose angrily.

Leave you out in the storm? If any one of us is going to fair poorly in the storm, it's going to be you three humans. The horses – if turned loose – will run to high ground and we would too, while you insist on staying here by an overflowing riverbank in the slippery mud and pouring rain. Her eyes twinkled with a light fueled by the need to protect her pack-sister.

You're right. But what high ground is there? There isn't anything near; it's all flat land!

A hand on my shoulder interrupted me. I turned around. Niyol was gazing down at me with concerned eyes, Silver watching from a few feet away.

"Kohana, staying here isn't smart. The river will certainly overflow and we will be caught in the waves if we stay. If we can't get to high land, we at least should leave the banks," he said. I nodded, cursing myself silently for being stupid enough to be corrected twice at the same time.

Silver started gathering the horses' reins so we could walk to safer ground when a deafening roar sounded above. It wasn't thunder…it was too concentrated, too loud, and too angry to be anything natural.

All heads turned to the sky, and although I'm sure Silver had an idea, only Goldensun, Niyol and I really knew what was happening.

Chu`si was back. And she was quite unhappy.

In the same instant, Silver and I drew our bows. My quiver was stocked with new arrows, but I had no feathers for fletching. The arrows wouldn't ever fly straight, making them utterly useless.

Niyol pulled out the sword that Tokala made. When I was knocked out a few days ago, he must have taken it from me. As I thought about it, I remembered the boar he had a run-in with, and how he came back with the sword covered in blood. I wondered why I hadn't pieced it together until now. He held it off to the side, as if anticipating an attack.

Goldensun, get behind us. She is going to try and take you guys, and if we can protect you, she won't get the chance, I told her. She glared at me as if to argue, but another roar that sounded above changed her mind. She, Haunt and Echosong leapt behind us and crouched low, growling yet trying to become invisible.

"We have to protect the wolves and the horses!" I shouted over the pounding rain. Silver handed me some arrows.

"You have a better shot than me! Bring her down and I will take care of the horses!" she yelled. I nodded uneasily as she dashed off to control the nervous horses, which were whinnying and bucking and trying to get rid of the reins that tied them to the tree.

I saw the golden fur flash through the trees above, and I notched an arrow. It felt better than I thought to be holding this weapon once more.

Lightning lit up the sky. Thunder cracked overhead. Rain pounded down. Chu`si's shadow was momentarily visible in the lightning, but it disappeared before I could strike.

"Can you see her?" I roared over the noise. Niyol, with his back to me, either didn't hear me or didn't respond loud enough. But the next thing I knew, I was knocked over by a heavy weight equipped with sharp claws and fangs.

"Niyol! Help!" I screamed. Chu`si was snapping at my throat, not wasting a moment trying to wipe me out. My bow and arrows were flung to the side when she attacked me, and were far out of reach. Silver was way out of earshot. I closed my eyes and prepared for the end.

Out of what seemed to be nowhere, gray, gold and red blurs knocked into the demon all at once, causing her to stagger and release her death grip on me. I scrambled out and grabbed my weapons, taking aim. But I couldn't fire. I could hit one of the wolves, and I wouldn't forgive myself if any of them were caught between my arrows and my target.

Kohana, shoot! Goldensun howled at me, both mentally and audibly.

I can't! I might hit one of you!

SHOOT!

I did. I heard a wolf yelp, but the demon continued her fight.

I crinkled my nose, grabbing another arrow and notching it. I was shaking, trying to get a good aim. I shot again, but the arrow soared over my target and landed in the flooded river.

Chu`si had enough. She shook the wolves off of her, also sending a spray of water and blood into the air. Goldensun and Echosong landed backwards on their paws – where I saw an arrow sticking awkwardly out of Echosong's right haunch – and Haunt skidded on her back in the mud. She nearly spun into the river, but gained her footing just in time.

The demon turned to me, hissing. "If I can't have you…" she growled, "I'll just take *him* instead!" Chu`si spun to Niyol and took a flying leap at him.

"*NO!*" I screamed. Time slowed down, and with inhuman speed, I drew another arrow and struck the beast. The momentum was still too much, but thankfully, Niyol had moved aside. She landed heavily in the mud next to him.

A pained roar split the air, and the beast lay heavily on the ground, twitching in the final moments of death. The wolves trotted over, panting, all three of them plastered with rain and blood. Goldensun's ear was torn and bleeding, Echosong had a cut across her muzzle, but the arrow was sitting in the mud where she had been standing. Haunt had a shallow slash along her whole flank. But all three were wearing triumphant smiles and wagging tails.

Niyol rushed over. The rain was still pounding the air. "Kohana, I don't…I don't know what happened. I couldn't…" I ran over to him and embraced him. I think he took that as me accepting his mistake, realizing that he couldn't manage.

Silver stood gaping from the tree, not believing what she saw. The horses were somewhat calmer. They were no longer bucking or screaming like a fierce wind, but they were all eyeing the river nervously and had ears laid back, ready to flee if that's what it took.

A grumbling laugh sounded below me. I let go of Niyol and saw Chu`si, in her demon form, still bleeding on the ground. An arrow stuck out from her muscular chest, and the fur was stained red; not even the downpour could wash out the heavy flow.

"You still haven't won…" she growled. A wicked smile grew upon her face. "You may have brought me down, but my companions are still there to carry out my deed. Your wolf friend is still going to die, and that will be just the beginning!" She cackled, closing her eyes and smiling. Out of context, you'd think one of us had told a joke. She then began coughing, spewing blood from her throat.

"Your knife is still going to do everything we need it to. You haven't won a single thing by bringing me down…you only think you have." She screeched again, like a batty old witch.

"Where is my knife?!" I shouted. She grinned wider, eviler.

"You will never have it. I doubt any of you will even live to get to Galdur Fjall! I was only the first of many attacks you will have to face!" Chu`si shrieked in her maniacal way and then the light faded from her eyes, even if the only light possessing them was an evil one.

Niyol stared blankly down at the demon. His brow furrowed in a way that made it clear he was confused and hurt at the same time.

"She's gone," he said torpidly. He let out a long, troubled sigh, and sat down in the mud. I opened my mouth to ask what was wrong, but he answered before I could ask. "I know she was a demon the whole time, and I know she was evil and all. But I grew up with her. My parents abandoned me when I was only a few days old; I don't even remember them. She was the only family I had. And…I guess I wanted to believe she still had some good in her."

A small raindrop trickled down his cheek. Or maybe it was a tear. A silent, ignored, fought-against tear. I could imagine him trying to keep his voice straight and the stinging wall of tears welling up in his eyes, but he wouldn't let them fall. I sat down in the mud with him and rested my head on his shoulder.

"I know exactly how you feel," I said.

We both cried.

Chapter 8
Truth Revealed

The rain continued for a long time, but its intensity diminished considerably. It was as if Calleo was letting out a gentle sigh of relief at being ridden of the demon.

But according to the deceased evil fiend, there were many more.

More that would come to get us soon.

Niyol sat by her for a long time. Eventually I stood up and went to help Silver set up camp. We told him to come under the shelter we had made, but I don't think he heard us. Niyol sat there all night. Only the gentle nudge from his horse could get him to look away.

We hadn't been together long, but the two new horses were forging strong bonds with their riders already, just like I had automatically with Jaci. It excited me to see them adapting to their new lives so well, but it also terrified me. Somewhere deep in my gut I knew that they wouldn't last long living with us, and I was scared to have to become attached to them if they might die soon.

The day after Chu`si's death, at what I assumed was around late morning but not quite noon, Niyol stood up and walked over to us.

We were fixing brand new arrows. Silver had scavenged around for something to use as fletching and found an old cardinal's nest lined with the scarlet feathers. She brought them back and was helping me decorate my arrows and bow with them. We even added the plumage to the tips of the bow, just for display, of course.

"I want to bury her," he said. Silver and I both looked up with bewildered expressions. "I know she was a demon, but she was my family too."

I shared an uneasy glance with my friend and we both reluctantly nodded.

The ground was soft from the rain and we buried her right where she died. I wasn't completely comfortable doing so, for two reasons. One, the obvious one, she was a demon. She always had been, and Niyol had just been manipulated by her. He only *thought* she still had goodness in her, when truthfully she never did. Two, I was the one who killed her. It felt weird burying an evil beast whom I had murdered. Something about that just wasn't right.

After we lay her in the soft mud, we started to pack up our things. My quiver was full of beautiful arrows again, and it bounced surely and comfortingly on my back as I walked around.

However, the same problem still faced us: how were we going to cross the flooded river?

Niyol took Blaze and Haunt downstream and I went with Jaci and Goldensun upstream. There had to be a fallen tree or some other mean of crossing. Silver, Sky, Doli and Echosong stayed at the makeshift camp, to keep an eye out for coming trouble.

I searched for a good three hours. We ran up and down the slippery bank several times, and there was nothing. Only on my fourth search upriver did we find something.

Jaci had taken me farther upstream than our previous searches. Although it was dangerous, considering guards were more likely to be upstream, we found a bridge. It was an old, solid, wooden one stretching all the way from flooded bank to flooded bank. It almost would have worked. The only problem was the men patrolling it.

Jaci and I stayed hidden in the forest, watching the men march on the other side. They had a different air to them, a tougher, more don't-mess-with-me kind of tone, and it made me nervous. There were three men. Two were tall, one medium height. They all carried bows, quivers, swords and knives. This way was not going to be the way to cross.

I turned Jaci around and we started returning to camp at a fast gallop. Silver heard me coming and drew her bow; arrow notched, but saw Goldensun ahead and realized it was okay.

"Anything we can use?" she asked. I shook my head.

"There is a bridge, but it's guarded. They're heavily armed. We wouldn't stand a chance, even if luck was on our side. This is exactly the type of border patrol we want to avoid. "

Silver sighed. She sat up on Sky's back, and stroked her speckled neck. "Well, I guess we just hope Niyol found something. If not, we are going to have to find a shallow spot and swim."

Niyol came back with similar news. He had run a good three miles or so downstream and found nothing. He told us of how he was almost captured by border patrol, but Echosong had run off to divert their attention. She came back moments later, as if on cue, panting and smiling.

"That's it then," Silver said. "Swim across it is."

I shook my head. "I know we have to get across, but something about swimming in a flooded river in the middle of autumn doesn't exactly scream 'good idea' to me anymore. We need to think of another way across," I said, hoping they didn't realize how I was countering my earlier position. Before, it seemed like a much better idea, but now that the river was flooded, we had too many odds stacked against us. Swimming was a bad idea.

"We could try to run a line between the trees," Niyol suggested. "You know, by shooting an arrow into a tree on the far side, and kind of climbing across."

"What about the wolves and horses? They would freeze or drown in the river," said Silver.

We went back to brainstorming. Nothing came to mind. We couldn't wait much longer; so much time had been lost with my head injury, and we spent more days here than planned.

The clouds started clearing later that evening. We climbed the trees and saw the sunset, which to me looked even brighter and more vibrant knowing we didn't have Chu'si to contend with anymore.

But as I looked at Niyol next to me, his eyes cloudy and distant, I knew he didn't feel the same way.

The day after our first sunset in a few nights, the Zomer river had started to recede from the banks. Perhaps we could still try to swim across. I suggested it the next morning, again contradicting myself. Silver nodded in agreement, saying we couldn't waste any more time. We had only three weeks left until the Red Moon. I found it strange how easily it had slipped my mind; I'd hardly thought about the event in days.

The river was cold. I touched my hand to the surface and knew we would all be in for an unpleasant swim. The task at hand, however, wouldn't be getting in ourselves, or getting the wolves to follow, because we could communicate with them and tell them what was going on. We were going to have a problem getting the horses across, because horses don't like swimming, and we couldn't tell them why we were leading them across a freezing cold river.

We galloped along the riverbank as close as we dared to the bridge that was heavily guarded, looking for the shallowest spot possible. We had to split up, to cover the most ground quickly.

I certainly regretted that.

I don't know why I didn't see it coming. A couple of kids camping out in the woods not even two miles from a guarded area was bound to bring trouble, even if caution was taken.

I was riding Jaci downriver with Niyol, Blaze, Echosong and Goldensun. Silver had taken Sky, Doli and Haunt upriver, in hopes to find a shallow crossing before she got close to the bridge.

We slowed to a trot. "Niyol, we haven't found anything. I say we head back to the camp and meet Silver. If she's got nothing either, we'll just have to cross there," I said. Niyol nodded, still scanning ahead as if a shallow area would appear if he stared hard enough.

I turned Jaci around and cantered back. Niyol followed at a slightly slower pace, eyes peeled. The wolves were sniffing the banks anxiously, and when I asked Goldensun what they were doing, she responded with, *Just sniffing.* But I could tell by the apprehensive looks in both wolves' eyes that they were more than 'just sniffing'.

We returned to the campsite to find Haunt pacing frantically. When we trotted in, she raced up to Goldensun and whined anxiously. Goldensun's eyes grew cold and angry, and she looked to me. My companion's icy stare was something that I had seen only once in awhile; it was made of anger and burning desire.

Silver ventured too close to the bridge. The guards saw her and shot down Sky. They took Silver while she was trying to get up, she told me.

I groaned. We weren't even over the border, and already our chances were slipping.

It just wasn't happening. There was just no chance. But if we couldn't save the world, we could at least save my new friend.

"Niyol, come with me," I said. *Goldensun, tell Haunt and Echosong to come too.* My golden friend twitched her ear in understanding.

"We don't have much time," I said, both out loud and in my mind. I trusted Goldensun was relaying my words to the other wolves, but frankly I didn't care if she did or not. They would probably pick up the tone of my voice and realize I was saying something important or motivational.

"Silver is in trouble. We are going to go rescue her, and we have to do so with strategy and a plan. If we go in without thought, this could happen again. Or perhaps the consequences could be worse. We are going to catch up to them, and follow. Do not act until the plan is in place. Niyol, have your weapons ready because the bridge will still be guarded, and we will have to fight to cross."

I pulled up on Jaci's reigns, and she, catching my mood as well, reared high in the air. "Now let's go!"

I turned her around and galloped, full blast, bow notched with a cardinal-fletched arrow, and rode through the forest without gripping Jaci's reigns. Niyol unsheathed his sword and stood up in Blaze's stirrups. The wolves ran beside us, dodging hooves and flying clumps of dirt, darting in and out between the horses and steering them the right way. In the short time we had all known each other, we had become close, like the knots that tied the string to the bow. If one comes loose, nothing is functional. We were all a team, and finally acting as one.

The bridge came into sight. I tightened my grip on the bow and saw the first guard. A heavy man with a thick red beard. I shot my arrow and it pierced his heart. He fell, and three others emerged from the foliage into our sights. We thundered across the bridge, seemingly louder than even Chu`si's furious roar from a few nights prior. As I passed the first man, I leaned over and snatched my arrow from his chest and re-notched it into my bow.

There was a little blood on the tip. But it was still sharp and still in one piece, so I was using it again.

My second victim wasn't as lucky. The arrow hit him in the shoulder. He wrenched it out and snapped it in two. All around me now, battle was raging. There weren't many participators, but it was still quite the skirmish.

All three wolves were ganging up on a small, skinny guard. He looked to be our age, maybe a year or two younger. His golden-yellow eyes screamed for help, but his companions were engaged in fights of their own.

Niyol had jumped off Blaze and was fighting another man with his sword. The man had a blade out as well, but every move he made to stab Niyol was deflected.

And Doli, the smallest of us, was flying around, dive-bombing anyone within her range. She would dive, scratch and peck for a moment, and before her victim could gain their bearings, she would be flapping above their heads again. She was like a small, courageous fighting-machine, and it surprised me the effort I saw being put in by what I thought was a small, gentle creature.

I took in all of this in close to two seconds. Then I turned back to the man I was fighting and smiled deviously. I jumped off Jaci and notched another arrow. He drew a sword. For not the first time, I regretted not having my dagger. A bow and arrow were practically useless in close-range combat.

The man was well trained. Somehow, I managed to keep my grip on my bow and dodge his strikes. Up until one stab attempt, when he knocked my bow out of my hands. It tumbled through the air, landing on the ground a few yards away, and sporting a brand-new scratch on it.

But then I saw it; the white body with the blue-gray speckles laying, bleeding on the ground. It was Sky, and I saw the faint rise and fall of her stomach. She was alive!

And that was all I needed. There was a beautiful creature still breathing, still waiting for someone to come save her. I knew she was fighting, and I knew she was slipping away. But if I could get this man away from me and get over to her, I might be able to save her. Or do something. Or just be there, so she won't die alone.

The man stepped closer. I stepped back. He stepped closer. I took two steps back, and tripped. Tripped over a tree root. I then lay in the grass on my rear end, not sure if I was pretending to be afraid, or if the terror in my gut was real. He smiled the same wicked grin I had given him moments ago, and stabbed at my chest.

The only thing was, in that same moment, I whipped an arrow from my quiver and rolled backwards, leaving him to catch his sword in the ground. He pulled and pulled, but it was stuck. I jabbed the arrow at his chest, and it pierced his heart, just like the man before him. He fell to the ground, the arrow bent. Unfortunately for me, that made it useless.

I looked around. The wolves were panting over the twisted body of the young soldier. Niyol was pulling his blade out of the guard's chest. Doli was sitting on a nearby branch, preening her feathers in both excitement and anxiety. Jaci and Blaze were standing over Sky, snorting and nickering to get our attention. I rushed over and skidded to the ground on my knees, just at the fallen horse's head.

She was covered in sweat. Her eyes were focused on something far away. Her pretty mane was oily and damp, and was strewn all over. She had been so beautiful not an hour ago, with a rider to match. I looked for the cause of her injury. If she had been shot by an arrow, I could pull it out and wrap the wound. A knife would be a clean cut and easy to wash. A sword would have caused too much damage.

It was an arrow, but it was lodged still in her throat. Without being told, I saw the scene in my head; she would have been shot with the arrow that might have been meant for her heart, and fell down. I could see that from where it was, located, the projectile made it harder for her to breathe. Removing it wouldn't help; she'd then have a hole in her throat that would whistle while she suffocated. Sky wasn't going to survive.

The wolves and Niyol came to stand beside me. Goldensun leaned her head into my shoulder. I stroked Sky's neck, and whispered words of comfort to the dying horse. She panted and gasped for breath, and I sang the song my father had taught me so long ago.

I sang it so quietly that I don't think any of the others even heard. The words formed in my mouth and died on my lips. But I knew that the horse was letting go. I wanted to wish her well on her journey up into the heavens.

I moved my hand to her cheek. She glanced at me for a moment, but the look in her eyes told me she didn't see me at all. "Sky, don't worry. We'll be fine. Silver will be alright. You can let go now. Let go, and you won't feel the pain anymore," I said. She nickered one last time, and twitched her ear to the sound of my voice. Then her eyes clouded completely, and her stomach fell. Only the wind stirred the horse's tail now.

Sometimes, things are more beautiful in death than in life. Sometimes, they are prettier because you learn to appreciate them while they were living. You learn that they really were a thing to marvel at because they were special, and nothing can ever be put back in your life that was quite like them. Sky was the one thing. I always knew she was beautiful in life, but it was as if the world was grieving for her death. I didn't know her well or long. But she was special; she was a living creature who didn't deserve to die.

I numbly stood up and sang my song again. This time, I sang it louder. This time I sang it so her soul could hear it and take it with her on her voyage. When I finished, I hung my head and walked to Jaci. I jumped into the saddle and said, "Sky is gone...but there is no changing it."

Niyol cast me a horrified look, but calmed down when he saw the anguish in my eyes that still remained. The wolves were still sitting with their ears back and tails limp, and the horses looked mortified. Considering they had both grown up in captivity, I assumed neither my mare nor Niyol's stallion had even seen death. The little bluebird sang a sad song, but her eyes were cold and hard, and she was ready to fight her little battle again.

"Now, I think it's time we made sure Sky didn't die in vain. Let's go save Silver." I spoke with a hard tone to my voice that not even I knew I could use, but as I stood up in the stirrups and turned Jaci towards the forest, I realized I had more strength in me than I used to think. I guess I had just discovered how empowering I could be, for behind me rode a man, a horse, three wolves and a bird.

And they were following me.

We rode through the forest, having the wolves run in front and track Silver's scent.

She had been taken on a horse, by three men. The men were wearing the 'scent of excitement', as Goldensun put it, and had run off northward.

She's wanted...we all are, I thought, remembering the parchment with our names on it. *But could news of our thieving really spread so quickly, Goldensun?* I asked her as we tracked down Silver and her captors.

Goldensun gave me her version of a shrug. *I don't know, but I've learned to stop underestimating mankind. Your gossip spreads like wildfire. It wouldn't surprise me.*

I groaned. It still didn't make sense. I mean, it was bad enough that I was wanted. I just had to drag my friends into becoming wanted criminals too. What was wrong with me?

Goldensun lifted her nose from the mud long enough to give me a sympathetic glance, for even though I wasn't talking to her, she still could hear my thoughts. Then she turned back to tracking and stuck her muzzle in the ground.

I felt myself slump in the saddle. I felt crushed, for this was entirely my fault. Had I not gone to the Mountains, Niyol and Silver wouldn't be in this mess, and I would still have my knife. I wouldn't have dragged anyone down with me, and life would be normal. All my fault.

Riding beside me atop Blaze, Niyol glanced over and asked, "Kohana, are you okay?"

I wanted to say, 'yeah, everything is fine', but I couldn't pull it off. I shook my head. His eyes pleaded with me to tell him more.

"It's all my fault," I whispered. "Silver wouldn't be in this mess, and you would be back with your, um, grandmother, and neither of you would be considered criminals and I would just be Outcast again. Life would be much, much simpler, everything would be back to normal, and you guys wouldn't have gotten dragged down by me."

Niyol steered Blaze closer, and I looked up. His pretty, sea-green eyes were calm and full of understanding, and despite my searching, he wasn't hiding any emotions, it seemed.

"Kohana, don't beat yourself up. This has been the adventure of a lifetime! I mean, in just a few months, I have met a girl who can talk with her wolf, stood up to Dragons, learned my grandmother is a demon, stolen more things than I ever imagined, and fought hand-to-hand with a guy twice my size. You didn't drag me down, you pulled me up to do things I never thought I could!"

I tried to smile, but I couldn't. Niyol was lying, he had to be. But again I tried looking past the emotions his eyes showed, and that was all there was. Just understanding, calmness and a hint of…of something I couldn't quite name.

"I'm serious. And I am sure Silver feels the same way. Because not only have you given us something to fight for, but you gave us something to believe in."

I looked up questioningly. He smiled.

"You told us your story, and we didn't back away. We didn't leave you because we know you are right!" he said.

I furrowed my brow. He wasn't making sense. "Okay, you have something to fight for. *Why* are you fighting for it though? I mean, like I said before. I'm just a stupid, Outcast princess. Plus, this all started with my knife—"

"*My* demon grandmother," he interrupted.

I continued without paying the comment much attention. "So I don't see why you are helping me." Niyol rolled his eyes, as if I was oblivious to the obvious.

"Don't you get it? We fight with you because we *know* you. The real you, not the 'Outcast princess'. We know you, Kohana Silvermist, the one who is a superb archer, and smart and beautiful and one-of-a-kind. We fight for you."

He smiled a blinding, white smile, and it struck me down like a bolt of white lightning. And I smiled too. I couldn't help it. The thought had entered my mind and filled me with such gratitude and happiness that I just couldn't contain it.

He looked ahead, blushing slightly, the smile slowly fading from his face as he returned to the world around us. And I looked on, but not failing to notice that I felt my cheeks burning too.

We came to a large clearing in the forest. Sunlight streamed in and lit up the side of a wooden tavern; windows aglow with candlelight and muffled laughter sounding inside. The grass was dark green and lush, despite the coming of winter, and the colorful trees all around made the scene look like a painting from a fairytale. The clink of glasses and more laughter filled the air, and a large man stumbled out the door. He vomited in the grass right next to it, wiped his beard, and returned inside for more.

I looked to Goldensun. *They took her here?* I asked doubtfully. This didn't seem like the place to go to turn in a 'criminal'.

Her scent leads in there. So I would assume so.

I scowled at the tavern, so alight with happy, drunken men. I was about to turn around and have the wolves check her scent again, when I saw the horses tied up outside.

There were four horses, all jet-black, and one had a rope tethered onto another's saddle. Two were large males, the other females. The one that was tied up to the other horse was a young horse, and she had pretty white patches all over her hide.

Niyol glared at the tavern and the wolves were growling angrily and pacing. *What's the plan, Kohana?* Goldensun snarled. I looked down at her, startled by her assumption that I actually had a plan.

I shrugged. *Wing it?*

She looked up to me with sarcasm flitting in her eyes. *Here we go again...* she grumbled.

Another man, different than the one who vomited, slammed the tavern door open and shouted something back inside. He had a long beard and scraggly black hair, and he began to untie the four horses. He was followed by two more men, who looked very similar to the first. One was carrying a girl in his arms.

Dark brown hair fell in a braid from the girl's head, but her face was turned towards the man's chest. Her hands and feet were bound by a coarse rope. Her hands were tied up behind her, and were dangling underneath her body in a way that couldn't have been comfortable. Her legs drooped from the man's arms.

The girl's carrier deposited her roughly onto the ground. Of course, being unconscious, the girl fell onto her back and let out a light groan. She rolled over and exposed her face, but I already knew it was Silver.

I jumped off of Jaci's back, and prepared to shoot an arrow when Goldensun grabbed my boot. *If you attack without thought, prey often gets away,* she said, speaking very old words of wisdom shared by wolves.

I glared at the men, and put down my bow down without responding to Goldensun. She did have a point, however. I would wait.

The men were talking to each other in low voices, and I could catch only a few words.

"Desaria…higher price…others…" one of the men said. A few more garbled words were exchanged, then the biggest and obviously leader of the group shouted a few profanities at the man, and punched him in the gut. The second one tried to break up the fight, but was pushed aside.

Out of nowhere, with little provocation, it seemed, the two men were now fighting. I figured it had to be the recent consumption of alcohol that made them this way.

The second man, now on the ground, rolled his eyes and went to check on Silver. The others were shouting and taking wicked blows at faces, guts, shoulders; anything that was in reach was now a target. It was clear that the bigger man was going to win, and the smaller was already bruised and bleeding from a cut in his lip.

"We should get her now, in the confusion," a voice whispered in my ear. I whipped my head around in shock, to see Niyol crouched next to me. I hadn't even heard him dismount or come over here. But he was right. I took aim and, ignoring the guilt that dropped in my stomach like a stone, let my arrow fly.

Unfortunately for Silver's captor, he stood up from his original position and found himself with a long twig with crimson feathers sticking out of his stomach. He howled in pain and crumpled over, but the other two were far too busy fighting to realize their comrade had been hurt. So I shot again. This arrow hit him in the heart, and he slumped, lifeless, onto the ground.

But what now? The fighters would surely see us if we went to take Silver back. But Niyol didn't realize that, and before I could stop him, he was running across the clearing towards the tavern. The men fought, Silver started to gain consciousness. But in an instant, everything changed.

The large man sent a punch to the other's face that made him finally give up. He stumbled backwards and fell. He groaned and didn't get back up.

The man still standing saw Niyol trying to pick up Silver. He roared and ran towards my friend, and in the split-second we all had to react, something strange happened. Stranger than the typical unusual things that have become a common occurrence in our group.

What appeared to be an actual piece of the sky rocketed down towards the man. It was fringed with darker and lighter blues. It was too fast to make out the shape, just a varied blue blur. But the man about to hit Niyol like a bull was the missile's target, and it hit dead-on.

The man screamed and tried to swat away his attacker, but the blur was incredibly fast. Niyol stood there, awestruck, with a half-conscious girl in his hands, while the rest of us were frozen in the trees. It was Haunt who barked loudly and snapped him out of his state.

Niyol stumbled towards us and laid Silver down on the soft forest grass. We tried to ignore the man's screams as he was bombarded again and again by the blue blur, and despite the obvious danger of it, I was extremely curious as to what it was.

The four black horses, spooked by the man's screams, kicked out at the post they were tied to and pulled at the reigns. One of the blows broke the post, and they all pulled away, neighing and whinnying. My heart sunk as I watched them get away. I had assumed we would take one to make up for Sky. Now, we were one horse short.

"Get her on Jaci. I can run. Don't wait up for me if I fall behind. Understand?" I said. He looked at me in frustration.

"Kohana, we aren't going to leave you behind. You–"

"Well what do you propose we do?" I asked, cutting him off mid-sentence. He glared at me for one more moment, gave a defeated sigh, and turned back to Silver.

"Wake up, Silver. Come on," he mumbled, while I cut the rope that bound her. "Kohana is cutting the rope off of you and you'll be free in a moment or two, but we need you to wake up. Come on..."

She fluttered her eyelids, but she clearly wasn't going to gain consciousness anytime soon.

"We have to tie her to the horse. We will go as fast as we can and tie the horses together, but she isn't going to wake up and we need to get out of here."

Niyol nodded his assent and we set to work. Still the man in the clearing was fighting the sky-attacker, and nasty red marks were appearing all over him. They almost looked like burns. Scratches joined the marks and blood oozed from several limbs. His face and arms wore the worst of the wounds, and his screams of pain, terror and confusion made me want to vomit up my last meal.

Finally, all was safe. It had only taken a few minutes, but it felt like hours. I slapped Jaci's rear end when Niyol was ready to go, and we all dashed off into the forest, heading northeast and away from the tavern, the man and the strange blue blur.

Nobody talked the whole time. The silence was glass, and none of us wanted to shatter it. I ran on foot while the others rode the horses. Silver had finally regained consciousness. The wolves ran at my feet, lunging forward and backward in long strides. Running with them, I truly felt as if I were part of a pack again, like days past when I ran with East River pack.

I think we didn't talk for another reason. Everyone was thinking about something. All eyes were absent and lost in deep thought, and I could imagine that mine were as well. Questions about the blue smudge rang in my head, a swarm of angry bees reverberating through my skull. *What was it? Who sent it, if anyone? Why did it attack the man? And why did it seem like it was saving us?* Hundreds more accompanied these, and only the loud yelp of a surprised Goldensun brought me out of my reflection.

She had completely stopped running, and was looking up into the clear sky, a look of pure bewilderment spread across her face. I shouted for the others to stop, and the people pulled on the horses' reigns while the wolves skidded in the forest floor.

We had run into a clear forest, not like Dark Forest. The trees all had bright colors, and their trunks were spread apart, leaving ample room to see the sky. As I looked up with my companion, I noticed a cobalt speck among the lighter blue, and as I looked harder, I noticed it was getting bigger.

"Hinto!" I whispered to myself. Goldensun growled, stepping closer to me. I didn't know if it was for protecting me or defending herself. Niyol had somehow heard me and narrowed his eyes, looking skyward like us.

The other wolves, picking up on our mood, started pacing anxiously. Doli took cover near Silver, who just looked perplexed. I pulled my bow from over my back and notched an arrow in it, but didn't pull it taut or aim at the Dragon. I simply wanted to be ready.

A thundering roar sounded and the smudge got closer. I could now make out the sliver of fabric that was the Dragon's wings, and the glint of his claws and scales. He was rapidly descending; now the yellow of his eyes were visible and each tooth was clear. He spread his mighty wings wide and landed with all the grace and power that a beast as himself should have. The air buffeted all around us from his wings as he landed.

"What do you want, Hinto?" I asked with much defiance in my voice. I flung my words at him with scorn, seeing as he was the one who took away my life in the Mountains. His electric gaze swept over me and my friends.

"Kohana, is it true?" Hinto's cobalt blue nostrils flared, but I don't think it was in anger. His eyes were bright with curiosity.

I glared at him. I had no clue what he was talking about.

"Are you really going to stop him? Tatsuo, who wishes to control us?" The blue Dragon couldn't hide the contempt from his voice, as if he was ashamed and insulted that someone as low as me would be the one to try and do it. I responded with boldness in my voice,

"Nobody else would want to. I don't even want to. But if nobody else will, I guess I'll step up and do it, seeing as everyone wants me dead anyways." I surprised myself how I wasn't afraid, and how not even the flare of anger in Hinto's eyes set me off guard. I meant what I said and this Dragon didn't scare me.

"You're quite courageous, then. Or perhaps it is stupidity. Regardless, I–"

Niyol jumped off Blaze's back, drawing and brandishing his sword in front of the Dragon. "She is *not* stupid!" he shouted. Hinto growled and tried to control his anger. He then smirked, lowering his face so that he was eye-level with Niyol. Smoke spiraled up from his nostrils in small, thin clouds.

"Remember, boy, Kohana has an important destiny to fulfill…but you still have plenty of room to be roasted like a pig," he growled.

I placed my hand tentatively on Niyol's shoulder. His eyes still flashed in defiance, but he took a step back.

I turned back to Hinto. "So why haven't you left yet? You know it's me, coming to save you all despite what you have done to me. And I'm not doing it for you, I'm doing it for everyone who would suffer if this 'Tatsuo' guy got out," I said, disdain filling my voice. I still wanted him to know that frankly, I was not thrilled to be doing this. I was even less thrilled that it was following along with some master plan that only he knew of. It made me feel like I was doing it for him.

His shining sapphire tail swished along the forest floor, kicking up piles of dead leaves and barely missing the trunks of two nearby trees. His long neck swayed and his eyes seemed to be surveying me, just like when we first met. Hinto let out a deep, troubled sigh that echoed through the trees and seemed to make the branches shake with the wind. It almost sounded like a growl, but the defeat that filled his electric eyes told me otherwise.

"Kohana," the blue Dragon said, bowing down low, "Get on my back. I must show you something, but we must fly there."

I looked between him, Niyol, Silver and Goldensun, wondering what to do. I couldn't leave them here in the middle of an unfamiliar forest in an unfamiliar Kingdom. And how would we even find each other again? But Hinto had found us before, and we hadn't even seen him.

Niyol gave a tiny nod, Goldensun remained impassive. Silver shook her head; her eyes screamed, *don't do it! It's a trick, don't get on!*

But I reached out for the beast's shoulders, unsure of how to do this. I swung myself on like I would a horse, straddling his shoulder blades and right at the base of his long, serpent-like neck.

Hinto stood, and it shocked me at how high up we already were. My eyes were higher than the lowest branches of the trees.

With a swift glance back to make sure I was ready, Hinto spread his massive wings, and pumped them three times. The first flap got us to the treetops, the second high above them, and by the third we were so aloft that my little vagabond team were like small splotches below me; Goldensun was howling nervously while Niyol and Silver waved in an awkward way. I was about to wave back but Hinto started to rapidly beat his wings and we rose even higher above the forest, so high that the trees were miniscule and my friends were gone.

I could see the Zomer river to the south, glinting in the sunlight. The little clearing with the tavern was a little closer. Beyond the Zomer river were the dark green treetops of Dark Forest, but that was as far as I could see in that direction. Everywhere I turned, I saw treetops and forest, some water possibly. When the wind blew, they all danced in unison to the same music, same beat. It was beautiful.

And then Hinto sped off to the southwest, back to Desaria, as fast as the wind would carry us. His cerulean wings flapped like mad, trying to get me to wherever we were going. My unbraided hair whipped behind me, and I knew it would be a pain to untangle. It would take time I didn't have. Along with that, it was cold. The air rushed against my exposed skin like water in a mountain stream; drenching me in its chill. I needed winter clothing, and instantly regretted not wearing enough. It was freezing up here, and I had to decide whether or not I wanted to grip the Dragon's scales or clutch my arms to keep me warm. I went with the scales.

Shortly after we began to fly, a stream of black clouds appeared on the horizon. A few short minutes later, we were at the source. It was a forest fire. Orange flames licked at the trees, which would suddenly explode into a scorching blaze. It contrasted terribly with the cold air, and I would experience hot and cold bursts, which was extremely uncomfortable. I wondered if Hinto ever got cold flying up so high.

"So? It's a forest fire, they happen all the time!" I shouted. Hinto whipped his head around in shock.

"This is no natural occurrence," he snarled. Electric eyes shot daggers at me, and for a moment I was genuinely afraid. "This was man-made! They lit this forest on fire in order to 'flush out' the Outcast! They still think you are in Desaria!"

I gaped down at the burning trees. I could practically see their spirits flowing into the sky.

"Why did you show me this?" It seemed as though Hinto was indicating that somehow this, too, was my fault.

Hinto was silent for awhile, hovering over the burning forest. Then he said, "King Tse issued this. He wants you dead, Kohana. He needs you out of the way, because only you can figure out who killed your family and clear your name. If you can do that, you will take the throne from him. King Tse will not settle for that. If you can't stop him, he will fear nothing and rule with an iron fist."

"Why do you care?"

Again, there was a moment of contemplation.

"Things are very complicated, Kohana. I'm not sure if you've realized yet, all of the strings your fate is tied to. There is something building, something bigger than you can comprehend at the moment. Tse is at the heart of it, and that is all you need to know."

This answer didn't satisfy me. I crossed my arms and arched my eyebrows in disbelief.

Hinto curled his lip a bit. He then sighed, closing his eyes and drooping his neck. "Fine, maybe I do care a little bit about humans. But only because they are interesting creatures, and because our races share a complicated past. But, that isn't important. Just get rid of Tatsuo, then we can talk."

I smirked from my spot on his shoulders. Then, recalling something he had said a moment ago, wiped the grin off my face.

"Wait…Hinto, who killed my family? Why would he be so concerned that I knew…?" The thought formed in my head. "It can't be. Are you saying that Tse was the one who poisoned them?"

Hinto looked back with a grim face. "He wanted the throne and wasn't prepared to wait. He would have killed you too, had you been there. This is why you cannot let him be King any longer than you must. He rules without sympathy and is unfit to be King."

I couldn't process. I couldn't think or do or say, and it took all my strength to stay atop his back, and not plummet into the flames below. Sensing this, Hinto rapidly turned and headed back towards where we came from.

I barely noticed anything. *Tse killed them. He was the one who killed my family. I trusted him, and he killed my family. Tse killed my family. This can't be right. The Dragon is lying. He never liked me. Yes, he is playing some sick joke on me. He just keeps trying to ruin my life. He is lying.*

"I'm not lying. Not pretending. Tse killed your family." Hinto said it like he would state something normal, something that doesn't involve emotion.

He must be mistaken. Tse couldn't have…wouldn't have…it wasn't him.

I didn't notice when we landed, or when Hinto spoke to Niyol, told him to watch me carefully. That I wasn't feeling well. Probably didn't want to talk. I didn't notice when Silver rushed to my side and placed her hand on my forehead, or when the wolves started pacing nervously in front of me. My state of shock was too intense to be able to notice anything.

Tse killed my family.

Tse killed my family.

Vengeance wasn't just optional. It was necessary.

Chapter 9
Reality

I was stunned. I couldn't believe what Hinto had said, I mean it just couldn't be true. Not Tse. I couldn't stop thinking that something had been mistaken, as we often do when something goes awry.

That night, I dreamed. I dreamed of horrible things; of murders and shadows and nightshade. I dreamed of my family, suffering by the hands of the deadly plant, and I dreamed of Tse laughing wickedly above them.

I am running through the castle halls, oblivious to the scene I am to encounter. I have a handful of red, purple, pink and white wildflowers that I had found growing just a short walk outside the castle, and as I run along, a few petals flutter down around me. Mother will chastise me for picking them without reason, but she won't mean it. She will take the flowers from my hands and put them in with the bouquet that is already placed on the table. Maybe she will put one in her hair, and she will give one to Father. Or Father will pluck one from the bouquet and give it to Mother, bowing down like a true King, and she will take it with a curtsey. They will maybe hug or kiss or hold hands, and Chayton and I will make disgusted faces at them. Secretly, I will smile, because I love how in love they are.

My feet hit the cold stones and I fantasize about what they will do. My laughter echoes through the castle. I burst through the doors in exuberance, but the smile dies on my lips when I see them all on the ground.

Suddenly, a shadow descends upon me. My body changes; I am no longer a little girl, but as I am today. The black mist caresses me and changes the scene, but not before I hear my own cries of panic. I feel the tears streaming down my face as they did all those years ago. The shadow talks to me, but I can't understand its words. "I can't hear you!" I shout, and I don't know why. The air grows cold and sinister, but still I cannot hear the garbled words that the shadow says.

Then, without any warning, I am upon Hinto's back. His yellow eyes are sympathetic, but I can barely see them. I am falling towards the smoke, into the fire. It burns my skin, and I scream, but nobody comes to save me.

"You should have died with them," the shadow's voice says. It flits about the flames like a fairy, laughing and always just out of reach. "You suffer and you burn, but if you had only died with them, you'd be free of pain. Free..."

I scream again, but this time in utter frustration. "Let. Me. GO!" I bellow. The shadow's face is momentarily visible, and it is full of shock. It drops me from the fire as if I have become too hot to touch, and once again I am falling.

I have the strange sensation of floating, now. As if I am in a deep pool of water, completely submerged, yet totally able to breathe. I see Tse through a murky blackness, strolling through the castle with Father's robe on. He sits at the throne, he eats at the head of the table, he sleeps in the bed that once belongs to my parents. He trains in the courtyard with guards that used to serve my family, he rides horses through town that belonged to us.

He approaches a man who is tied to a post. His back is exposed, and a guard hands Tse a leather whip. I close my eyes, but the crack of it and the scream of the man are still audible. I pull myself away, forcing myself back into the waking world.

I woke with a jump and heavy breath. My blanket felt wet above me, the spirits shone with a watery brightness. I felt my forehead and it was soaked with sweat.

Kohana, are you okay? Goldensun asked from a little bit away. She had obviously been sleeping, for her fur was ruffled and her eyes held a dreamy look to them.

I nodded and closed my eyes, trying to push away the snippets of the nightmare I could remember. *Just a bad dream.*

Goldensun stood up. She walked over to me and sniffed my forehead. Her cold, black nose felt good against my hot skin.

Hinto came by while you were sleeping. He is very concerned for you, believe it or not.

I rolled my eyes, knowing I was smart in choosing not to trust that statement. I would have to see it with my own eyes to believe it.

I sighed. As much as I wanted to march down to Enin, shoot all the guards if I had too, and kill that awful Tse, I knew that I owed my time to the Dragons, and to that Tatsuo guy.

Goldensun nuzzled her head under my chin. *I'll always be here for you, Kohana,* she said. *Come wake me if you want to talk.*

She took a few steps back to where she had been sleeping, curled up, and with one last apologetic look at me, fell back asleep.

Truthfully, it was the best thing she could have done. It felt good to know she was there, but she wasn't going to force anything out of me, especially if I wanted it to stay in.

I couldn't go back to sleep. The claw scratch of a moon shone in my eyes and haunted me, reminded me of the precious time ticking away. We had approximately twenty days before the Red Moon. Approximately twenty days to get the knife, save the Dragons. Or else it was game over.

I crawled out from under my yak hide and grabbed my bow and arrows. I then climbed one of the trees and perched in the highest branches, watching the sliver of moon and the forest below me.

Movement caught my eye. Just a rustle in the branches a few trees down. I assumed it was a bird and shifted my gaze back to the moon.

Ever so faintly, the rustling noise came again. Out of the corner of my eye I snatched a glimpse of something scarlet-red, like a flame, but when I turned to look at it, the color was gone.

There were a lot of spirits out tonight. The sky was filled with them, and although I searched and searched, I couldn't find the group of them that I thought was my family's. I sighed and pulled an arrow from my quiver. The arrows clattered. But another sound accompanied the wooden noise from inside. It sounded like some leaves had fallen in.

I looked down into it, but it was all shadow. The wisp of moon gave no light, and the spirits weren't much help either. So I stuck my hand in and was surprised to find not leaves, but a piece of parchment. I pulled it out, to see it had a light, thin scrawl on the front.

Kohana

I scowled at it. I unfolded it and squinted at the words inside, trying to make out what they said. It took quite a while, but soon I had read the entire note.

There is danger afoot. You don't know me, but I have been watching you closely. When you need me most, I will come. Until then, continue on your journey. I wish you the very best of luck, for you will certainly need it. Don't give up yet, for there is still time. You will not fail; I know it. We are cheering for you.

F

P.S. The night is always darkest just before dawn.

I read the note several times. None of it made much sense, besides the 'danger afoot' part. I knew that. The Dragons — everyone in Calleo, really — were in danger. But nothing else actually made any sense.

"When you need me most, I will come," I murmured. *Who's 'F', and when will I need him or her? And why did they mention "the night is always darkest just before dawn?"* I'd been told that before…I was beginning to wonder if the saying itself was going to haunt me for the rest of my journey.

And someone was watching me closely. Did that mean someone was following us? Or perhaps someone like Fae was watching me through an orb or something? If it was Fae, I suppose it would make sense, for her name started with 'F', too, but this did not look like Fae's handwriting. It was somebody new, someone I didn't know. It made me feel unsafe, vulnerable.

Either way, it confused me. How did the note get there? Who put it there? And why?

Again, I glimpsed the red flash. But as I looked back to where it came from, I saw nothing but the dark shape of the tree.

Not a sound came from it, either. Was it just my imagination? Or was there actually something fiery in the tree, something…or someone…moving in the branches and watching me?

I groaned and shook my head. Things were getting too complicated. It didn't help the fact that I couldn't shake the crushing weight of knowing Tse killed my family.

I heard more rustling behind me, but not the stealthy kind. It was more of just an approach. I turned around and saw the shadow of my 'favorite' blue Dragon.

"I see you are having trouble sleeping," Hinto growled in that deep voice. His head was peeping through the canopy, but he had to crane it to reach that high, considering last time I saw him, his head rested somewhere among the branches.

I nodded and turned back towards the moon.

"Kohana, there is more that you must know, in order to defeat Tatsuo," he said. I glanced back at him to show I was listening, and he continued.

"You see, it isn't just supremacy that Tatsuo wants. He is envious of our magic and power, yes. But he also is envious of our freedom. He created us. My ancestors were crafty and free thinkers, and they didn't like being controlled by anyone. They came to think for themselves instead of being workers as Tatsuo had intended. They refused to be controlled. So they set up an intricate plan that worked over the count of many years, and eventually managed to escape him. And he has spent many centuries looking for the right time to bring us all back.

"Now is the time. Previously, he had no strength to return. Not even his loyal demons could bring him back without the help of us. But then they caught wind of the magic knife that had been created by Dragonfire. With this knife, Tatsuo realized he could be freed. He could be set loose on the night of the Red Moon, with a knife made with the breath of his own creations' children.

"We are all anxiously awaiting his return, too. He will find all of us, no matter how we hide. And that is why we rely on you, Kohana. He knows all of our strengths and weaknesses. A whole weyr of Dragons wouldn't stand a chance against him."

I still was gazing up at the moon. It was ever so slowly falling towards the west, sinking in a pool of black night. It looked like the stars were supporting it, making a pillow for the thin moon. I looked back to Hinto.

"So, what you are saying, is that the reason you can't fight him is because…"

"He would know what our intentions were before we even did. The fight would be unfair, for his control over Dragons is absolute. As soon as he is in the same realm as Dragons, the fight is over. We need you Kohana."

I tilted my head to the spirits and the moon, drinking in the very little light through my eyelids, letting it soak through my skin and light my brain with knowledge. Let it color my hair a pale white and give me wisdom…but when I opened my eyes again, everything was the same as before.

"I never said I wasn't going to help you," I said. I thought I saw a smile twitch at the corners of the Dragon's mouth, but when I glanced over, it was gone.

"Kohana, I am truly sorry about your family, and Tse," Hinto rumbled. His electric yellow eyes sparked with, to my surprise, genuine sorrow. "I didn't want to tell you. But I had to. You had to know the truth and stop hiding behind lies."

I nodded and tried to hold back the wave of fresh tears I felt coming. But the real reason I didn't cry is simple. I think I knew it was Tse the whole time, but never even let myself know. I did hide behind a lie without actually knowing it.

I said nothing. Hinto was silent. He let out a long breath, but I couldn't tell if it was a growl, or a sigh. He spread his long, pale wings and whispered, "I'm rooting for you, Kohana. Things are rough, but they will get better. This destiny is yours to see through, and although it seems sudden and unfair, it is the way the spirits have aligned." He paused again, before adding, "It might be dark now, but soon dawn will break, and only then will we see what we may."

And with a large gust of wind, Hinto was no more than a silhouette against a spirit-painted night.

Chapter 10
Firebird

I didn't sleep for the rest of the night. I stayed up in my perch and watched the dawn come. Lost in my thoughts, I didn't hear Niyol calling me until he was just a few branches down the trunk.

"Kohana! Come on, we have to get moving!"

After a quick breakfast, we started walking. Silver rode on Jaci, but you could see the pain in her eyes. No physical pain, but I knew that her heart hurt. Poor Silver. Poor Sky.

The day dragged on forever. We ran into nobody, never heard the slightest crunch of leaves or twigs coming from somebody in the forest. We were completely alone, all day.

I let the others believe that. Because as silent as the forest seemed, there was still the fact that *I* knew I was being followed.

The note from the hidden 'F' burned like a forest fire in my quiver. I wanted to rip it out and read it again, and see if I had missed any clues. Scorch marks or water marks or stains from leaves or berries. Anything to give me a hint would have been favorable.

And how did one write like that? The scrawl on the note was perfect; not a single word misspelled or misshaped. I envied this anonymous author. They had perfect handwriting, while I could barely remember how to hold a quill.

Jealousy bubbled up inside me like a boiling pot of soup over a fire. I don't know why I felt such sudden anger at the writer. Perhaps the muscles in my hand wanted to do more than shoot arrows, more than thrust swords and knives. They wanted to create, not destroy.

I tried to shift my thoughts to something else; the beauty of the day, whatever Goldensun was trying to tell me, Doli constantly staying by Silver's side, feeling her companion's pain, the splendor of the leaves that fluttered to the ground all around us, forming piles by the trunks of the trees.

What drew my attention was the splash of blue in the forest. Too pure and too low to be part of the sky, too bright to be clothing.

"I'll be right back," I said. Everyone looked strangely at me, all eyes filled with several questions. But no one protested, and I veered off into the woods.

I started making my way back to where I saw the flash of blue. I found nothing. No tracks, no clumps of fabric, fur, or feathers. Nothing to suggest anything was even there, or had been.

I was just turning back when I heard a soft rustle and a crackling noise, followed shortly by an astonished cry.

I looked up and to my right and saw a small fire burning in the topmost branches. Instantly, three things stood out to me.

One. There was a young man crouched in the trees, with messy, short brown hair and a face made for laughing, even though it was twisted into a look of shock.

Two. There were two birds in the tree. Screeching and cawing, while their owner tried to calm them down.

Three. They were no ordinary birds at all. They were Phoenixes. One was a muscular, bright crimson bird with black-tipped feathers, while the other was leaner and had blue feathers. Both had striking glowing eyes that mirrored their flaming plumage.

The boy had cried out when his red Phoenix brushed up against a leaf, and set it on fire. Naturally, the flames licked up at the other branches and twigs, and soon the whole tree was ablaze.

"Run!" he shouted, and leapt from the tree just as it his branch became engulfed in flames. His Phoenixes, immune to fire, swirled from the branches, looking pleased with the heat.

I turned around and dashed towards where the group was, and the boy followed me. His birds shadowed him, but stayed clear of any branches they could. We didn't need to add more fire to the one already spreading.

I saw Goldensun as I darted through the autumn forest and I shouted, *Follow me...the forest is on fire!*

As I buzzed past her, I heard her paws crunching on the dead leaves behind me. *Kohana! You leave for two seconds, and already you've found a boy and set the trees ablaze?*

Pretty much. You should stop expecting otherwise of me.

I was running full on, faster-than-wolf-speed now, and I was shocked at how fast the boy was running too. He kept up with me the whole way, and was barely breathing heavy when we reached the others.

"Niyol, Silver! We have to get out of here!" I shouted.

As if to stress my point, black smoke billowed from the sky and another eruption sounded. I could see the bright blaze of the fire chasing us through the foliage, and I could sense the bewildered souls of trees as they were toasted under the flames. Small creatures darted past us in their attempt to escape the inferno that now haunted their blessed home.

"Wait...who is that?" Niyol asked, as he pointed at the boy.

"We need to get out of here before the fire can catch up with us!" I exclaimed, ignoring his question. Truthfully, I didn't know, but a strong feeling in my gut told me it was 'F'.

I turned to the boy. "There aren't enough horses. Get your birds to fly over the trees. We'll just have to outrun it."

He nodded, looking somewhat scared, and looked at the red bird perched on his outstretched arm. The bird ruffled its feathers and zoomed upward, his blue companion following.

The group was off faster than a crack of lightning. Between the speeding horses, the wolves, the boy and I, we were clear long before the flames ever reached us, but the dead forest and dry air would only supply the fire with more fuel, so we had to keep moving.

Once we made it into the hills, where the trees thinned out into nothing, we stopped. The horses were tired, the wolves panting, and both the boy and myself were about to fall over from exhaustion.

In the bright red sunset, I could see the smoke billowing into the sky; a plume of choking blackness that was poison to all who inhaled it. I felt bad for a while; the beautiful forest would soon be reduced to nothing but skeletons of trees and ashes.

Silver and Niyol cast cautious glances over at the boy with us as they were unpacking our things for the night. I turned to him. I could feel their eyes on us as we conversed.

"Who are you?" I asked.

He stared at me with coppery brown eyes, like the delicate feathers of an eagle, with all the beauty and added depth to them. I stared back, taking in his features.

He looked to be around sixteen winters old. His skin, dark and tan, was smooth and soft-looking. The underside of his forcarm, where the wrist guard didn't cover, was lacerated with long, sharp scars. I could only assume that they were from his birds, which landed softly on his shoulders just then.

"My name is Falcon. Falcon Shadownight, if you want to get technical," he said. His red bird ruffled its flaming feathers at the sound of his owner's name. "And who might *you* be?" Falcon continued. A glint in his eyes told me he was hiding something. He was a bad liar.

I squinted at his last comment. "Falcon? Wait..." I said. 'F.' "Are you the one who wrote the note?"

He turned his head. "Um...well, yeah. I've kinda been watching you for awhile."

I felt Niyol and Silver's energy change. They were very interested in the newcomer. I still heard the sounds of unpacking, but they were slower, more quiet, so as not to block out Falcon's words.

His copper eyes were alight with excitement. "I want to join you."

I narrowed my eyes to as small as they would go.

Although I wanted to open my arms to him, to anyone who was on my side, I somehow didn't trust him. His light brown eyes dared me to do otherwise.

"I'm Kohana, but you already know that. That," I gestured to Niyol, "Is my friend Niyol. The girl is Silver." I also introduced him to the wolves.

"Who are they?" I asked, pointing to the Phoenixes.

Falcon smiled and reached out to stroke the red Phoenix's feathers. I twitched hand instinctively to stop him, but watched in amazement. His hand wasn't burned as he ran his fingers through the scarlet plumage.

"Their feathers don't burn me, don't freak out or anything," he said with a laugh. Falcon switched his gaze back to the Phoenix. "His name is Pheo. The other one is Sapphire, but she prefers Saph."

"Is Pheo your...?" I let the question trail off, as there were many different ways to call an animal one's companion. Not one, definite term but several, and most didn't know them all.

"Yeah. Saph just follows us around." He leaned in close and whispered, "I think she has a little crush on Pheo. But don't tell her I said that!"

I couldn't help but smile. I nodded. "Okay."

We all sat and ate together that night, and although the others took a little while to get used to him, we decided he should join us. Goldensun was the least open to letting him come along.

How do we know we can trust him? She asked fretfully.

We don't. We don't know if we can trust anyone here. But I think he is going to be a valuable member to our team. I told her.

She narrowed her eyes and turned back to the campfire.

Falcon told us a little bit about himself, and joked around. But he kept the details of his past to his own memories. Nobody pried farther than they thought they should, and everyone respected his silence.

We all had something in common, however, and that was a past that was uncomfortable to speak of.

We talked deep into the night. I wanted to ask him how he learned to write so elegantly, but I knew that would be part of the past he kept away from us. We joked and laughed and enjoyed one another's company, and one by one we went to sleep, until it was just Niyol and I. He tossed another log on the dying fire, and then sat down next to me.

I had to admit, he was good looking. He stared at the fire, his aqua eyes sparking and popping just like the flames.

The fire crackled in front of me, and shadows danced on the grass. I was sure my shadow darted to and fro behind me as well.

"Why are we allowing him to come with us so easily?" Niyol whispered. He didn't look at me; his eyes were still directed at the fire, engrossed in the rhythmic dancing of the blaze.

I looked over at him, and as I tried to calm my racing heart, replied, "I guess I'm not really sure. I just...I kind of have this feeling that he will be a good ally to have with us. I feel it in my gut."

"Do you trust him?"

I glanced over at the sleeping boy, but was silent. *Did* I trust him? Or was I just so desperate for someone who believed in me that I let random strangers into the group?

No matter why I decided he could be trusted, I did. He was in the group, and the only way he was leaving would be if he left on his own accord. I wasn't going to make him leave.

"Truthfully, I don't know," I said. "But I trust my instinct."

Niyol nodded, but he seemed distant. A question burned in my mind, one that wouldn't let go. I took a deep breath and said,

"Why do you care about me?"

It was Niyol's turn to be shocked. He looked at me with wide eyes, as if the answer was right in front of me. When he saw I wasn't joking, he answered me. "Why wouldn't I? Ever since you first showed up at my village, I knew you were special. And now...now look at us! Look at *me*! I thought I was going to spend my life in that little Mountain town...but now I am adventuring across the continent! This is more exciting than anything I had ever dreamed..." his voice trailed off. "But that didn't really answer the question, did it?" he laughed.

I couldn't keep the smile off my face. But I soon turned serious as I waited for another answer.

He thought about it for a minute. "I guess I don't really know. Besides the fact that you are special, you are beautiful, and you are brilliant..."

I felt my eyes widen considerably. My eyebrows arched and my jaw dropped. This was not what I had been expecting him to say.

Niyol smiled. He closed my mouth and said, "Close that. You'll catch flies."

And then, with his finger still under my chin, he tilted my head and leaned in close. He rested his forehead against mine, and whispered, "I care about you because you're *you*. You are smart, beautiful, brave, sweet...the list goes on." Then, he moved his forehead away from mine and instead, kissed me.

It was the sweetest kiss I ever had, the one by the campfire. It beat my autumn kiss with Tse, so many years ago.

The smoky smell filled my nostrils and his lips were sweet like honey. I threw my arms around his neck and let myself go. In the back of my mind, I tried to pull away, and tried to tell myself that this wasn't right. This shouldn't be happening. If I let this happen, it could be trouble, is what it told me. But I shut out that little voice, shut it out and felt the pure pleasure of that kiss fill my body and flow through me like a crystal clear river.

We broke apart and I fluttered my eyelids open. Niyol's were still closed, as if he were still savoring the last of it on his lips.

I turned back to the fire, unsure of what to do now. I was about to rest my head on his shoulder, but Niyol yawned and stretched louder than necessary. "Well, I'm going to bed," he mumbled through a yawn. He gave me a long, warm hug, and left.

I stared at the embers for a long time. Now that the moment was over, I couldn't believe I had let myself do it. What was I thinking? What was I doing, letting him now think that I felt that way about him…which wasn't an untruth. But I had to put the mission before emotions. I already had enough of them to deal with, anyways.

But even though I tried so hard to berate myself for that kiss, that one moment of pure, untamed delight…I just couldn't. I loved every second of it, and several times I replayed it in my head. Even with my eyes closed, I could feel the passion coursing between us like a heartbeat that made two people one. Something that tied us together in a way that couldn't be done with words.

When dawn came, I didn't know what to say to him. I made up my mind in the night that I would have to tell him what was happening; I had to tell him how I was prioritizing my life, and the mission came first.

Thankfully, I didn't have to.

"Kohana, I have to talk to you," he said in the morning. Silver and Falcon were packing up, and he dragged me a little bit away to speak.

I nodded to tell him I was listening, and he spoke again. "I think...I think we shouldn't have kissed last night. I'm...I don't..." I saw him tripping over his words and I thought I could save him.

"I agree. Sort of. We need to get the mission done. There isn't...time...to do anything but finish it."

He nodded, thankful for my words. "Kohana...I'm sorry. Please don't take that the wrong way. Everything I said last night was, *is*, true...but last night didn't feel right..."

Wait...what? I thought. *It felt perfectly right to me. I just don't want to divert from the mission...*

"What?" was all I could say.

The hurt must have shown in my eyes, because instantly, Niyol tried to take back his words. "I didn't mean that! I just think that now...with the mission..." he was stumbling again, trying once more to cover the blunder. But I could see it in his eyes. The way they were sad, trying to break it to me as easy as he could.

"No. I understand," I said bitterly. I stalked off. How could something that felt so right to me, feel so wrong to him?

I went back to Silver and Falcon, and packed up my very few items silently. I hadn't slept at all, but I had gotten out my blanket in the night when it got cold.

We started northeast at a slow pace. Falcon and I, both terribly sore from yesterday's run, needed a break. We walked alongside the horses and wolves.

Niyol tried to catch my eye and talk to me several times, but I refused to pay him any scrap of attention whatsoever. But, that decision decided to come back and bite me in the face, because not only did I *not* do it casually, but I also ignored him to the point where the group started to notice.

What's wrong with you and Niyol? Did something happen last night? Goldensun asked. I narrowed my eyes and kept on walking.

Nothing happened last night, I replied stonily.

You're lying.

How can you tell?

I can always tell when you are lying. You aren't very good at it. So, tell me what happened.

I tried to not sigh, as much as I wanted to let it out. But instead I just said, *He kissed me, and then said it 'didn't feel right'. I feel like I've been tricked. Happy?* I couldn't keep the bitterness out of my voice. But instead of being mad, Goldensun walked closer.

I'm sorry, Kohana. She said as she brushed against my leg. Her fur swished against the patched pants I wore and it felt nice in the coming winter chill.

The hills we traversed were wide and grassy. I could imagine that in the summer, they were bright green and dotted with flowers. But now, in the heart of autumn, it was dusty brown and dead-looking.

By nightfall, we hadn't made it far. Walking was not the fastest way of travelling, clearly, but even though we hadn't gone far, my feet hurt and my body was stiff from yesterday. Behind us, the forest fire from yesterday, that seemed so long ago, smoked as only a tiny pillar.

We set up a campfire similar to the way we did last night, but instead of having Niyol next to me and Goldensun at my feet, I sat next to Silver, and went to bed early.

Goldensun followed me to my resting spot with sad eyes. My pain was her pain, my thoughts were hers. She had experienced the kiss and the argument several times, only because I had been thinking about it all day. I felt bad for forcing her to feel all that heartbreak that I did, but I also felt relieved that someone knew how I actually felt, how upsetting it was.

Even though I went to bed long before the others, I didn't fall asleep. I stayed up and tried counting spirits and breaths that my wolf took beside me, but nothing could call sleep to me. I was both mentally and physically exhausted, yet I couldn't sit still.

I stood up and walked over to the fire. It was just embers now, left without fuel when the others went to sleep. Jaci opened an eye when I passed her, but she soon went back to ignoring me, pressing her head into Blaze's neck. *How sweet*, I spat to myself.

The night was dark. The moon was completely gone; the only light cast was from the spirits. The faintest glow on the horizon suggested that the forest fire was still burning.

I saw a shadow move in the darkness, and I looked over to where everyone was sleeping. I could barely make out the silhouette of Niyol, as he dropped his head into his hands and murmured something.

He then looked over to me by the dying embers, which still emitted the faintest glow. I knew his face was serious as he stood up to come talk to me.

"Kohana," he whispered. I looked away.

"You don't understand. Please, let me—"

I cut him off. "No, *you* don't understand. You let me think that something would come from that. You let me think that you meant something from that. Apparently, I was wrong. So you can try to defend yourself, but I know what happened. I saw it in your eyes what you meant, and you just backtracked because you saw that I took it differently than you expected I would." I didn't yell and I didn't look at him. My voice was soft. But so much pain and power filled it that I knew I got the message across better than raising my voice.

Niyol sighed. I felt his hand hovering by my shoulder, but he dropped it in defeat.

"Kohana, when I said that this morning, I meant that I think…we shouldn't have. We need time to think things through. We need to finish the mission, too," he said.

"Niyol, that's not what you said before."

"Because I didn't know how to. And it all came out wrong the first time. I don't want to fight with you. You mean too much to me for that. Please don't do this to me, Kohana…" he sounded so hurt, so defeated…it was hard to stand my ground.

I tried not to cry. What would that show him? It would show him that I am weak and can't deal with things like this. I didn't want that to be his image of me.

"I don't want to fight either," I sighed. I looked up to him with a smile I didn't feel, and he sat down next to me in the dying grass.

Neither of us said anything. We didn't kiss, we didn't hug, we didn't rest our heads on each other's shoulders. We just sat in forced companionship and watched the night.

We both heard it at the same time. A kind of crackling noise, the sound of something stepping on a twig. In unison, we leapt to our feet and faced the noise.

Huge, scarlet eyes glared at us from the depths of darkness.

Chapter 11
Scarlet Snow

I panicked for a fraction of a second, before I realized who it was. I knew that Granite wasn't here on friendly terms. His eyes sparked and blazed like the fire in the forest. I just didn't understand how he had come so quickly, and from so far. Then I remembered our speed through the Mountains. He could have left only a few days ago and have caught up to us.

"Kohana..." he growled. I nodded to him, which seemed to infuriate him more.

"What do you think you're *doing?!*" he howled. Somehow, the others didn't wake. "The Outlands! You will not last a day once you cross over!"

I heard Silver turn in her sleep. The Phoenixes' glow got a little brighter, but dimmed again as they returned to normal sleep patterns.

I stumbled over my words as I spoke. "Well, I just...I have to...nobody..."

"You *have* to? Kohana, that's why you aren't going to survive! You have to *want* it, because then you have a drive! A reason to do it," Granite growled. I couldn't help but wonder why he was here, because his eyes showed more reason than just to scold me about my mission.

"I do want to! Well, I want my knife back, and I want Fallenoak back, and if this is what has to be done to get them, fine, I'll do it! Why does everyone keep fighting me about this? I'm kind of saving the world here, what's with all the complaints?" I threw my hands in the air, exasperated beyond description.

"What are you doing here?" Niyol asked, cutting us off.

Granite sighed and walked into the glow of the embers. The first thing I noticed was how skinny he had gotten. He was thin as a branch; each rib visible. I could count them. His fur was matted and looked as if he hadn't groomed it in a while. I could practically hear his stomach growling from where I stood a few yards away.

151

"I am here for you. My kind is being affected by the rise of Tatsuo as well. The Dragons have no need to eat much, seeing as they can go several months without a meal. But Tall Wolves cannot. The food supply is scarce, for the demons that serve him have been stealing and gorging themselves. We tried to make peace, but demons know of no such thing. We tried to reason with them, get them out of the Mountains, but they refused to listen. Then we tried to fight, but the casualties were great. We need your help."

I shook my head. "Granite, we have less than three weeks until the Red Moon. I can't go help you; I am barely going to make it to Galdur Fjall in time at this pace!"

He nodded. "I understand. The way you would help us is by ridding the world of Tatsuo. But you have to know what you're up against."

"What do you mean?" I asked. He was just ruler of all the demons, how bad could it be?

"Tatsuo cannot be killed with mortal weapons."

My eyes went wider than I thought they could. "What do you mean…'he can't be killed with mortal weapons'? Does that mean that arrows, knives, swords…"

"Won't work on him." Granite finished for me. "He is immune to them. He is of hatred so strong that no man-made weapon can destroy him, or even wound him."

"What about my knife…?"

"It may be enchanted by Dragonfire, but it is still man-made."

"How do I kill him then?"

Granite sighed. "Demons are the very essence of hatred, fear and anger. Weapons are made with spite; they're made to kill, and killing is an act of hate. *This* is why they will not work. They are part of who he is."

"So, are you saying I just have to find a weapon crafted by love, or something?" I asked, hoping for an answer even simpler than that, but knowing there would be no such thing. After all, things for us were never simple.

"It means what it means."

"How do you expect us to kill him without weapons, then? It was nearly impossible before...but now there is no shot at us being able to beat him!" I slumped to the ground, putting my fingers to my temples. I didn't know what to do anymore. The task in front of me was just too much to bear.

"Kohana, you can't give up now, this is your destiny," Niyol whispered.

"But I'm just one girl, how is any of this fair?"

Granite shook his head. "Life isn't always fair."

I glared at him with such ferocity that he took a step backwards in shock.

"Life isn't always *fair?* Look at my life! My family was *murdered.* I was blamed for that! Sent out to live on my own, with no clue how to do it, at just twelve winters old! Then, when I finally built a life somewhere else, it was shattered too! Sent on my own again, with only a vague idea of what I was supposed to be doing. Then, obstacle after obstacle came and tried to shoot me down, but I've kept going. Now, I don't think I can face another thing...I can't deal with one more thing working against me on this quest!"

There was no sympathy in the wolf's eyes. Niyol was clearly sad for me, but Granite had emotions of...well, granite.

"Kohana. Not everything in life is going to be easy. In fact, there will be more struggles than easy rides. But you have to think about the consequences of giving up. You are the only one who can kill him. You cannot pick your destiny."

"That's not the first time I've been told that," I growled.

Granite stuck his nose up so that he was looking down on me in the most condescending way he could. "And it certainly will not be the last."

With that, he walked off into the night, leaving me staring furiously after him.

I didn't sleep at all that night either. Niyol, being as faithful as anyone, sat with me all night. Part of the act infuriated me further, and part of it made my heart soar.

Morning came far too slowly. I was exhausted from three nights of no sleep, and it was hard to move in the morning and pack up. My movements were slow and jerky, my eyelids constantly drooping.

As questions swam through my head, the one at the forefront was *How are we going to get there in time?*

Nothing I thought of would have worked. But as we picked up our pace, I heard something that was entirely new to me, and all thoughts of Galdur Fjall vanished.

The noise that confronted me was like thunder and a lion's roar, jumbled together. The smell was of salt, and I saw the world abruptly end before there should have been horizon.

I steered away from our course and took off, full speed, towards the sounds and smells that I would soon come to associate with the ocean. The others followed, and I was vaguely aware of Niyol telling me to 'watch out'.

A large, tall, rocky cliff yawned before me, and I skidded to a halt, my body leaning over the edge. Below me, water crashed on sharp rocks.

I panted. That was too close.

I heard the others pull up on the horses beside me, and I could feel how tense Jaci was by the energy she emitted into the air. She pawed the ground nervously.

"What is it?" I asked. Both Silver and Niyol looked at me in utter disbelief.

"You mean you've never been to the ocean?" Niyol asked. I shook my head.

"Have you?"

Both of them nodded. Silver spoke first. "I went once when I was very little. Fae and Tokala took me to the Enyd Cliffs, but wouldn't let me get close. They said it was too dangerous, and I could fall off." She absentmindedly reached for the pendant around her neck, and gazed off into the ocean-horizon, lost in memories.

Where I was used to an uneven horizon, dotted with treetops or hillsides or mountaintops, this was the complete opposite. The ocean met the sky in a perfect, straight line.

"It's beautiful," I whispered. "When did you ever go?" I asked Niyol. As far as I knew, he had been in the Mountains his whole life. I guess I was wrong.

Niyol's face turned stony. I looked away, and didn't ask anything else. Although he knew I didn't need an answer, he continued.

"Chu'si took me when I was little. We saw a little fish trapped in a tiny pool, and just as he looked like he was going to run out of water, a wave came and swept him back to sea. Chu'si then told me that even when things looked grim, there would always be hope." He said no more.

I watched the ocean with wonder. It was vast, and I could sense the power held deep below the water. I could almost imagine a force stronger than Dragons, stronger than Tatsuo even, lashing its anger out on the cliff side with the frothy waves; bigger than anything that ever lapped at the beaches of Crystal Lake.

I wondered what other shorelines looked like. Many nights ago, when we were back in Desaria, Niyol and I had agreed to go to the beach after we completed this mission, but now I wondered what he meant. Was he picturing this, or perhaps the soft, sandy one on the edges of Crystal Lake?

Goldensun craned her neck forward, sniffing at the breeze. *It's very salty,* she said. I nodded.

It's different.

I wonder what's on the other side of it.

The question was odd. It was different than anything Goldensun had said before, and it made me wonder, too.

Maybe there are people like us, I offered. *Maybe wolves and Dragons and whole kingdoms of land.*

Well, everyone is always talking about it, Goldensun replied. *And you said the man who sold you the map came from across the seas. And Tatsuo will extend his reign far past Calleo. So, I would assume you are entirely correct.*

We camped a few yards away from the cliffs that night. I was insanely curious about the ocean. But I knew that I wouldn't be smart to go investigate.

That night started similar to the night of the kiss. The others went to sleep while Niyol and I stared at the flames of yet another campfire.

"What happened to your parents?" I asked him, the words tumbled out of my mouth so fast that I couldn't stop them, and I knew it was wrong to ask him such a thing. It was a private matter and I had not right to be butting into it, and yet I did anyways like a nosy girl hungry for gossip.

Niyol was silent for a long time. At first I thought he was just ignoring the question, but then he took a deep breath and said, "I never knew either of them. The village just woke one day to find me crying in the streets, only a few weeks old. Chu`si said she would be more than willing to take me in, and then I just grew up with her. I just called her my grandmother because it always seemed to fit."

I nodded. I kept my mouth shut, trying not to pry, but he clearly knew that I wanted to know more.

"When I think of my mother or father, I can't remember anything. I mean, sometimes I think I can; Mom had really silky hair, and Dad always smiled, and they loved each other very much. And Mother had really teal eyes, like mine. But, I was only with them for a few weeks; it's probably just my imagination."

I wanted to tell him how sorry I was that he couldn't remember them. Instead, I said, "Does it hurt more knowing that you never really knew them, or that you don't have them now?"

He shrugged. "I don't have many feelings towards them, because while they were my parents, they were the ones who left me alone, and who unknowingly left me in the care of a…" he let the sentence trail off. I knew the word that would have completed it though.

Demon.

"What about you? Do you miss your parents?"

I nodded. As I looked up into the spirits, I searched wildly for my family's, yet couldn't find them. A stray tear trickled down my face and I quickly brushed it away.

"My father," I said, "He was the King. He was a great man, and he loved me so much. He always told me stories and let me play with our hunting falcon and took time away from his duties to make sure he could spend time with my brother and me. My mother was a great woman too. She was wise and happy at the same time, and was even more connected to nature than someone who spent their whole life in it. I used to pretend she could talk to trees, but when I think about it, it isn't too much of a stretch. My brother, as much as I wanted to strangle him sometimes, is the one I miss the most. He was always there for me when I needed him, and was my only friend throughout my entire childhood. And I know that had only our parents been killed, he would have led Desaria with a strong heart and an open mind." I fought the tears that burned my eyes, but I was too tired for it to work. They spilled over and I cried silently, still searching for their spirits. Three sleepless nights piled up on me, and suddenly I felt as if I could sleep forever.

I stood up just as Niyol was trying to put his arm around me, trying to comfort me. I felt awful, but there was no time to apologize. I ran to the cliffs and stood there, with a gentle breeze blowing my hair back and drying the salty tears to my face. I then tilted my head back and howled, as only a girl as heartbroken as me could.

I don't remember falling asleep, but the next thing I actually remembered was opening my eyes to a cloudless sky, in a sleeping Niyol's warm embrace. I didn't fight it, and as I leaned my head against his chest, I fell asleep again.

I woke with a cold wolf nose in my face. It scared me and I jumped, hitting the top of my head on Niyol's chin. He shouted and fell backwards, and all I could do was slip off his lap, hitting my head on the hard ground.

I sat up, rubbing the back of my head. *Goldensun, what was that for?* I asked accusingly.

She ignored my comment, wagged her tail and replied, *Snow is coming!*

I widened my eyes. *What?!*

She sat down, not expecting me to take the news this way. *I can smell it coming. It will be here soon, and it will be very deep snow. Why aren't you happy?*

I groaned. *Because I don't have any winter clothing! We will all freeze!*

A soft growl came from Goldensun's throat. *Why do you not have any? Isn't it your job to be prepared for this kind of thing?*

No.

Niyol sat up, also massaging his skull. "What's that about?"

"Snow. She says it's coming soon."

I looked down at my tattered, patched up brown pants, my boots, my forest green shirt and my light jacket. Everything I wore, I had made by hand. I had become Outcast in a frilly pink dress, but shortly after, I realized that it wouldn't suit me well in the wild. So I hunted, made new clothes, and made more as I grew up. But I hadn't thought to make new winter clothes. I had the ones from last year...but the chances of them fitting were miniscule.

I looked south, down the length of the cliffs, searching for the infamous peak that we were headed for...Galdur Fjall.

I couldn't see anything. The rolling hills proved to be too large, and I knew it was too far anyways. But as we set off south, running today, we saw something starting to loom in the distance.

But it wasn't a mountain like we thought. It was a wall of storm clouds, blowing vicious, freezing wind towards us. We stopped and put on as much clothing as we could, and kept going.

I was right. I had grown a solid four inches since last year, and my winter pants didn't fit me. The rabbit-skin gloves didn't cover my hands. My current boots were lined with fur, but not fur for winter. The dark cloak I had worn into town that day with Silver was the warmest thing I owned, and just about the only thing that fit.

The snow started the following day. That night, I had been more than grateful for the yak hide blanket, although I still shivered underneath it.

The frigid air bit my face when I woke up. Fierce winds ripped across the landscape, blowing dust and snow as far as we could see. I shielded my eyes from the bluster, but snow still whipped in and scratched my face, like tiny icicles. Despite our best efforts, we didn't make it too far that day.

How much longer will the snow last? I asked Goldensun. She couldn't tell; *everything* smelled like snow.

That night, we all slept closer together. We huddled to share warmth, and the horses stood on the edges. The blizzard raged and was relentless. I was colder than I ever had been in my life, and I didn't know how long any of us could take it. We were inadequately prepared for such weather, and I was afraid we were going to suffer from it.

The next day, the storm calmed, but didn't stop. It became gentler, silent snow that fell slowly and delicately. As we traversed south, we noticed the snow becoming wetter, more sticky, and that the ground underneath was more rock and less grass.

"I wonder if we are crossing into the Outlands yet?" Silver asked, her voice cutting through the silence like a blade through the air.

I shrugged. My fingers fumbled inside my pack until I heard them brush across the rough paper of the map.

I pulled out the map and pointed to some cliffs towards the northeast corner of Aliyr. "Those look like where we were earlier." I traced my gloved fingers down the coastline, towards the border of the Outlands. The terrain turned to rock near there. "We are probably around this region. I would say that if we continue at this pace, with the current weather conditions, that we would cross into the Outlands by tomorrow."

Falcon was looking straight ahead, not saying a word. He and I walked next to each other, while the other two rode on the horses.

"Falcon, are you okay?" I asked. He looked at me and sighed.

"Well...I'm not quite sure what we are doing. I mean, I know that Tatsuo is rising, but that's it."

I glanced towards the others, but neither of them looked at me. So I told our new friend the story.

His eyes lit up as I explained what had happened to me, to Niyol, to Silver. How Chu`si stole my knife, how she kidnapped Fallenoak. Our journey as a family, almost. I then told him of my past, as princess. Of my deceased family, of the blue Dragon who liked to visit. I took all day to tell him everything. I never stopped to make sure he understood, and he never asked questions. When I finished, he smiled. "You make my life sound easier than breathing."

Pheo swooped down onto Falcon's shoulders. His scarlet flames warmed me even from the few feet away he was. Saph landed on Falcon's other shoulder, and I closed my eyes to the welcome heat.

Falcon looked to Pheo and just stared at him. I realized he must have been talking to him.

"They went to fly above the storm," he told me. "They say it goes on for quite some time, and that the weather probably will continue in this pattern for a while. Will we make it to Galdur Fjall in time?" he continued, not missing a beat.

I shrugged. He caught on so much quicker than Silver had. "Hopefully. We still have two weeks…" But my voice trailed off as I did the math. Pulling out the map, I saw that at our current pace, we might just barely make it, but only if we were lucky and moved faster.

I nodded, trying to reassure myself more than Falcon. "Yeah, we'll make it. We'll be fine…"

That night was cold as well. We had only the fire of the Phoenixes, and had to huddle close again. I tried not to notice the wolves shivering. And something was wrong with Silver's fingers. They were covered in red, yellow, and pale white patches. I knew about frostbite, and I knew these were the first stages. In a few days, if it was cold enough, Silver would be dealing with serious problems with those fingers.

I couldn't help but ask myself if I was leading all of them on a suicide mission. We brought down Chu`si without much problem, but she was just one demon. What would we do about the others she promised on her deathbed?

As if my thoughts had summoned the very thing itself, a terrifying snarl rattled through the land. It seemed to come from everywhere at once, but through the snow, I couldn't see a thing.

The wolves and Phoenixes simultaneously leapt to life, growling and screeching a warning towards our attacker. But whatever it was, it paid no attention to them, for its rumbling growl echoed through the snowfall. It was getting closer.

I drew my bow, as did Silver. Falcon unsheathed a blade longer than a knife but shorter than a sword, and Niyol pulled out the sword from Tokala.

Silver fumbled with her arrows; her fingers were too numb. A shadow streaked across my vision, too fast to make out, and Silver fell with a scream.

I rushed over to her. There was a long cut on her arm. It looked deep, and it was already starting to bleed. "Falcon!" I shouted above the din, "Start patching her up! Niyol, keep on your guard!"

Both nodded. Falcon came over and pulled a cloth from his pack, which seemed to have an unlimited supply of anything we might need. Niyol scanned the skies for any other sign of the black shadow.

It came again, but time seemed to slow down. I saw the thing come again, streaking across the sky towards Goldensun. I drew and shot an arrow at a speed I didn't know possible.

A furious screech filled the air, practically shattering my eardrums. The shadow slowed and hit the snow, sending up a shower of white powder.

I rushed over to look at it, and before me was a very strange, jet black creature.

It had piercing, red-orange eyes that sparked and burned with both evil and pain. Yellow and orange flecks inside its eyes made it look like fire was actually burning inside them. The creature itself seemed to be like a griffin, however only its head resembled that of a bird. The rest of the beast's body was that of a midnight lion. It was entirely jet-black, save for the fiery eyes.

Scarlet feathers stuck out of its chest at an odd angle, and it took me a moment to realize that they were the fletching of my arrow. I had somehow managed to pierce its heart, and it was dying as I observed it.

"What are you?" I asked, more out of curiosity than anything else. I didn't even really expect a reply. But I was shocked to receive one from the beast that looked like shadows.

"I am a Nymer," it said, in smooth voice. At the same time, it was almost like a hiss, and it sent shivers down my spine.

"We serve only Tatsuo," he hissed. "He is the only one. Soon he is coming; soon he shall vanquish you and all your little friends." The Nymer cast a haunting look to my group, and his blazing eyes lingered on Silver. "She will not last...my talons are poison." He laughed and shuddered, then lay still, just as Chu'si had on the day of her death.

The air hung heavy with silence. I could feel the stillness of the air beating on me like a drum, pounding my ears and making my heart thrum faster. I stared at the body of the Nymer numbly, and then closed my eyes.

I had been right. I was leading my friends into a death trap, and we were all going to die if we continued on. He had said Silver 'will not last'. Already, her skin was pale and sweat was forming on her brow as Falcon cradled her head in his lap. Her arm was bound but she was clutching her elbow, as if the pain was too intense to bear. Blood still pulsed through the cloth, dripping onto the snow and staining it scarlet.

Falcon looked up. "She isn't looking good. Whatever that thing said...well I think he was right. She..." he trailed off and changed venues. "The arm is already getting infected. We need a healer, or some magic, or something..."

He trailed off as Pheo landed on his shoulder and peered over at the sick girl. Falcon smiled as a small, tiny trickle of water started from the Phoenix's eyes. The little drops splashed down onto Silver's arm, and the strangest thing started to happen.

The blood on the cloth started to disappear, retreat back into Silver's arm. The stained fabric was now just sliced with a scarlet line; the gash that the demon left. Her arm instantly started to shrink back down to normal size, and the puffy redness started to disappear as well. Silver started breathing normal and stopped sweating. I wiped the perspiration off her brow, to keep her from freezing. Color started returning to her cheeks. It was as if she was healed in an instant.

Falcon's face opened up into a huge grin. "Pheo! You genius!" he exclaimed.

I was still staring at the wound. Just moments ago, it had been a bloody, sticky, wet, red mess, and now it was healed. Silver now looked as peaceful as a sleeping child.

"Phoenix tears..." Niyol whispered behind me. I started, not realizing had been standing there.

"They can heal cuts and wounds. Anything with blood, really," Falcon explained. Silver rolled over, her eyes closed and a dainty smile spread on her face. Falcon still held her head in his hands, and he didn't move. There was a look in his eyes that was completely unique and nearly impossible to describe; one filled with gratitude, wonder and even a touch of amazement. But the twitch at the edge of his mouth told me he was fighting back a smile, fighting the urge to show anything other than subtle joy. I didn't know why he resisted, but he obviously had a reason I was oblivious to.

I smiled too. Falcon was new, he was still going to have to get on everyone's good side, but I knew he could be trusted. The way he cradled Silver's head, the way he was so gentle with her, told me that he cared. Cared about people he hardly knew the names of, a person who was in need. I knew he was going to be good for the group. And right then and there, he had my trust.

Chapter 12
Taste of Battle

The snow continued for two more days, and when it stopped, it left an eerie silence that unnerved me more than I would have expected. Every crunch of every boot sounded malicious, every whisper of wind sounded like the breath of a Nymer ...or something worse.

By now, we knew we were in the Outlands. The snow, as deep as it looked, actually could be swept away to reveal dry, rocky ground, which corresponded with the details of the map. The Outlands were composed only of the least forgiving soil, where farming was impossible. The people who lived here had to hunt and kill the giant animals with fangs and claws to match; animals that could easily turn the humans from hunters to hunted.

A memory surged into my head faster than a striking snake; poisoning my paranoia with dark storm clouds of anger.

I point the arrow at the man's face, and he has a throwing knife ready. We both have the power to kill the other, but neither makes the first move.

"Why are you hunting me?" I say. Before now, I could live on my own, without the threat of being killed. As long as I stayed away from society, I was left alone.

The man laughs without taking his eyes off of me. "Stupid girl, haven't you heard? The Council has changed their minds. They want you back, so they can send you away. They've decided a life in the Outlands is more suitable for a delinquent of your nature."

I try to hide my surprise. Why do they want to send me to the Outlands? I am only 13 winters old! *I think.*

"I don't believe you," I hiss. The man smiles.

"Of course, when they say alive, they mean it quite loosely. I'm sure by killing you, I've done their work for them, and they'll pay me even more." He throws the knife. It flies past my face, missing me by mere inches. I let go of the arrow. I don't stick

164

around to see if I hit him; I take his grunt and the loud thud as an answer.

I had no other memories of ever being confronted with news of the Outlands. To now be stepping foot in a place where I should have been sentenced to felt very strange. It felt like a memory from the past, returning to haunt me. In fact, I suppose that's what it was.

I shook my head and kept walking, trying to shoo the thoughts from my head.

It didn't work.

I kicked the snow, sending a large amount of it flying into the air. I couldn't shake the feeling that I was both supposed to and not supposed to be here. Something in my gut kept chewing away at me.

We had entered a scrubby part of the land. Little bushes dotted the landscape; the only things tough enough to grow in this soil. And they bore no food; berries or other. I accidentally walked too close to one, and it clawed through my pants into my skin. The fabric didn't rip, but it left small scratches on my leg.

Later that day, the fierce wind resumed, blowing the snow on the ground up into our faces. It was hard to tell if it was snowing or just blowing. The sky was dismal and gray; the same color as Echosong's fur.

We started to get tired as the sky started to get darker. Silver was struggling to keep up; we couldn't ride the horses, for they, too, were treading through the snow with heavy hooves and heads down.

Silver stumbled and fell, but Falcon caught her before she hit the ground. Her face was bright red and her eyelashes were frosted shut. Her fingers were starting to look more frostbitten than before, and when we pulled off her shoes, we noticed that the frostbite was worse on her toes than her fingers.

I watched as she shivered in Falcon's arms, and he looked up at me, wondering what to do. Niyol turned to me as well.

I realized that I was in charge of our group, but I didn't want to be. I didn't want to be the one responsible for these people; I didn't want their lives to be in my hands. I was so incapable of leading them, why would they trust me to?

165

Goldensun came over and put her in my hand. It was cold, the snot frozen. I felt two comforting pelts beside me and realized that Echosong and Haunt were sitting close to me too.

Kohana, don't give up. Tatsuo is trying to deter us from the mission, but we have to show him that we will keep on going.

I looked to my pack-sister, and although her fur was sticking up at all angles in the cold, her eyes still sparkled with determination and encouragement.

I placed my hand on the top of her head. *I love you, Goldensun,* I said.

I love you too.

We made camp early that night. We dug into a drift and made snow-caves; something Niyol had learned how to do in the Mountains. He said we couldn't build them earlier because the snow drifts were not deep enough. So, in a strange way, I was grateful that the snow kept coming.

The caves were warm, or at least ours was. If we made them too big, the roof would cave in, so we made two. The girls slept in one; Silver, Doli, Goldensun, Echosong, Haunt and I. Echosong and Haunt slept on Silver's fingers and toes in a feeble attempt to warm them up. Goldensun and I stayed up late talking. Niyol and Falcon carved their own just to the right of ours, along with Pheo and Saph.

I don't know, I said, *I just don't anymore. I am afraid I'm leading you all on a suicide mission.*

Goldensun shook her head in the darkness. *Kohana, do you think none of us are scared? I know that the other wolves are terrified, and so are your friends. I can assure you that you're not the only one afraid of what might happen.*

Was that supposed to help? I stared at the ceiling. It was pitch-black, just like the rest of the snow-cave.

What if something happens? What if one of you gets hurt or... I looked over to where Silver's sleeping form should be. Tears welled up in my eyes. *Or worse?*

She laid her head on my arm. *If we didn't believe in you, we wouldn't be here.*

I smiled even though she couldn't see me. I fell asleep soon after.

We woke to the first clear day in awhile. The sky was bright blue and not a cloud was in sight. The sun reflected off the snow in a way that was painful to look at.

But the first thing we noticed wasn't the day. We noticed the horses, or rather the lack of them.

A long trail of hoof prints led away from the snow-caves, suggesting that they ran away sometime in the night. Goldensun growled and paced in front of the caves. "What are we going to do now?" Niyol asked dejectedly.

I realized it was my job to tell him.

"We haven't been using them for transport anyways," I said all too optimistically, "And we couldn't catch them. We don't have any time to go on a horse chase; we need to get to Galdur Fjall before the Red Moon."

I tried to ignore the fact that the rest of our provisions were in the saddlebags. Granted, not much food was left in them anyways, but even a little bit would have been better than nothing.

We set off again, but this time with no provisions, no transportation, and a late autumn sun beating down on our necks.

Around midday, the terrain started to turn a little more hilly, rather than just flat, barren wasteland. Some patches of ground that weren't swamped in snow were visible. The weather was a little warmer, which I'm sure was some relief for Silver.

Out in the distance, I saw the slightest tinge of gray that suggested mountains. Maybe we were getting close.

I heard him before I really recognized what was happening. It was almost impossible to hear, and surprisingly, even the wolves didn't register it. But the soft, *whap, whap* of the wings were all too familiar to me.

The blue Dragon was just landing behind us. His neck was waving gently, his electric eyes filled with calm sparks of light. His whole essence gave off a tranquil feel.

Hinto dipped his head politely to us, but his eyes lingered curiously on Falcon, whose brown eyes were wide in fear. He reached for the handle of his blade, but I stopped him.

"I see you have picked up a new member," Hinto rumbled. Falcon's Phoenixes screeched in the sky above us, and the Dragon glanced up at them. "Or three."

I nodded cautiously. "What are you doing here, *again*?" I asked. I didn't want to talk to him anymore. I was all but fed up with this Dragon. Was he staying or going? Maybe if we got far enough away, he'd leave us alone for good; I didn't like his unpredictable visits and his equally random mood swings. It seemed like every time he came to us, he was an opposite side of the emotional spectrum.

"I was coming to ask your permission," he grumbled. He asked very politely, but I could tell it caused him emotional stress to be asking a favor from a being he considered lesser.

"Permission for what?" Silver boldly questioned. Her hands shook as she asked him, but I couldn't tell if it was from the frostbite or from nerves. The Dragon tried to keep himself calm, but his tail lashed out behind him, sending up a shower of snow.

"I would like to join your group. I realize that none of you are exceptionally trusting of me, but with my visits becoming more and more frequent and your unfortunate lack of any food, water, shelter or warmth, I think that joining you would be good for all of us."

"What if I say no?" I dared.

He peered down at me. "I would leave. It is your destiny, Kohana, and therefore you may control who you let tag along."

I scoffed at the idea of controlling my destiny. But despite the fact that I wanted to be as far away from Hinto as possible, I found there was no other choice. I sighed loudly, turning back to the group.

"Well, what do you think?"

Goldensun asked the wolves, who all agreed it would be best for us. Niyol and Silver skeptically said yes, and Falcon flat-out denied Hinto's acceptance.

"Falcon, you don't even know him," I whispered.

"But I know the stories about Dragons. They are vicious and blood-thirsty and violent and—"

"Not this one." I cut him off. "Hinto might be a pain, but he isn't violent," I said, then added under my breath, "Usually."

Falcon shook his head. "I don't care. I think it's too dangerous!"

Niyol put a reassuring hand on Falcon's shoulder and started talking to him in a low voice, trying to sway him in our direction. While they were talking, Silver and I walked over to speak with Hinto.

"What's the real reason you want to come along with us?" Silver accused. I looked at her, shocked. She was quite courageous to be so openly hostile towards the Dragon. Although, according to Hinto, that was considered stupidity, not bravery.

Hinto smiled, but I could tell it was fake. "My wings are tired. You lot are a pain to keep up with, and none of the other Dragons are exactly willing to fly across two Kingdoms and into the Outlands just to track down some humans."

I glared at him still. "I don't believe you."

The Dragon wrinkled his nose in the beginnings of a snarl, and for a moment I thought I had gone too far. But his features relaxed again and he dropped his head to our height.

"The truth is, you will not survive without a protector. There are not only savage humans in the Outlands, but ferocious cats, vicious wolves that travel in massive packs, and Dragons so unruly and brutal, that nobody knows anything about them. The Dragons are what I fear the most for you. When they attack, they kill. No hesitation, and rarely even for food. They are larger than me; at least twice as big. And hardly anyone – human, Dragon or other – has lived to tell of them."

"Reassuring," grumbled Silver.

His yellow eyes flashed to her. She looked back at him with steely resolve. "Do you want my help or not?" Hinto snarled. Silver wisely said nothing.

I heard footsteps behind us and saw Niyol walking calmly over. He clearly hadn't heard any of our conversation. "Falcon is somewhat willing to give him a shot," he said. "But he isn't too keen on it, so I would try not to screw up, okay?"

Hinto glared at Niyol and stiffly nodded his head, not forgetting a sarcastic, "How very kind of you."

Then, to everyone's great astonishment, Hinto spread his wings and flew away. His blue, scaly hide soon became nothing more than invisible against the sky. As quickly as he had come, the Dragon was gone again.

I stared blankly at his disappearing form. Then, frustrated once more with the Dragon, I moved back towards the wolves, Falcon, and his newly landed Phoenixes.

"What is that all about?" Silver exclaimed. "I thought he wanted to *join* us?"

"I don't know," I snapped. "He's probably just toying with us. Come on, we need to get moving."

As we walked along, the scraggly bushes became more common. We saw them everywhere. A sudden idea struck me, and I started collecting pieces of the dry bushes by breaking them off and holding them under my arm, despite some of the scratches.

Niyol looked at me as if I was crazy. "Kohana?" he asked. "Yes?"

"Why are you doing that?"

I handed him a branch. "Feel how dry that is? We will be able to use these for a fire, even if it doesn't last long. We'll be warmer tonight, regardless."

He passed the branch back to me, and then the others started collecting them too. By the time dusk fell, we had gathered enough branches to fuel the fire all night, even though our hands ended up bloodied and hurt.

I put a good amount in a pile and crouched down, trying to light it. I struck my flint rocks on each other several times, but the sparks didn't do any good.

I sat down all the way in frustration. If we couldn't light the fire, we would have to spend another night in the cold. But with no snow to build caves out of, we were stuck outside.

I heard a heavy rumble behind me, followed by a snort and clanging. I knew without turning around that Hinto was back.

"Hinto," I said calmly, but not without some bitterness, "Around here, we like to stick together, not run off without telling everyone else where you're going." I felt like a mother scolding her child.

"Sorry," he growled. Something was in his mouth, because his voice sounded muffled and different. "I just thought you would like some food, considering your horses ran away with all of it."

I turned around to see him with a large moose in his mouth. Blood stained his claws and teeth, and his eyes still sparked with the thrill of the hunt. He dropped the body down on the ground, and then stretched his neck over to where I was trying to light the fire. He gently blew some of his own fire onto the branches, and a wall of flames exploded from them. I scrambled backwards, barely avoiding being toasted.

Falcon was trying to drag the moose over to the fire so we could cook the meat. "I don't know about you guys, but I think I like him already!" he shouted with a smile on his face. Even though I hadn't known him long, I could tell Falcon was one who was quick to trust and quick to forgive.

Although the sun was already set, the light of the smiles and laughter we shared that night didn't extinguish so easily. We listened as Hinto told stories. He told us about his home, his sister Kai, and his leaders. He even told us of a fabulous journey in where he traversed to the Southern Islands…and beyond. No human can sail past those islands, for none know where the next stop would be, how much food to bring. We were all amazed at his bravery.

"I have done it before," Hinto boasted, obviously loving the attention. "And I have journeyed past the Northern Islands as well. But I had to turn back, for it became so cold that the ocean was solid ice at *least* as thick as you are tall," he said, pointing to me with his snout. We too, shared our stories, but none matched Hinto's. Soon, we didn't even bother, but instead listened with rapt attention as the blue Dragon weaved tales of bold adventures with his sister and his friends, of fighting knights in shining armor and flying high above the clouds. When the time came to sleep, he curled up in a tight ball, but flicked his tail in our direction.

We all slept under his wings, for they were large enough to conceal us all and keep us from the frigid weather. Hinto put out the fire, and the world became silent.

I awoke to the sound of thunder and lightning. Cracks and flashes filled the air, and I realized instantly that Hinto's wing wasn't above us. I sat up, trying to shake away the remnants of sleep. What I saw though, was far from any storm.

Bodies crashed and heaved against each other, and I promptly noticed that they were huge. The flashes of light illuminated the scene; but they weren't from any cloud or storm or natural occurrence.

Claws scraped on scales as the Dragons clashed in the hills. The thunder was actually bodies striking each other and their heavy landings; dead or alive, I couldn't tell. Clattering scales sounded like rain, and lightning. Sparks and shocks flew from the claws as they attacked Dragon hides with a fury unknown to man.

I had only a few seconds to take everything in. I grabbed my bow and arrows, noticing sadly that my supply was diminishing. A small, human body ran into mine and I grabbed its shoulders.

"Silver!" I gasped. She looked around wildly; her brown, braided hair whipping behind her head.

"Kohana! Thank goodness! I can't find anyone! None of the wolves, or Hinto, or Niyol or Falcon or anyone! And it's even harder considering I have to dodge these Dragons!" she took a deep breath. "Where did they come from?"

I shrugged. "I just got up seconds ago. I don't even know what's happening!" I shouted over the din. "We need to go find everyone!"

We locked hands, and started through the storm of Dragon roars and stomping claws, of lashing tails, falling bodies and whipping wings. An electric yellow Dragon reared above us, at least twice as big as Hinto, and was about to breathe fire down when a dark object slammed into him. He spun around and ensued in battle with the new opponent, leaving us to escape.

I saw snatches of golden fur and flaming birds, but between the blazes of Dragon-fire to the sparks of claws, I couldn't tell what was real and what was just my eyes playing tricks on me.

We continued our mad dash through the battle, but not to much avail. None of the others in the group were anywhere to be found; not even Hinto, who had so recently joined us. The fire and sparks lit up the battlefield, the lightning in this storm.

A small, blue projectile hurtled towards us through the horde. It hit Silver in the chest, and she clutched it tight as soon as she realized it was Doli.

I heard howls and barks. Grabbing Silver's hand, I dragged her in the general direction of the noise, trying to locate the source and hoping it would lead me to the wolves, or at least someone else in the group.

The Dragons parted in their dance of war, and through the gap I saw more than I had expected.

Goldensun, Haunt, and Echosong were crouched under a big blue Dragon that I immediately knew as Hinto. A shockwave of gratitude flew through me as I realized he was protecting them. He was battling the larger, fiercer looking Dragons all around them. The beasts surged and lunged, but Hinto refused to back down. He shot jets of orange fire at any Dragon who came close, and they would reel back screeching, disappearing into the mass.

Falcon and Niyol were fighting back-to-back. Niyol clutched Tokala's sword, while Falcon held his blade. Being smaller than the enemy, they attacked and dodged the Dragons whilst remaining unscathed.

Pheo and Saph streamed from the sky like falling spirits. They used a similar strategy. They would race down, burn and claw a Dragon's face, then swirl back into the sky before the enemy could retaliate.

I wanted to run at Niyol and throw my arms around him. I wanted so bad to just lose myself in his strength and the comfort he had always provided. But now was not the time to let emotions cloud my actions.

Silver and I ran over to our friends. As soon as we were close, the smell of fresh blood assaulted my nostrils. A thought in the back of my head had already assumed the worst; someone was dead, or dying. But I shook it away and instead shouted, "Who's hurt?"

It's Echosong, replied Goldensun. Her voice sounded drained, and her eyes lacked their usual spark of determination. She was afraid for her sister.

What happened to her? Can she move? We need to get out of here.

No. She was cut, and it's deep. It runs down the whole of her flank, and it has been bleeding since.

I cursed. Echosong just couldn't be hurt. She was part of the team, and the team had to stick together. I knew what I had to do.

I raced over to Hinto's shoulder and laid a hand on it. He didn't turn, and instead shot another jet of fire towards an attacker.

"Hinto!" I cried over the sound of battle. "How many can you carry out of here?"

His long blue tail lashed in contemplation. "Only a few. I could carry all of you humans, but the wolves would then have to stay," he replied between assaults. "But we can't exactly leave. I'm being attacked from all sides!"

"Well, we can't exactly stay!" I screamed up to him. He grumbled something that probably wasn't very nice, but it didn't matter. An escape plan was already forming in my head faster than I cared to let on.

I left his side and ran over to Falcon, who was breathing heavily by Niyol and Silver. All three were now attacking the beasts with their man-made weapons, and I knew I should have been doing something to help. But instead, I grabbed Falcon's arm and drew him close to the wolves.

"Come on," I said. Barely audible over the shouts and roars of the Dragons, I told him, "We are going to fly out of here."

Falcon looked at me as if I had just started speaking a different language. I groaned in exasperation; there wasn't much time to explain. I grabbed his arm and pulled him away, dragging him through the mass of scales and claws. *Get everyone ready to leave, and tell Hinto that Falcon and I are finding our own way out,* I told Goldensun. She didn't respond, but I had to hope she heard me.

I knew what I was looking for now. I could picture the exact kind of Dragon in my mind. It was a snakelike beast with an incredibly elongated body, with both front and back legs. It had long, swirly whiskers and its tail was tipped with a plume of fur. It seemed calmer and gentler than most of the Dragons here. I had seen her. I had to find her again, for she was our ticket out of here.

I stuck close to Falcon, and we worked as a team through the fray. I needed to get back to the place where I had woken up, because not only were my supplies there, but so was my blanket and the map of Calleo. Survival was back there.

The only problem was; I had no idea where I was going. I was just leading Falcon where I thought was the right way, and hoped I was right. He watched my back as we searched, but without any landmarks to guide us, it was hopeless.

Falcon nudged my shoulder, snapping me out of my thoughts, and pointed at something on the ground a few yards away. I rushed to it, forgetting that we were supposed to stick together.

It was my pack. Somehow, by some miraculous reason, it hadn't been trampled. My blanket, just a few feet away, had been stepped on my something large, but it was still in one piece, and still completely usable.

Just as I turned around, holding my pack up triumphantly, a large, clawed hand hit me in the side, sending me flying through the air. I don't remember screaming, but my throat burned. I caught a glimpse at Falcon as I was thrown into the air, but his face was of utter shock as he followed me with his eyes in my flight through open sky.

The ground rushed up at me, all snow and dead grass, and I hit it hard.

I heard a loud crunch noise, and a lightning-hot pain shot up my body from my hip. This time, I heard my scream, and I didn't like the way it sounded. I saw Falcon at my side in no time, standing over me like a welcome friend or a protective brother.

For a moment, I was thrown back in time.

I cry on the rocks, clutching my scraped knee. Goblet the fish swims anxiously in the pond, avoiding the drops of blood as they splash into the water.

A shadow falls over me, and I look up, tears blurring my vision. He is standing in front of the sun, but it doesn't matter. I would know his shadow anywhere.

He crouches down and examines my knee carefully. He is only a few years older than me, but he acts so mature. I wonder if I will ever be like him.

175

"Come on, Kohana," he says gently. He offers me a hand and pulls me to my feet, and provides a shoulder to lean on as we walk back to the castle.

"Come on, Kohana."

A voice from the present jerked me back, and once again I was in the world of shooting pain and bellowing Dragons.

Falcon's voice was smooth and welcoming. He tried to pull me to my feet, but to no avail. I couldn't stand.

Falcon stood up, still defensive of me, and made a strange, birdlike call. It was very unnatural at the same time as it was beautiful and mesmerizing. It sounded like the sound of rain, the whisper of the wind, the crackle of a fire, and the clatter of stone, all put together into one unearthly sound.

But I knew we were as good as dead. We would get stepped on, torched, bitten or clawed. A tail would fly by and slam into someone. Some already thrashed above me, too close for comfort.

I was aware of a sudden heat, and at first I thought we were getting attacked. But through my half-shut eyes, I noticed that the firelight was hovering, and was both red and blue.

I felt needle-sharp pricks through my boots and strong, warm hands on my back. I started lifting into the air, but the prickles on my lower legs disappeared without warning. Before I could shout in surprise, I felt a solid arm catch me from under my knees.

It hurt to breathe and to move. My chest and hip hurt, and every time I shifted positions, a shock of pain jolted through me. My chest hurt much more than my hip.

Falcon's voice seemed distant. I wrapped my arms around his neck, despite the pain it caused me. "What did you say?" I mumbled. Talking hurt worse than breathing.

My vision cleared enough for me to see his big brown eyes staring at me like a big brother would watch his sister. He reminded me so much of Chayton, even though they looked nothing alike.

"I said you're going to be fine."

But even I could hear the doubt in his voice, and I could tell he was having a hard time believing himself.

I woke up to silence. It seemed louder than the storm of the Dragon battle that we just left.

I tried sitting up, but an excruciating pain bolted through my chest. My hip throbbed numbly; a strange yet welcome sensation after the torturous feeling from earlier.

I looked around from my position on the ground. I was in a snow cave, but I could hear the *drip, drip* of it melting. A soft blue light filled the cave. Its source was Saph, sleeping peacefully in a corner. She glowed like a dying blue ember, as Phoenixes did when they slept.

"Saph?" I asked. My voice was raspy and my chest stung when I talked.

She opened an eye, and for a moment looked irritated. But then realization hit her, and it was apparent in her beady eyes. She screeched loudly, and dashed out of the cave.

"Guess what?"

I opened my eyes, and realized I must have fallen asleep. The snow cave ceiling was a lighter color; the sun must have risen.

A head, nothing but a silhouette against the roof, took up a good portion of the view. Not that there had been much to see, anyways. Both blue and red lights flickered in the room too, and the *drip, drip* seemed faster than before.

I groggily rubbed my eyes and tried to sit up, but a firm hand on my shoulder held me back.

"What?" I groaned. My eyes adjusted a little and I came to recognize Falcon as the silhouette above me.

"I saved your life! Oh, thank goodness you're alive!" He bent down and gave me a hug, in which I squeaked in pain. He drew back, eyes flashing with concern. "Oh your ribs. I'm sorry…I didn't mean to," he said.

I nodded, with eyes squinted shut and chest burning like a Phoenix's feather. I waited a moment for the pain to subside, then forced out, "Wait, why wouldn't I be alive?"

Falcon's face hardened to stone, but his eyes appeared to be fragile, brown, stain-glass. "When you were sleeping…wait. Let me start over," he said. "You got hit, and I mean, really hard.

177

That Dragon came out from nowhere. But I carried you out of the battle. I don't know what happened to the others, either. And I grabbed your things," he motioned to my pack, bow, and quiver in the corner and continued, "But you were semi-conscious while I made the cave. I brought you in here and laid you down, and then your breathing turned really light. I couldn't tell most of the times if you even *were* breathing. I thought..." he looked away, obviously trying to hold back some tears. He took a deep, ragged breath. "I thought you were dead four times. The only reason I knew you were alive was the fact that you sometimes talked."

I looked at him, bewildered. I couldn't remember a thing from after his false reassurance the other night. "Falcon, I wouldn't–" but he cut me off with a hand in my face. He was still staring blankly at the walls of the cave, seemingly unwilling to look me in the eyes.

"I know you wouldn't have given up, Kohana," he said. "But sometimes, you don't have a choice. You can't fight forever, and when death calls, you don't have any other option but to answer."

I nodded. "I know what you mean, Chayton."

My hand flew to my mouth. I didn't mean to call him that, but something just clicked in my brain, the similarities between them. They had the same crooked smile and the same laugh. Chayton and Falcon both had an air to them that suggested that they could be as serious as they wanted to be, but would prefer joking around. And even though they were different colors, both of them had the same light in their eyes that showed they had spent their short lifetime laughing. And I knew that had he lived, my true brother would have spent the rest of it smiling.

Falcon's gaze flickered to mine, confusion plastered on his face, a mask that I wanted to peel back. Before he could ask, I said, "He's my brother."

The mask tightened. Confusion swallowed up his eyes, too. "I thought your brother was..." Falcon let the sentence hang there, and I made no attempt to pick it up. My silence was the answer in itself.

We were quiet. The Phoenixes pulsed gently, their flames still flickering as they started to drift off.

"What did I talk about?" I asked suddenly. A spark of curiosity had lit inside my head, and the words just tumbled out.

Falcon smiled devilishly. "When did you and Niyol kiss?"

I was so taken aback by his question that I sucked in a nervous breath. He laughed and continued. "You *only* talked about him. You said his name a few times, and apologized. But nothing really made much sense; the only recognizable words were 'Niyol', 'sorry' and 'kiss'."

I felt my face turn bright red.

"I think you should tell me what happened with you guys. I mean, after that one night, you just started like, hating him and not talking to him. You acted like he was invisible...and it was..." his voice trailed off again as he put the pieces together. "He kissed you and had second thoughts, didn't he?"

There was a joking light in his expression at first, but as he realized what had happened, his face turned to stone. Again, silence was my answer. He frowned and said, "I'm sorry."

I nodded and closed my eyes. A wave of fatigue swept over me, and suddenly I was too tired. "Thanks for saving me," I mumbled. I was already passed out before Falcon could reply.

The next morning, I woke up to an empty snow cave. I sat up, doing my best to ignore the fire that lit up inside my chest. I blinked away the last bits of sleep, and got my first real good look at my surroundings.

I was up against one of the walls, with my yak-hide blanket on top of me. Falcon had scraped out the snow underneath, and I rested on top of some frozen grass. Despite the fact that it was dead and cold, it was still softer and warmer than just snow. It also gave me decent support, seeing as my body heat would have melted a floor of only snow.

The rest of the cave was to my left. On the other side of the cave, there was another blanket and a scoop in the ground, where I assumed Falcon slept. Two smaller indents next to it were glassy and looked like ice. I guessed that Pheo and Saph took those as their beds.

Falcon had moved my things to rest just at my feet. My bow and quiver were propped up against the wall, and the pack lay snuggled in the very corner. The map peeked out from the drawstring opening. From the look of this place, it was safe to say we had been here a few days.

I painfully got to my knees. The cave wasn't tall enough for me to stand, so I crawled out of it, looking for Falcon, Pheo or Saph. Some part of me hoped I would find Niyol or Goldensun or Silver, but I knew that they were gone.

I stepped outside, expecting the sun to be bright and the snow to be blinding. Instead, I was confronted with a dark, dismal sky and a chilly wind. A shadowy figure sat crouched a few feet away, with a cloak wrapped around his frame.

I walked over to him, trying not to cry out with the pain in my chest. There wasn't much time until the Red Moon, and I had to deal with the pain whether I wanted to or not.

I sat down next to him. He glanced over at me, and I smiled at him. My smile vanished as quickly as it came though, because gazing out from under the hood were not two brown eyes as I had expected, but two icy blue ones.

I leapt to my feet and looked around for any weapons. The only one was my bow and arrows in the cave, but the figure had already drawn a sword and pointed it at my throat.

"You are the girl, are you not?" he hissed. I took a few steps back, and he took a few forward. I didn't answer. The man drew back his hood to reveal an angular face. He had eyes the color of ice; not quite blue but far from white. His hair, a golden, shining mess, looked like he hadn't spent any time with it or cut it in a long time, seeing as it hung well past his ears, which were pointed like an elf's. When he talked, his mouth revealed shiny white teeth, but with frighteningly long and sharp canines. As he spoke, his eyes shifted into a bright, screaming red color.

"Who…who are you?" I stammered. He took another step forward. I reversed. My back touched cold, and I realized I was cornered to the back of the snow cave.

"Answer my question first, girl." His voice sounded snakelike, and his eyes – now blood red – sparked with irritation.

"I don't know what you're talking about!" I whimpered. He stepped closer, the blade of the sword now just a small ways from my neck.

"Don't lie to me! I know you are the girl!"

I shook and felt my teeth rattle. "Please, I don't know what you're talking about," I said again. He thrust the sword right up to my chin, the cold, needle point beginning to dig into my throat.

"You are the one with the knife, who wants to kill Tatsuo and the rest of my kind. I know what you are, don't pretend you aren't. I can smell lies!"

The rest of my kind. He must be a demon, I thought to myself. I swallowed, making the point scratch me. "What do you want with me?"

He smiled. A cold, dreadful smile. "Tatsuo would praise me. I would be his *favorite* if I killed the only one who can stop him!" he shrieked. "I would be-" he stopped mid-sentence, the sword dropping from his hands. The light in his eyes faded instantly, and he fell forward. He landed just at my feet, and I saw a knife sticking out of his back.

I looked up to see Falcon, standing coldly on the other side of the fire. His birds rested on his shoulders.

"Falcon!" I said delightedly. My voice cracked with both gratitude and utter astonishment.

He narrowed his eyes, but whether it was at me or at the man, I couldn't tell. He stiffly walked over, took the knife from the dead man's back, and went to go clean it with some snow. I followed him, even though I could tell he didn't want me to.

"What was that?" I asked. I felt the pitch in my voice rise, and I reminded myself of a two-year-old.

"An Ahghari. They're dangerous crosses between human and demon. They're not very common. Some of them can shape shift, like that Chu'si demon you told me about. Some of them can only change some of their features. You're lucky I was here for you, *again*." Falcon let the last word drop in such a way that it sounded like he didn't *want* to save me.

"What do you mean by, *again?*" I asked, my voice cracking once more.

He spun around with a spark in his eyes that I took for fury. "You're supposed to be saving the world from this 'Tatsuo' guy, but do you even know what you're doing? If you can't look after yourself, how do you expect to defeat him? I mean, we only have one week to get there, and we still have to cross *mountains*!"

"We don't know how high the mountains are," I mumbled to myself. He heard me.

"Right. Because that's a good thing. What if they're taller than expected? What if it's going to take two weeks to cross them, or three, or four? We don't have enough time for you to keep getting yourself into trouble."

"So if you're so concerned about me not being able to take care of myself, why don't you look back to the past three years of my life? I'm pretty sure I lived on my own without anyone telling me what to do or how to do it!"

I was breathing heavy. Falcon looked taken aback by the fact that I openly admitted I was living on my own. And the mark on my wrist still showed the sign of an Outcast, as it would forever.

A forked path, two dots, and a star.

The mark on my wrist had healed, but it had been cut deep enough to leave a scar.

Falcon saw me looking at my mark. He curiously tilted his head at it, reminding me of an inquisitive bird. He reached out to look at it, but I shrunk away.

"What's an Outcast?" I ask.

Father looks up from the book he was reading by the fireplace. His eyes go hard, as if the question unnerved him.

"They are undesirable. They are people who have been cast away from society, unfit to live with us. They are the sinners that can only live with others of their kind; can only live amongst savages."

I nod. Then I say, "What is the mark of an Outcast, Father?"

He is silent. I wait for him to answer. He breathes a sigh, deep and full of thought. Before I can say that he doesn't have to answer, he does.

"It is a mark that burns forever, and while the design is similar for all who bear it, there is always a certain quirk to it that defines the person. Some think that it causes bad luck, and whoever bears the mark of an Outcast will die at a very young age

due to misfortune." He pauses. "Kohana, where did you hear about these things?"

"I read about them, Father."

He sighs again, a faint smile tugging at the corners of his mouth. "Don't worry yourself with the Outcasts and their ways, Kohana. They will never mean anything to you."

I snapped out of my daydream, suddenly aware as Falcon tried to say something to me. I shook my head and looked back to him, still clutching my wrist to my chest.

"Kohana, all I'm trying to say is that whether you are Outcast or the Queen, you're still the same person. You're my friend, and you remind me of..." his voice trailed off. It was my turn to tip my head to the side.

It was clear he didn't want to talk about it, but I said anyways, "Who?"

"Aylen," he whispered. I tilted my head further and felt my loose hair fall around my shoulders.

Falcon looked up at me with sad eyes. His birds, sensing his emotions, tried to comfort him by rubbing their burning heads on his cheeks. But it was evident that he didn't want to be consoled.

"Aylen. She was my sister. She was such a nice person, with so much good in her heart. She had the same color eyes as you, and she had the same laugh. You look and act and speak just like her," he said. The then looked up sheepishly and said, "That's why I followed you in the first place. I knew she had to be just a year younger than me, and you could have been her. I followed you at first because I saw the light in your eyes at the tavern. When the man came to hurt you guys...well, I sent Saph in to attack him, so you could get away."

I was silent. Despite the million questions that buzzed around in my head, the only one I could cough up was, "What do you mean she *was* your sister?"

He shook his head. "I ran away when I was little. My uncle was the King of Aliyr. We lived in a castle, like you probably did. But my father never had time for me, or Mother, or Aylen. So I ran away. And I lived with this gang for awhile. News travels though, and I found out that Father had died from some unexpected sickness. Mother couldn't take it, and she ran away with Aylen. That was the last I heard of any of them.

"My gang friends tried to feel sorry for me, they really did. But they were the kind of kids who stole because they wanted to, not for survival's sake. They weren't the best influence. So I left.

"I kind of ran into this girl later, but we didn't stick together long. I woke up one day, she was gone. There was this pile of ashes at the foot of where I'd been sleeping, and just before I left, this weird looking bird came out of them. Turned out to be Pheo. I just wandered from then on. Saph here found us not too long ago, about a year. She's still…adjusting," he said.

Saph, at hearing her name, cooed and ruffled her flaming feathers.

"Falcon, I'm so sorry. I know why you don't talk about your past," I said. He nodded.

"Don't be sorry. The world is full of people who are sorry."

"If it means anything to you, you remind me of Chayton, a lot. Everyone thought I-"

"Don't say it. I know the story."

"Oh."

We stood there in an awkward silence. Then I took the three steps over to him and gave him a hug. "It's the least I can do, after you saved my life twice," I whispered in his ear with a grin. I felt his cheeks stretch in a smile, too.

For a split second, when I let go, I expected to see Chayton and his big blue eyes staring at me.

Part Three

Galdur Fjall

Chapter 13

Mission First

Despite my broken ribs, we still only had one week to get to Galdur Fjall. Falcon wanted me to take it easy for a day or two and make sure they healed, but I insisted on leaving. There wasn't time to take it easy. So we packed up our precious few belongings and set out. We didn't know what we were doing, other than the original mission that was permanently burned into the back of my mind.

As we walked, Falcon studied the map, and the horizon, then went back to the map. Finally, he leaned over and said, "We are about here, in these hills." He drew his finger along the small-looking mountain range. "And this, up here," he grumbled, pointing to the highest peak in the range, "Is Galdur Fjall. We can't see it right now because there are some smaller mountains in front of it. But we should go as fast as we can, considering we have no mountain gear whatsoever, and our only chance at survival is probably somewhere in these mountains."

"Chance of survival?" I asked stupidly.

He responded with a curt, "The others."

"Oh."

We walked in silence for the rest of the day. He sent the Phoenixes scouting several times, but they found no sign of our friends. By the time night was falling, the hills had gotten much, much larger, and I could see snowy summits peeking out just behind them.

We didn't have the strength or the snow to make a decent snow-cave. So we slept out in the open around a very small, very cold fire. It burned out quickly, and we both shivered. My stomach growled most of the night.

Saph slept on top of my blanket. She pulsed like a dying ember, but provided enough warmth to last through the night. Pheo did the same for Falcon, and when we woke the next morning, both of us were cold but alive. As we headed out again, I couldn't get my teeth to stop chattering.

A fierce wind blew the next day. It kicked up snow and powder into our faces in an attempt to deter us. But we forged on.

As we got closer, the wind grew stronger. There was real snow falling from the sky, too. Between the white stuff on the ground and the snow in the sky, it was all Falcon and I could do to see each other.

"Where do you think the others are?" I shouted above the blizzard. He looked like he shrugged, but I couldn't tell.

"I don't know, but wherever they are, they are safe with Hinto!" he shouted back.

We kept pushing. I don't think it was even noon yet when Falcon collapsed, shivering violently. I crouched down and tried to get him up, but he shook his head. "Go on," he muttered. The only reason I could understand him was by reading his lips. I refused and sat down close to him, sharing what little body heat we both still had.

"I'm not leaving you!" I yelled. As the words left my lips, the wind picked them up and carried them away, and I don't think they passed over Falcon's ears on their way out.

We just sat there shivering. The Phoenixes tried to warm us up, but even their fire was starting to flicker more than I thought was normal. Pheo rested his head sadly on Falcon's chest, and Saph curled up between my stomach and my knees, which I had pulled up toward my chest.

Kohana?

A voice made me start, sending Saph squawking off my lap. It came again, faint but stronger than the first one. *Kohana?* It sounded like it was searching.

I have known Goldensun for three years. Her voice was imprinted on my brain. She and I never left each other's company. But in just two days, I wasn't able to recognize her voice when I first heard it.

Goldensun! Goldensun where are you?

Falcon's eyes were closed and he was stroking Pheo calmly, as if freezing to death was suddenly okay with him. I shook his arm, startling both of them, and I said, "Goldensun! She is talking to me! Falcon, she's close, and she wouldn't be without the rest of the group...we're close!"

Communication with a companion is a tricky thing. It was just like communicating vocally; the more distance between, the fainter the voices became. Most companions could only talk if they were within earshot, as a general rule of thumb, but it really varied depending on the pair. There were many factors, including the strength of the companions' bond, each individual's sense of sound, age, and time in one another's company. Goldensun and I could speak farther than the average pair, but still had to be relatively close in order to hear one another.

A spark flew through Falcon's eyes, and he seemed to care again. He stood up stiffly, and said, "Where is she?"

Looking for you. We haven't seen or heard or smelled anything from you since the battle. I was afraid I wouldn't ever find you...I couldn't bear to lose you too. There was both relief and pain in her thoughts.

Too?

And like only we could, only a person and an animal with such a strong bond as us, she showed me.

Her real sister. I saw it all through her eyes.

She stood there, or rather, I did. Echosong's eyes were dull and her breathing was labored. "Don't go, Echosong," I said. Or Goldensun did. It was strange to bark and understand it, to hear Echosong whine and know exactly what she said.

"Goldensun, it's my time." She bent her neck upwards and gave me a kiss on my wolf nose. "Don't worry; we won't be apart forever. Someday, we will live once more." Her tail wagged faintly. I didn't have time to wonder what she meant.

Red movement off to my side, and I looked to see Haunt sitting sadly next to her. An angry thought flashed through my mind. *What is she doing here? Echosong is* my *sister, not hers!* But the minute I thought it, I took it back.

"Echosong, you can get through this," she murmured. She touched her nose gently to my sister's gray hide. Echosong flinched. Then her eyes became vacant, and she said, "Just give me one more minute, Mother. I must say goodbye to my friends." She nodded as if she had received an answer, and then turned back to me. "I love you very much, sister. And although I've been jealous of you and Kohana sometimes, I am glad you found her. I know you can do great things. I know she's such a pure person at heart, and if you were a human, you would be just like her."

She switched her gaze to Haunt. "I know I barely know you. But you, too, have good in your heart."

A great, shuddering sigh echoed through her, and she was still.

I snapped out of Goldensun's memories. Tears welled up in my eyes, but I didn't let them go, for they would have frozen to my face. *Goldensun, I'm so sorry.*

She was silent. I could tell she would need a long time to get over it. So would I. As I thought about it, Echosong was as much my sister as she was Goldensun's. I suddenly found myself wishing I had been closer to her, that I had gotten to know her better or treated her better.

Howl.

The voice echoed through my head again. It took another moment for me to wake from my memories and to realize Goldensun was talking to me.

Howl, Kohana. I will hear you and then I can find you.

Even in the wind? I asked.

Hopefully. Howl.

So I did. I gathered up air and almost choked on snow, but I howled. I let the song fill me up and let me float through the frosty air, high above the storm. I let it drain me and take away all my breath until I could barely stand and my lungs felt drained, and still I called out to my pack-sister. I put all my pain and suffering, love and hate, smiles and frowns, all my memories and all my strength and all my weakness into that howl. I let my lungs shake and my ribs burn from the effort. And for a moment, I could have sworn that the wind died down, as if the world wanted to listen.

I didn't hear anything back, so I took a deep breath and howled again. Three times I had to call to her before she answered.

I hear you! Goldensun barked in my head. She then vanished from my skull, leaving it as empty and cold as before.

A few moments passed. They turned into a few minutes. Then, through the snow, five shadows began to materialize. Two tall, two short, and one flying above.

The first to get to me was Niyol. He held a light in his eyes I don't think I had ever seen before; one of immense relief and joy and something else that couldn't be put into words.

He nearly tackled me when he got to me, giving me a hug I never forgot. It was strong and warm, and reassured me that everything would be okay. I was barely even aware of my ribs hurting as he hugged me.

He stepped back and I wanted to kiss him. I almost did, too. But Silver was squeezing me from the side now, and crushing my ribs. This time I felt it, and I shouted out. She backed up. "Sorry," she said, but her face was still painted with a smile. I didn't even mind that she had squashed my ribs; she was back, and she was okay.

Goldensun and Haunt were all around my knees, barking and howling and wagging their tails. Hinto landed and the ground shuddered. He flicked his tail across the snow, carefully trying to avoid showing his emotions to us so openly.

I looked back at Falcon. Everyone was hovering around me, while Falcon stood alone awkwardly. I grabbed his arm and pulled him into the crowd. "I wouldn't have survived without him. He saved my life. Twice," I said.

"Don't you forget it," he said jokingly. Then all the attention was on him, and his smile was so bright that I almost reached to shield my eyes.

Niyol pulled me aside while the others were thanking and congratulating Falcon. Silver saw me and gave me a wink and a cheesy smile.

We stood a little bit away. The snow was still falling, but the wind had died down, granting us a moment of peace, and the ability to hear without shouting.

I wanted to say something. How sorry I was or how much I missed him or how much I wanted him. But he pulled me into another hug, holding my head to his shoulder and pressing my back with the other hand. In just one motion, he said it all. He told me that he was sorry, that he missed me, and he wanted me, too. That he was here and wasn't going to leave.

But he wasn't done. He let go of me, but then leaned in and kissed me. At first, I thought about fighting it, but I knew I wouldn't have been able to do so. So I just leaned in and let him lead. My eyes were closed, so I couldn't tell if anyone was watching. I didn't care. I was so glad to see him and know that he was okay, and I knew he had the exact same thoughts about me.

I heard my heartbeat quickening, and felt his racing to match mine. For a split second, I thought that we were one. I felt that even though I loved Goldensun and she was my only sister, that Niyol and I were closer than a wolf and a person could be. We shared a bond that could only form between boy and girl.

I closed my eyes and became calmer than I have been in a long time. Tranquility came so rarely now days, that I literally felt a weight being lifted off of my shoulders.

He drew back, a smile on his face. He grabbed my arms and hugged me again. I was so flattered that he cared so much, when I thought he was mad at me.

"Tell me you know what you're doing," he sighed. I almost didn't say anything, for I knew that my answer was unacceptable. But he deserved to hear the truth, for all that was worth.

"I don't, Niyol," I whispered back. "I don't think any of us know what we're doing."

He laughed. So did I. The halfhearted chuckle never reached his eyes.

Kohana, break it up, I heard Goldensun say. I laughed even harder, for real this time, as I realized that they were probably all watching us. But I didn't care. I felt so safe in Niyol's arms. I felt like I was indestructible.

We broke apart, and both of us smiled. His lips were right there, so tantalizing near that it took all my strength not to reach that extra inch or two so that I could taste them again. I wondered if he was having thoughts like this, too, or if I was the only one that felt this way.

I turned around, and to my surprise, the group was still talking to Falcon. Only Goldensun was sitting in the snow, watching me. Her back was straight and her ears were perked. Her tail was tucked neatly in front of her paws.

She looked at me in a way that usually fathers reserved for their daughters when they stayed out too late with a boy.

I laughed again. I couldn't help it. She wagged her tail and ran over to me, practically leaping into my arms. I knelt down, arms spread wide, and she literally did jump right into them.

I held her close, although she was very heavy. Her tail wagged limply and she whined, but her voice echoed through my brain. *I thought I lost you, Kohana. I never saw you after the battle...and I thought you were gone too.*

If wolves could cry, she would have. She nuzzled her head on my chest and tried to get as close to me as she possibly could. I hugged her awkwardly while still keeping her supported.

You know I wouldn't give up that easily.

She nodded, and laid her ears back. I knew that tonight, I wouldn't sleep. The sky felt laden with hardships still to come. Tatsuo was going to rise in just four and a half days.

Four and a half. That's how long I had to prepare for this.

I didn't think I was ready.

In fact, I knew I wasn't.

We braved the open air that night. Hinto helped us make a fire, and he kept it going throughout the dark hours.

I dreamed that I was up on Galdur Fjall. The moon shone brightly down on me, the world washed in its pearly light.

A terrifying beast loomed ahead of me, but it was only shadows. It had flaming eyes, and it came from a hole in the earth. From the hole, hundreds of other shadows poured out, some with animalistic frames and others just masses with unrecognizable features. Each and every one had the same beady, flaming eyes that chilled me to the core.

I stood tall and strong. I had my knife in hand, and it felt good. I lunged, and my knife hit home. I fought shadow after shadow, my strength never waning.

But the light started to become red. Slowly at first, but I glanced up at the moon between attacks and noticed it was scarlet. The sky, the mountain, and the demons were all bathed in the crimson light.

They gained power. My strength started diminishing, and the demons began to conquer me. One by one, they attacked, until I was overpowered.

I screamed, calling for help. I saw my friends; Goldensun, Haunt, Falcon, Pheo, Saph, Silver, Doli, Niyol, and Hinto, all fighting alongside me, even though they hadn't been there before. None of them seemed to notice I had fallen, but I could clearly see that they were outnumbered. Silver and Doli fell first, and the demons swarmed them.

Falcon and his Phoenixes all screamed at the same time, and I saw a three-headed shadow biting down on all of them at once. All six eyes were glazed over in pain, and became dim from their recent deaths.

Haunt and Goldensun went down fighting side-by-side. Hinto was enveloped in a horde of demons, and when they backed off, I saw that he was no more than a dark shadow in the shape of a friend I once knew.

Niyol held out longest. But the largest shadow from the hole swung at him, and he dissolved like mist.

I shrieked. The demons parted and let me up. I stood, ready to fling anything I could at them. Tears streamed down my face, which I'm sure was covered in dust and demon blood. A scratch on my face stung.

The largest shadow, the one that killed Niyol, faced me now.

You thought you could win, human? It asked. I stood taller and prouder, and replied,

"I know I can."

The thing laughed. Deep and malicious.

You stand no chance of defeating me! You saw how my followers took care of your friends. Time for you to join them.

I yelled, "Never!" and charged at him, knife in hand. But I tripped and fell into the hole he sprouted from, and I tumbled into blackness.

I woke up screaming. Sweat dripped down my hair, and it soaked my collar. I sat up, panting. My companions all woke with starts as well, and Falcon drew his knife groggily, saying, "Are we getting attacked again?"

I shook my head. The firelight danced on my friends' faces. "Sorry, I…I had a bad dream," I stammered. Hinto closed his eyes, looking irritated. Falcon put his blade away and did the same, while Goldensun snuggled closer to me. She hadn't left my side all day.

Silver sighed sympathetically, and rolled over. Niyol still sat up.

"Anything you want to talk about?" he asked.

I shook my head. My heart was still beating, and the clarity of the nightmare left me shivering under my blanket.

Niyol was still looking at me. I could tell that he knew there was something else bothering me, but I didn't say anything; I just stared at the flames.

I didn't sleep at all after that. I waited all night in the frigid air, keeping the fire alive to the best of my abilities.

I cried silently a few times that night, too. I knew I wasn't ready to take on Tatsuo. Maybe Fallenoak got away, and didn't need saving. Maybe all the demons got sick and died, therefore wouldn't need fighting. Maybe...

Stop it, I told myself. *No matter how many things you wish were true, the* real *truth is that you are going to have to fight him.*

And you have to win.

I fought with myself all night. I wanted to run away so bad, but I knew that if I did, I would just worry the others. And I would be leaving them to fend for themselves, when they were just there because I was.

But if I left, I might live.

I might find a way to keep living and hide from the wrath of Tatsuo and his evil army of Dragons, and maybe I could clear my name. I could do something other than throw away my life.

You're not throwing it away, I said. My brain had been arguing amongst itself all night. *You're not throwing it away; you're using it to save the hundreds of thousands of lives to come. Maybe even more.*

I scrunched my nose and told my brain to shut up.

I had spent so long staring at the flames and fighting inside my head that I was shocked to look up and see that the sky was lightening. Sometime during the night, the sky had cleared, and the moon shone dully from the horizon. I could picture the dream in my head again, and I tucked my legs close to my chest.

The orb was just over three-quarters full, and pearly white as usual. It was hard to believe in just four days, it would be crimson.

I heard thudding behind me, and turned around to see Hinto standing up, and stretching. He looked like a cat, the way his long neck laid in between his front legs, and his rear in the air, and his tail curled up in a scrunching of the muscles. The blue Dragon's mouth was wide open in a yawn, and his claws had left deep scores in the frozen ground.

They must be sharp, was all I could think.

He spread his massive wings and reached them straight up into the sky. As soon as he finished his morning stretches, he sat down next to me.

"Thinking?" he rumbled. I nodded.

"I'm scared. I don't know if I can do it."

Hinto sighed. His long neck swayed as he thought; an action I had come to find both calming and bizarre.

"I know you're nervous. But I also know that you can do whatever you set your mind to. The human race has the uncanny ability to do so."

I laughed. It sounded strange, coming from him, seeing as he constantly seemed to look at us as if we were lesser. I guess we did have some strength, considering the world used to be wild and untamed. Not a single village or castle or human. Nothing stood taller than a tree, besides a mountain or perhaps a Dragon.

"Hinto," I said, "Are you scared?"

His tail swished in front of his feet, twitching just at the end. His little tuft of fur brushed the dead grass. Once more, he reminded me of a large, blue, scaly cat.

He took a deep breath, about to speak, but then closed his mouth again. His eyes sparked and flickered like the fire we sat in front of.

"I hate to admit it. But I'm terrified. I know that Tatsuo already knows I'm here. The other demons surely know as well."

I looked up at him again, but said nothing.

We were silent for a few moments. Then, I said, "Why are you coming with us? Like, what's the point?"

He didn't reply. He just stared at the dawn and the fire, too lost in thought to bother answering me.

Goldensun twitched beside me in her sleep. I reached over to her and put a comforting hand on her flank. Ever since we first met, I always seemed to think that her fur sparkled like the night sky, or that she was like a shooting star in her speed and color. But now, her pelt was dull, as if her very mood made it change its appearance.

"Poor Goldensun," Hinto murmured. His voice made me jump, seeing as I assumed he was lost in thought. I was irritated for a moment that he didn't answer my previous question.

"I thought I had it bad. I never see my sister Kai, but I still know she's alive. To lose someone you have spent your whole life with..." he trailed off as he realized what he was saying.

"I know the feeling," I grumbled. I missed my family, and I loved them for the entire time I knew them. But I was tired of everyone feeling sorry for me and for people to stop talking in the middle of a sentence that had anything to do with family.

"You don't need to say it," I growled before Hinto could apologize, "I'm absolutely done with people feeling sorry for me all the time. I realize that what happened can't be changed. As much as I want it to, I can't do a thing about it. They're dead, and I just have to trust in myself and believe that they want me to carry on with the mission."

Hinto looked slightly taken aback, but nodded. "Alright then."

I pulled my knees tighter to my chest. Four days. And we didn't know what we were doing, hardly knew where we were going, and I could feel the exhaustion beating down everyone like a blacksmith beats a newly formed sword.

"You should go to sleep," Hinto said gently.

I shook my head. "I should train, is more like it. I don't even know what I'm doing; let alone how I'm going to beat this guy. And I need to make new arrows," I said, and cursed. "I need new arrows, why didn't I think of that?"

I stood up, grabbed my quiver, and looked around for something I could practice on.

A small pool of water dotted by some tiny trees hid itself in the foothills. I wrapped some lily fronds over the bark of one of the trees, and with some charcoal in my pack, drew a crude target. Then, standing about twenty paces away, I shot my arrows.

Again and again, I shot. I took them down once I had fired them all, and used them again, until I could get all of them in the center. It was midmorning by the time I was finished, so I gathered my things and returned to the campsite.

Everyone was packed up and milling around anxiously. Silver was the first one to see me, and when she did, she shouted, "Oh, she's back!"

She ran up to me and gave me a hug. "Stop disappearing without telling anyone, Kohana!" she scolded. But her heart just wasn't in it today. "Come on, we need to get moving."

We hiked up the foothills. I could hear all of our stomachs growling the entire day. Hinto flew away around lunchtime to see if he could find us food. We continued without him, and made it to the base of the mountains by sunset.

The sky was a million shades of scarlet, orange, gold and dark blue. We all made camp as quickly as possible, and then scrambled back up the nearest foothill to watch the sunset. The wolves, both being in such a sad mood, decided they wanted to stay at camp.

We were all silent as the sun set. It was brilliant; a rainbow of red and orange. It was something straight out of a painting. And as we watched it, I looked towards the peaks at my back. They looked dark. And sad. I wondered if I would see a sunset once I entered them, or if I would ever see another one period. I loved sunsets, and I always had. They reminded me of the brightness in life, even when there seemed to be none.

After that thought, a thousand others like it raced through my head. Will I ever get to hug Goldensun again? Will I ever get to see Silver laugh again? Was yesterday the last time I would ever kiss Niyol? Would Niyol and I survive, or would one of us die? Was he as determined to live as I was?

Who is going to live through this, and who was going to fall?

I tried to push the thoughts away, but it was no good.

Silver stared at the sky with rapt attention on my left, Falcon next to her, and Niyol looked spaced-out on my right. His hand was resting in the grass, unattended. I reached for it, intertwined my fingers with his, and sighed.

He smiled while still looking at the sunset, and I knew that I could answer at least one of my questions.

Yes, he was determined to survive.

So was I.

Hinto returned with very little. A very small, sickly deer was trapped in his jaws. It would barely feed Niyol, Silver, Falcon and I, let alone the wolves and Hinto.

Don't worry. Haunt and I can find something else. There have to be a few rabbits somewhere in these hills, Goldensun told me. Her thoughts contained a smile, but I could read her eyes like I could read tracks of prey. They were dull and sad. But she had every reason to be upset. I scolded myself for not being more upset; Echosong was almost my sister, too, and I seemed to just forget her like she wasn't important.

"How are you going to eat?" I asked Hinto.

"I did. There was a fawn with this one, and I ate that."

I stared at him in disbelief. "How do you plan on not being hungry if you just eat a tiny baby deer?"

He shrugged. "Dragons can go a few months without a meal. Think of it more like a snack, and I will have a meal when I need one."

I rolled my eyes and started skinning the meat. We made a small fire and roasted it, and it was delicious. But the air throughout the group was tense, as if the peaks themselves made us anxious. None of us told stories or laughed, although Niyol made some feeble attempts to lighten the mood.

We all went to sleep without hardly saying a thing, and the only issue on my mind was the days to come.

I had another nightmare.

This time, Goldensun and I were walking through the forest. I recognized the trees as the ones back home. "What do you suppose will happen?" Goldensun asked me. I was shocked that she was talking out loud, instead of through our minds like usual.

"What do you mean?" I replied.

She rolled her eyes, as if I was totally blind to what she was trying to tell me. "Well, you left Niyol, Haunt, Hinto, Silver, Doli, Falcon, Pheo and Saph all alone at Galdur Fjall, remember? You got too scared and left them all behind!"

I stared at her in disbelief. "I wouldn't have done that!"

She shook her head. "I didn't think so either. But nerves do get to even the best of us."

As she spoke, the sky became red, the clouds turning black. A terrifying screech filled the air and Goldensun chuckled.

"I guess this is what happens when you leave your friends to do the dirty work…" she said in a creepily cheery, singsong voice. As if her words themselves were poison, her fur turned jet-black and her jade eyes turned to burning rubies. Her fangs elongated and changed from a dull yellow-white to a sparkling pearly color. They sharpened and her claws grew much longer. She was no longer recognizable as Goldensun.

She advanced towards me with a menacing growl. From the forest, emerging with a deathly silence, a horde of wolves joined her. It took a few moments before I acknowledged them as Darkshadow, Fallenoak, Haunt and Stormchaser. They stalked up to me as if I were cornered prey.

More shadow-figures and blazing red eyes materialized through the black trunks, but this time humans. They carried bows and arrows, swords and knives. Among the humans, I identified Niyol, Silver, Falcon, Chayton, Mother, Father, and even Tobie from High Point.

Demons wheeled in the skies. Their shapes varied in size and shape, and I thought I even saw Chu`si in the mass.

Dragons and Tall Wolves came after the humans, advancing with menacing slowness. Hinto was the only Dragon I knew, but among the Tall Wolves I recognized Granite and Shayde, his friend that took Niyol and me back down to the lower parts of Desaria after everyone in High Point found out who I was.

Goldensun growled, deep and guttural; a noise I have never heard come from her. Rather, I have never heard her make that noise and direct it to me. "You have betrayed your friends. You have left them to die. You traded their lives for yours, and you left the Dragons, and the world, to die. You have chosen wrong, dear pack-sister," she hissed, "And now you will pay the ultimate price!"

She lunged, and the pack of black wolves that I once knew followed. I had nothing but my knife, and I fought. I didn't count how many I killed, and I tried to ignore the fact that my pack-sister, the boy who I had fallen for, and my best friend were among those trying to kill me.

Falcon, who carried no weapon for reasons unknown to me, directed Pheo and Saph at me for countless attacks. Their fires combined into an eerie deep red. The world had turned to one mass of black and red, and it didn't matter which was which; I was trying to kill it all.

A blinding flash of white appeared in the battlefield. An angel, in the shape of a wolf. She was all white, with feathered wings protruding elegantly from her back. Her pale blue eyes gazed through the crowd, straight at me. A white glow surrounded her whole body, and it lit the area around her with the pearly glow.

"Kohana," she said, "Don't let fear rule you."

I tried to talk and fight off my opponents at the same time. "But Echosong, I didn't run away!"

The angel of Goldensun's sister shook her head. "But fear is closing in. Don't let it. This might get worse before it gets better, but the night is *always* darkest just before dawn."

I stared in dismay as she dissipated, leaving the world to be just black and red again. Then the swarm overtook me, and I woke up screaming.

Chapter 14

Magic Brewing

Midnight came and went. I knew that sleep was out of the question for the remainder of the night, so I told Silver, who was keeping watch, to go back to bed. She nodded with sleepy eyes and crawled back to her blanket.

I sat on top of our watch boulder with my bow and arrows resting beside me. It was cold, and I sat with my legs drawn up against my chest and my hands wrapped protectively around them.

For the first few hours, nothing happened. I was honestly surprised, seeing as we were practically at the doorstep of a demon hideout. I even thought about trying to go back to sleep, when a shadow in the darkness caught my eye.

I couldn't distinguish any shape, but it slunk towards the sleeping figure of Falcon. It skirted around the light given off by the dying embers of our once-campfire, adding an element to its stealth.

I grabbed my bow and notched an arrow. Then, with just as much covertness as the creature, I crawled down the rock and got closer.

Eyes the color of ice flashed at me from the shadow. I barely had time to think, *Oh no...* when a weight that seemed heavier than a Dragon leapt at me and pinned me down.

I tried to shout, but the beast was crushing me. My half healed ribs screamed in protest, and tried to not break again. I writhed and struggled, trying to escape, but it was no good.

The creature leaned in close and whispered something in a foreign language. One unfamiliar to me in every aspect. I stopped struggling, realizing it was doing me no good anyways.

I tried to call for help. As soon as a sound escaped my mouth, Hinto lifted his head. He saw the beast pinning me down and leapt towards it in the blink of an eye, but the demon saw him coming. It grinned evilly at me and vanished into thin air, disappearing without a trace. No smoke or feathers or fur; the beast was just gone.

Hinto stopped mid-bound. With a low growl, he asked, "Are you all right?" I nodded, still shaken. His electric yellow eyes flashed a moment's concern, but he nodded and walked back to where he had been not a minute ago. He didn't go back to sleep, but kept dutiful watch like me.

I returned to my post, but nothing happened for the remainder of the night.

Three days, Kohana. You only have three more days...

The words echoed in my head as the sun painted more of the land, and my companions still didn't stir. It seemed as though hours had passed before I heard the click of claws on stone and saw Haunt climbing up the rock.

I hadn't ever particularly liked her. She always appeared to me as a wolf that held herself higher, even though she knew there was nothing to boast. She was nice enough, I suppose. And she worked hard in the group, and she cared. But the feeling of overall aloofness never left her side; a constant shadow to her aura.

But something changed when she sat down next to me, watching the sunrise. Neither of us said a word, but when I reached over to stroke her scarlet fur, she didn't fight it. Rather, she almost leaned backwards into my hand.

The silence was peaceful. Lost in time, I thought about my past, despite the fact that there wasn't much to look back on.

I run blindly through the forest. Branches and bushes and all sorts of foliage tear at my little gown, but I don't care. I'll never see my family again...I can't believe they're dead. This must just be a nightmare. Yes, maybe I will wake up in my nice bed and run downstairs and Mother and Father and Chayton will all be there to greet me.

But reality smacks me in the face and tells me that no, I won't see them again. This is real. And supposedly, somehow, in some way that I don't understand...it's my fault.

I run through the forest for who knows how long. I collapse in a heap of pink dress and blonde hair and little girl tears, and fall asleep that way, in a small clearing in the forest, a far away and in a place I don't recognize.

203

I wake and I see a shadow staring at me from the trees with bright green eyes. At first, I wonder what I am doing in the forest. Then I remember, and have to try with all of my heart not to cry again. I know that I won't survive out here, and whatever creature is staring at me from the undergrowth is sure to make a quick meal of me.

But it doesn't attack. We stare at each other, my blue eyes blending with its green.

What are you doing?

I almost shout. A voice had just invaded my head!

The creature steps forward to reveal a shining, golden wolf. She looks little, about my age in wolf years, maybe a little younger. Her small tail sweeps the air in a friendly gesture, but I am still fearful. Although wolves aren't frowned upon in my society, a lone wolf still seems dangerous, even if she is young.

I'm Goldensun, if you can hear me, *the wolf tells me. I shout again.*

What are you doing in my mind? *I yell and think. She smiles, the broadest wolf smile I have ever seen.*

You can hear me! Pack-sister…you must be my pack-sister!

I frown. What does that me-

"Kohana!"

Silver's shout woke me from my memories. I turned to her, and Haunt did the same, ears perked high.

"It's almost midmorning! We need to move!"

I looked around, cursing myself for letting time slip by like that. I scrambled down from the rock, bow and quiver in hand, and rushed to pack up our things.

The first day was brutal. We battled the rocky cliffs and climbed the steep slopes, with nothing more than our hands and feet. Hinto carried most of our supplies, seeing as we had very little, but we all bore our own weapons.

I was especially wary of the hills. The last time I had climbed mountains, I had been attacked by Mountain lions. It didn't help that this time, I was without my knife.

The winds battered us and tossed us against cliff walls, and soon after we entered the pass, snow started to fall. Soon, we were caught in a full-on blizzard again. I knew that the good weather wouldn't have lasted.

Silver's frostbite, which had been healing up nicely, seemed to return with new vigor. Her fingers looked pale and waxy, and it didn't help that I had to drag her along by her hands. I once again gave her my rabbit-fur gloves, leaving my fingers exposed to the biting winds and driving snow.

Several times, one of us collapsed. Once it was me, once Niyol, twice for both Falcon and Silver. Every time one fell, it took all of their strength to get back up. I didn't know how we expected to do anything.

Silver fell for the third time, and she refused to get back up. Doli poked at her, little blue feathers frosted over. She had long lost the ability to fly, seeing as the snow coated her small body and made her too heavy. What she said to her sister, I will never know. But whatever it was couldn't get Silver to move.

I told the rest to keep going. With reluctant nods, only Goldensun, Doli and I stayed with Silver. We were to catch up later.

"Silver, you have to get up!" I shouted over the storm. She mumbled something; I saw her blue lips move. But her dark eyelashes were crusted shut with snow and her hair was more white than brown now. I knew that there wasn't much of a chance for her, but I still had to try.

Trying to find the words, I crouched by her side. I knew that every second I delayed would be one second closer to when she would stop breathing. I knew that time was of the essence, but I just sat there beside her for what felt like a long time.

"Silver," I finally said. More like shouted, considering I couldn't be heard at a normal speaking volume. "Don't do this. You need to get up. We can't do this without you! If you let go now, then Doli won't have a chance. And then, you'd leave me, and Niyol and Falcon and Hinto and everyone all alone! Think about Sky, and how she died for *you*. You can't give up!"

I never was much of a motivational speaker, but this seemed to get the job done. Silver struggled to open her eyes. She looked up and I offered her my hand. I clasped my cold, stiff fingers around hers, protected inside gloves, and pulled her up.

We walked, and she stumbled several times. I offered her my shoulder, and we lurched along, side-by-side.

A shadow appeared through the blizzard. It didn't take long before I recognized it as Niyol.

"Niyol!" I called. Soon he was by Silver's side, and he picked her up and carried her the remainder of the way.

I didn't realize how long we had been gone until we got to the makeshift camp. A small alcove in the cliff side provided just enough shelter to hide us from the winds, if Hinto sat between the rest of the mountains and us.

A fire tonight was out of the question. We all sat huddled together as close as could be, and one by one, we dropped off into a deep, cold, snowy sleep. I know I was awake longest, for when I finally did close my eyes, I could hear the blowing wind and a Dragon's snores.

I had no dreams that night. My mind left me in utter darkness. I woke feeling well-rested, but the moment my eyelids fluttered open, I was attacked viciously by a wave of anxiety. *Tomorrow. Tomorrow night was the Red Moon.*

I can't do it.

Yes you can.

An internal battle raged within my head. It felt like it was going to burst, split right down the middle from the conflict. But a third, sweet, gentle voice interrupted the crossfire.

Kohana, you and I both know that you can *do it.*

I looked over to see Goldensun laying regally in the alcove, green eyes fixed on me. *Stop debating, and decide. If you can't do it, then let's leave. If you can do it, then we need to keep going.*

Remembering my nightmares that plagued me the nights before, I shook my head. Even if it was fantasy, the angel Echosong sent words that chilled me to the bone. *The night is always darkest just before dawn,* she had told me. I wanted to know why everyone kept saying that to me, and at the same time, I wished the words would just go away.

I took a deep, thoughtful breath, and then looked up determinedly. *I will keep going.*

As we continued our journey that day, I couldn't get the thought out of my head; there were only two days left. I had today and tomorrow, but tomorrow night was the Red Moon. A thought occurred to me as we continued our trek up the mountains, and it wasn't long before I realized it was a serious problem. So I voiced my concern, hoping that the others knew the answer.

"Do any of us know which mountain it is?"

All eyes turned to me in surprise. I dug around in my pack for the map. When I pulled it out, I scanned the little mountain region, but it was so much harder to tell where the terrifying peak was, when we were knocking on its doorstep.

Falcon came over and surveyed the map with me. We decided on a peak that was a bit higher than the rest, and all together much more menacing. Unfortunately, it was still a good distance away. We'd have to keep moving.

That morning, we had awoken to find Silver alive, but not by much. She was pale and clammy, and she hadn't much heat about her. When I tried to get her up, she barely stirred. We knew that we had to keep moving; we had no time to waste. We hardly had any time as it was.

Hinto came up with the solution. He helped us settle her on his back, and she had been there since. It was only midmorning, and thankfully, the snow had stopped. But I knew that we were still short on time and short on direction. If Silver wasn't moving by tomorrow night, then we would be one weapon and one ally short in the battle.

We hiked all day again. Hardly any conversation took place, and when it did, it was to try and find a way to take down Tatsuo. But if he couldn't be hurt with mortal weapons, what was the point in bringing them, and what could we possibly fight him with? I didn't know if it was even worth continuing; our only chance of survival was rendered useless against our mysterious foe.

An idea had formed in my head, though. Just one, and it was the longest of all long shots. But if it was a chance, I was going to take it, for it was probably the only hope we even had against Tatsuo.

207

I suggested it during the climb, and Niyol instantly pointed out the flaw in my plan.

"Yes, your knife is special, Kohana," he told me, "But remember what Granite said? It's a manmade weapon; it won't do any good, whether or not it's been enchanted by Dragonfire. Plus, how would we get to it? I'm sure that the demons on the mountain will have it under lock and key."

I tried to hide my irritation. Niyol didn't know anything about my knife. He didn't know the things I could do with it, and he didn't know the powers it possessed. I stuck firm with my plan, although the edges of the picture now seemed faded.

Everyone was silent practically the whole day. I tried talking to Goldensun a few times, but her answers were brisk. And only the occasional glimpse of her thoughts wandered through to my head; she guarded her mind well. She still needed to teach me how to do that.

Doli fluttered anxiously around Silver and Hinto all day and night, too. The concern was printed in her little beady eyes, and I could sense it wasn't just for Silver. She could sense the impending danger just as well as the rest of us.

Falcon looked to be having a conversation with Pheo for the majority of the journey, so I was left to my own thoughts, and the occasional wisp of Goldensun's.

"Father," I say, sitting by the pond with him. Recently, he has been busy with his duties, and hasn't had time for me or Chayton. Today, he told the war chief, his advisor, and practically everyone who's been badgering him for the last few weeks that he needs to spend time with his children. But since my brother is out with his friends, it's just me and the king. "What's the hardest challenge you ever had to face?"

I look into his blue eyes, but he avoids mine. Something is on his mind, so I look out to where his gaze rests as well. To my surprise, my fish friend Goblet is swimming around, directly in the line of sight of Father. He grumbles something about the fish being too large, but doesn't say anything else.

"I don't know. As king, I face many challenges. But I can assure you, you will never have to deal with something worse than calming a riot or distributing food evenly for the town." He smiles

at me, and it's a warm smile that's so full of promise. He's always had that effect on people, that makes you want to smile back.

I laughed cruelly. *Yes, Father,* I thought, my mind full of disdain, *I never did have to deal with riots or distributing food. Instead, I have to run from riots and find my own food. And I have to save the world, too.* Almost as soon as I thought it, I regretted it. I loved my father very much; he and I were closer than I was to Chayton or Mother. I missed them all terribly, and it wasn't fair for me to be scornful of them; they only did the best they could to raise me, and it wasn't their fault that they died. It wasn't my fault either.

For a moment I forgot that Goldensun could hear me, and Father probably could too from his perch in the heavens. But I ignored both possibilities. To think, that day was just a few weeks before I became Outcast.

I thought back to what Silver said that day when we were hunting on Golden Plains.

You can run faster, think quicker, hunt smarter, all because you are Outcast.

I thought about what that meant. Maybe it would get me an answer. Doubtful. Then, I thought back to the message given to me by the Echosong angel and the Night Cat, and also in Falcon's letter. But what did it mean?

The night is always darkest just before dawn.

I thought about asking someone. But Hinto was obviously striking an engaging conversation with Saph and Doli, and Falcon was doing the same with Pheo. Niyol was too lost in his own thoughts to answer, I couldn't talk to Haunt or Silver, and Goldensun wasn't in the mood to talk. Maybe I'd ask tonight. But as we continued our same pace throughout the day and into the darker hours, I wondered if I'd have the chance.

We were still hiking well past dusk when I decided to break the silence. "Falcon," I said warily. He snapped out of whatever thoughts he was in, and slowed down to walk with me. Pheo slept soundly on his shoulder, and glowed faintly.

"Yeah?"

"How willing would Pheo or Saph be to do some scouting?" Pheo's color brightened at the sound of his name and he opened one eye, clearly irritated, but closed it as he realized the conversation didn't include anything terribly interesting. He was soon dozing off again.

Falcon rubbed his chin thoughtfully. "I would assume that Saph would be up for it, but Pheo would certainly need a little coaxing." He turned to the scarlet bird on his shoulder and whispered something into his ear. Pheo brightened and ruffled his feathers, screeching angrily. The look on his face plainly stated that he didn't want to do this, but he flapped his great wings a few times and lifted off, calling to his blue companion as he went.

Falcon watched them until they disappeared over the next peak. "I told him to look for a way up to the top of the tallest mountain, and also to keep an eye out for demons. That'd be a dead giveaway, don't you think?"

I nodded. "Why did he look so mad?"

Falcon smiled. "I woke him up. He doesn't like that."

"I can tell."

Silence followed, cutting through the cold night air like a blade sharpened to perfection.

Despite the lack of our flaming, feathered friends, visibility was no problem. The almost-full moon shone down on us, providing near-perfect vision.

The moon had always seemed so welcoming, but now her glow washed over me with a seemingly cold, cruel light. *The next time I see you,* I thought to the moon, *you will be blood-red and giving power to my enemy.*

As expected, the moon didn't respond. She didn't apologize or console or laugh or taunt, but instead just stayed there, silent in the sky. I could have sworn that the silence was worse than an actual reaction.

We walked until we could no longer move. Falcon was the first to collapse, and Niyol and I followed shortly. Hinto claimed that he was wide awake, and he took the shift to guard. When I suggested waking up in a few hours to replace him, he strongly refused and told me that I definitely needed the sleep. I lay down to close my eyes, certain that sleep would be all but impossible, but in the early hours of the morning, the weight of slumber washed over me in seconds.

I woke to a soft, gentle heat by my side. I opened my eyes a crack and saw a red and blue glow, and Falcon was sitting up. His gaze was fixed intently on Pheo as he must have told Falcon what he knew.

Falcon smiled broadly and looked up to the peaks, just turning pink in the dawn. I mustn't have gotten more than three or four hours of rest, but it had rejuvenated my body that was weary from a day and a half of straight hiking up steep hillsides.

Although there was no morning meal, and we hadn't eaten all of yesterday, everyone seemed to be in higher spirits. Falcon told us what his birds had discovered as we were preparing to leave, and I pretended to not notice how fragile Silver looked as Niyol carried her up to Hinto's back.

"They found a way up! It's gravelly, but they say the rocks looked solid enough to climb, and that there's a path that leads up to the gravelly bit, which is only near the top," he told us. A broad smile stretched across Niyol's face, and I felt one tugging at my lips, too.

"They said that the mountain just beyond this one, which is very tall and steep, had many shadows that were moving across the peak and it felt...dark. Plus, Pheo says it was the tallest one visible."

"That's great!" I said, but I couldn't get the forced excitement out of my voice. While finding Galdur Fjall was definitely a crucial part in the quest, this now meant that we were one step closer to what was possibly all of our dooms.

The Red Moon is tonight, I kept thinking. It seemed so impossibly far away and so tragically close at the same time; an obstacle that was just in front of me but too large to hurdle.

Niyol came over to me as we set out, the golden-pink light touching even the deep crevice of the pass. It climbed upward, between two mountainsides, and I was sure that beyond them lay our destination.

We walked in quiet companionship, similar to yesterday when we moved along in absolute silence. But with him by my side, I felt somewhat reassured that everything was going to be okay. I laced my fingers through his and held on, because I didn't know how many more times I would get the chance to do so. He squeezed my hand in an attempt to reassure me, but it did little.

As we neared the top of the pass, Hinto slowed. He told us that Silver was stirring, and we should lay her down. When she was in a deep sleep, she was more stable on his back, but not so much anymore.

Just as Falcon was setting her down on the ground, her eyelids fluttered open long enough to reveal her chocolate eyes. She looked around at us and whispered, "I haven't missed it, have I?"

I smiled, but it was fake. "No, you haven't. Why do you ask?"

She mumbled, "Because I won't give up until I know you have won…or until I know there's nothing to wake up to."

I kneeled down next to her, and I gave her a hug. One she weakly returned. "Silver, don't worry. You'll be just fine, and whether you fight tonight or not, you will still have done enough to move mountains."

She gave me a feeble smile, and her eyes closed. She sunk back into her deep, dark sleep.

I stood up. Her dark hair contrasted with her pale, fragile-looking skin. She looked so thin, but as I gazed around at the others, I realized that we all looked rather lean.

Falcon and I carefully returned her to Hinto's back and we set off again.

We paused at the very peak of the pass. Beside us lay two mountains that were still towering. Before us rested a taller, thinner, rockier peak with an almost flat top. I looked as hard as I could, but in the midmorning light I couldn't see any movement on the summit.

But Pheo and Saph were right; even from our distance away, I could feel the dark magic brewing.

Chapter 15

Red Moon Rising

The downhill trek was easier than uphill, but by early afternoon, we were on the ascent again. The gentle pass through the peaks had all but ended at the foot of Galdur Fjall, and when I asked, Falcon explained why.

"Few actually attempt the journey here, and even fewer survive. Galdur Fjall is the best – and pretty much the only – place to perform complicated magical spells. Some people try to revive the dead here. Others use it for sacrificial purposes. But let me tell you: Galdur Fjall is hardly ever used for light magic. Dark magic is used so commonly here, that sometimes, people in Aliyr referred to it as Dimma Fjall."

I looked at him curiously, considering I didn't speak the old language very well. He sighed. "Dimma Fjall means 'Dark Mountain'. It is almost *always* used for dark magic, and some people think it practically emanates darkness."

"Yeah, but why isn't there a path up the side?" I asked stubbornly.

"There haven't been enough travelers to cut out a path. The pass we used until now is used by the Outlanders who need to get from the north to the south and vice versa, but hardly anyone goes deeper into the mountains from here. Stories say that the east side of these peaks is infested with demon-like creatures and beasts so terrible that just their looks will cause you to die of fright."

"Well, where are they all?" Niyol questioned.

Falcon shrugged. "Maybe they're waiting for us to get to the top, so they can throw us a surprise party."

The tone in Falcon's voice made me shiver, even though I knew it was supposed to be a joke.

I would have tried to hold Niyol's hand on the climb up, but the terrain wouldn't allow it. The slope was steep and rocky, and most of the time we were climbing with both our hands and feet. My knees became scraped and bloody, yet I barely felt the pain due to the adrenaline. My heart was pumping not only with the increasing altitude, but also with the idea of what I was going to have to do tonight.

Hinto was jumping from boulder to boulder, nimbler than a mountain goat, when Silver moaned. He stopped and I helped her off, set her down on the rock, and she started talking again.

"I'm going to walk," she groaned. Her chocolate eyes shone with determination as she struggled to stand. Silver used my shoulder to help herself up, but it was obvious that she couldn't climb on her own. As it was, Falcon, Niyol and I were breathing hard; and we were in top form.

"Silver, stop, you can't do this. You can barely stand! You won't be able to climb this!" I said. But Silver shot me a look that clearly read 'Kohana, shut up', and I knew that she wasn't going to let any of us stop her.

"I want to fight with you. I have been waiting for this moment since I found out what we were actually doing, and I need to know that I didn't just travel so far away from home for nothing. I won't let anyone else die, and even me fighting in my weakest state is better than me not being there at all."

Goldensun and Haunt watched from a boulder above Hinto. Small gravelly rocks skittered down the hillside as they scrambled up to the next one.

I obviously wasn't aware of the possibility of another injury, because I didn't think that someone could fall on the hillside.

A yelp sounded above, and I looked up just in time to see Haunt lose her footing on the gravel. Goldensun reached for Haunt's scruff with her teeth…

But she missed. Her reach was off by just a whisker.

Haunt tumbled down the slope in a russet blur, scrabbling for anything she could gain footing on. There was nothing for her to stable herself on, so the wolf plummeted downward with surprising speed. Before anyone could react, she was below us.

Even above, we all heard the sickening crack. Haunt hit her head on a boulder, and lay still.

Goldensun scrambled down the slope, slipping and sliding on the pebbles. She hit the brakes, slamming to a halt at the boulder where the red wolf lay.

My golden friend's stillness told us all we needed to know. Her tail drooped and her ears flattened, and she then let out the most mournful howl I have ever heard.

We all stood in a shocked silence. Hinto's breathing, just a few feet above me, seemed to be loud enough to hear from Enin, and I thought I could feel its heat on the back of my neck. Silver's eyes were swollen with tears, which quickly spilled onto her cheeks. Despite how I thought I had felt about the red wolf, I felt my eyes burning and my cheeks becoming moist.

Falcon stared open-mouthed. Niyol took my free hand in his and squeezed it. The message was clear; *which one of us is next?*

The only ones who moved were the three birds. Doli wiggled out from Silver's backpack and glided down to Haunt and Goldensun, with the Phoenixes in tow. They all stood in silence as Goldensun let loose another cry so mournful that I couldn't begin to imagine what she sounded for Echosong.

I turned away from Niyol, for once shunning his warm, solid protection and instead reaching for Silver's frail, skinny body. I embraced her like I did Goldensun, and she hugged back.

I don't know how long we waited and stood there in our shocked state. But Goldensun soon began to trudge up the hill, and I noticed how dull her eyes looked. As if someone had taken the little bit of energy she had left and sucked it out of her.

What will Fallenoak say? She thought. I don't know if it was to me, or to herself, but I answered anyways.

Say to what?

He and Echosong...they had something special. I... her voice trailed off, and without really thinking about it, I realized that she had finally accepted her sister's death.

I thought about it, too. As soon as Echosong realized that we were going to rescue Fallenoak, she had jumped onboard without a second thought. *And look where that got her,* I thought bitterly to myself.

We climbed in absolute silence for the rest of the day.

Night came, swift as a shadow, and we were waiting near the peak. A small cave, proven deserted, had become a perfect hiding place and a perfect resting place. I sat guard outside, and it was just after moonrise. I had already gotten my sleep, and was as well rested as could be for the impending battle.

I stood outside the cave, and decided that if this were to be the end, I would go looking as I did in my finest. My long hair flowed freely from my head, but I began the long process of braiding it. By the time I was done, it was pulled sharply from my face, not a single strand astray. I felt it rest between my shoulder blades and smiled coldly.

I sharpened my arrows. I oiled my bowstring. When the moon came to a point between its rise and midnight, I rallied the others.

I helped Silver braid her hair, too. It made her look stronger, and I was a heavy believer in the power presented by your appearance. Braiding my hair always made me feel like I was tougher, and that I had more room to move around, seeing as my hair wouldn't get in my way.

Hinto sharpened his claws and teeth, Falcon his long blade, Niyol his sword. Silver prepared a few extra arrows from a stash she had (unknown to me, I could have really used it awhile ago) and sharpened those points as well. Then, we were ready for battle. The moon was almost at the highest point in its journey, and before we left, I found all of my friends looking at me expectantly.

I realized they wanted me to say something. So, I said what I had wanted to say, and had prepared to say since this morning.

"We don't know what we're going to face. We might have an army of rabbits, or an army of Dragons. It's a mystery to all of us. And we're probably more than a little outnumbered. But that doesn't matter. We are a team; we have fought together and ran together and hunted and lived together; a family of different bloods." I hoped I sounded more convincing than I felt.

"Some of us might not survive. Some might end up giving their lives in this fight today. But that doesn't mean I want any of you to die. Whether we win or lose today, we need to fight our hardest. We need to put our all into this battle, and win or lose, we need to know that we did the best we could."

The cave was silent. I was just starting to think that I had made a complete fool of myself when Silver stood up shakily. "I didn't give up when I was sick, and I'm not giving up now. At least, not until I get a few arrows into demon hide," she said with a crafty smile. I grinned back, showing my full support in the only way I could.

Niyol nodded his head and stood too, pulling Falcon up with him. His Phoenixes made strange, growling noises in their throats and flared up bright. Goldensun's fur practically shimmered in the birds' light, and her eyes flashed like jade swords for the first time in a while. She stood and growled, hackles raised and teeth bared in anticipation. Hinto stood with his head lowered upon his long neck and his eyes carried a sharpness to them that I wouldn't want to test.

Echosong and Haunt will not have died in vain; I will avenge their deaths one hundred times over on each and every demon I sink my teeth into, Goldensun hissed to me. The fury in her voice almost made me pity her future opponents. Almost.

With a swift nod of my head, I motioned for my friends to follow me, and we headed out of the cave.

We emerged onto the peak as one, completely illuminated by the full moon's light.

I don't know what I expected. Perhaps the red-black nightmare-land I had envisioned, or the pile of bones and bodies of loved ones from my dream in what seemed so long ago. But whatever I expected, this wasn't it.

The peak was barren. Completely and utterly desolate of anything living. The only thing – besides rock – that was here was so abrupt and angular that I doubted it was natural.

A pedestal, about four feet tall, sat in the center of the ground. It was carved into a rectangle, and its flat top had a slit in it just big enough for a blade. I stared curiously at it, before glancing between my friends. They all shared the same confusion as I felt.

I stepped towards the pedestal, knowing this wasn't the brightest move but hungry for something to happen. My nerves were so high strung that Goldensun's click of claws sent me spinning around in her direction, an arrow already drawn and pointed at her heart.

She stared at me, shocked. I bit my lip and lowered my weapon. *What's wrong with me?* I accused myself angrily. *How could you just point your weapon at your pack-sister? You know that a demon would be silent, and you know that it wouldn't have come from that direction without some sort of attention!*

I turned back to the dais. It drew me as if a rope were attached around my waist. I reached out and touched it, but despite my hunger for battle, I wish I hadn't.

A roar louder than anything I have ever heard filled my ears. It wasn't that of an individual; it was as if all of the underworld had split in half and was screaming at me. I covered my ears, but the noise still came, louder than before. I saw images of horrible things flash before me, and I writhed on the ground that I could no longer feel. I was stuck inside a nightmare worse than anything I had ever dreamt now, and words couldn't further describe the things I saw. I didn't notice that my screams had been added to the din. All I could think was *How long have I been here? When will this nightmare end?*

Suddenly, the vision dissipated like smoke. I lay trembling and shivering and sweating on the ground back by my friends, away from the podium. Strong, warm arms were wrapped around me, but I couldn't stop. I was rocking back and forth, moaning at every noise. I couldn't tell if it was tears or sweat that soaked my face, or if it was a mixture of both. Silver's brown braid swept over my face, and in the moonlight her skin looked even paler and sicklier than it had before.

I was barely aware of her murmuring, "Demon magic. The pedestal must be cursed."

No sooner had she uttered the words then a screech filled the air. The noise made me cringe. Niyol released his warm grip on me and drew his sword. "Kohana's touch must have summoned the demons," he growled. For a moment, I thought I had upset him.

I shakily tried to stand, but Goldensun's warm fur pushed me back. *Stay,* she said gruffly. I obeyed.

Silver shot an arrow at a black streak coming our way, and it fell from the sky, skidding to a halt on the stone. It looked like a Nymer, but I couldn't tell. More noised filled the air, and this time when I tried to get up, Goldensun didn't keep me down.

I shakily drew an arrow and notched my bow. "Stick together," I said. I could hear my voice cracking from the still-present fear of the nightmare I had just endured, "Stay back-to-back. They can't us separate that way."

Mumbles of consent followed and soon I felt the warmth of my friends pressing close to each other. Goldensun and Hinto gave terrifying snarls, practically at the same time, just as a mass of at least forty demons landed and appeared in front of us. They, too, gave opening statements that gave me the impression that they were just as serious as we were.

Without a second thought, Goldensun threw herself at the nearest demon; a thing that looked like a black mountain lion with deer's horns on its head. She thrashed her head, breaking its neck, before merging back in with us. Hinto reared and torched the close demons, making the scene heavy with the smell of burning flesh. Then, more appeared, and the war began.

I fought through the crowd, firing arrow after arrow. I felt Falcon beside me, slashing at anything that came within three feet of me. Niyol on my left had a similar thought process. I could only hope that Silver was faring well, seeing as she was behind me in our tight circle.

Pheo and Saph were visible darting in and out of the horde, sometimes flitting overhead and always audible. But most of the demons screeched like them, so whether or not they were the cause of the din was a mystery to me.

A few times, I thought I caught the glare of ice-blue eyes, and I could only think of the strange demon that had attacked me in camp just a few days ago. But as soon as they would appear, they would dissipate once more.

Goldensun, I thought to her, trying to get a feel for how she was doing. But either she was too wrapped up in battle to answer or she was gone, for she was silent.

Arrow after arrow flew from my bow, and I retrieved as many as I could from the fallen beasts, but I knew that I wouldn't get anything done once they were gone. I needed my knife, but all I had were arrows.

Something sharp prodded me in the side. I glanced down to where Falcon was trying to hand me a small dagger. I smiled. Finally, something I could use.

In one quick movement, I slung my bow over my shoulder, swiped the knife from my friend's hand, and jumped into the battle. I would lunge and attack, slaying one demon after the next, and then fall back into the group. Lunge, dodge, attack, return. Lunge, dodge, attack, return. I followed this pattern flawlessly.

I barely noticed as the bluish light of the moon began to turn pink, then red. But as soon as I did become aware of it, I took a moment to glance up.

Just as in my nightmare with Echosong, the moon was blood-red. The sky was red and the mountaintop was stained scarlet. The demons, almost all of them black, had a red glow reflected off of their sleek pelts and feathers and hides. Their eyes now burned with hatred; a blinding, neon orange in the world of black and crimson.

I didn't notice a demon slink towards me and attack, but I reacted with speed that would make a cobra proud. A long gash ran down my arm; my own scarlet blood adding to the crimson ground now below me.

I gasped, trying to push it to the back of my mind. I needed to focus on the battle, not the blood. Yet I found the pain almost unbearable. I gripped my arm and prepared to fight again.

Things started going south. The pain made it hard to think. My lunges became sloppier, and some of the demons fell upon me. I felt them scratch and bite and strike out at me, and I tried to fight them off with the dagger. There were two on my back, then three, until I fell, struggling to turn around and attack. I heard shouts from my friends as they worked together, and one of them cried out in pain. I didn't know who.

They don't see me, I thought as I continued to struggle against the demons. *I'm going to die here, they don't see me.*

Suddenly, I felt some weight retreat from my back. It was enough to throw another monster off, and stab the third in the chest. He slumped, now dead, on my blade, and as I pushed him off, I saw Goldensun fighting bravely against one of my previous attackers. The second demon took my moment of distraction to attack me, but I blocked him with my forearm and sent him flying into the mass. Goldensun was then at my side with a bloodied muzzle. *Thank you,* I said.

You're not dying on my watch.

We then threw ourselves into the battle as a team. My wolf guarded my left side, where the gash was, and she took down more demons than I did. I did my best, and took down three or four more, before something strange happened.

The creatures drew back. They surged and moved like a wave, practically spitting Goldensun out at my feet. The Phoenixes and Doli circled back to their companions, landing with grace on shoulders. As I looked around, I realized that Hinto was nowhere to be found. However, I had no time to dwell on that fact.

A black shadow stepped towards us. "We will give you one chance," it said with a voice like nails. It had the body and legs of a horse, and the head and neck of a snake. Long, jagged spikes ran from its snout, down its back and to the tip of a reptilian tail. Skeletal wings sprouted from its shoulders, but they were tucked tight against its hide. "One chance to leave and we will let you go."

I bared my teeth in what had to be the most wolfish display I could muster. "We will not back down!"

The demon shook his head and gave me a 'tut tut' that is usually reserved for mothers scolding children. "Well, then. I suppose we have no choice but to kill you."

The battle resumed with more vigor than before. The demons kept coming and coming, whereas our forces were rapidly exhausting. The pain in my arm was immense, and the wetness of my blood made me anxious. I was losing a lot of it.

A terrifying screech split the air, and the demons stopped once more.

"It is time!" called a Nymer from the skies. It beat wings that were silvery white, to match the rest of its oddly colored body.

Then, all of the demons that we had been fighting vanished in a cloud of black smoke. The ones we had killed went with them, leaving nothing but our small group. If not for the bloodstains on the rock, I wouldn't believe a battle had ever happened.

Now that we had a chance to pause, I noticed how strange this red world was. Even though the demons were gone, shadows played tricks on my eyes. They grinned with pointed teeth and glowing eyes, darting away every time I turned to look at them. Dark, evil monsters danced at the corners of my vision. They were everywhere, but the mountaintop was empty.

The Nymer landed at the podium, bringing me back to the matter at hand and thrashing its tail. "Don't even bother," it said as Niyol ran at it with a sword. "The barriers will keep you out."

Niyol, not trusting a demon, ran at it with full force. But before he could get there, he crashed into something that sounded extremely solid and very pain-inducing.

He stood up and rubbed his head, then stabbed at the barrier with his sword. The sword wobbled as it struck the invisible wall, but nothing happened. Meanwhile, the demon had pulled from thin air an object that I had longed to see for well over two months, since Chu`si had taken it from me up in High Point.

The blade was sharp as ever, but the black seemed to have lost its sheen. The knife looked weathered and old, as if it had been far too overused. The handle was still beautiful, but it, too carried the look of too much strain. The rubies in the hilt sparkled with an unnatural, red light, given to them by the moon.

The Nymer raised the blade over the podium, talons glistening along with the blade. It then began to chant, quiet at first but then louder, until I could hear it clearly from where I stood, even over the clash of Niyol's blade against the invisible barrier.

"Rivers of fire, lakes of ash.
See the Master, let him pass.
Bring him strength, bring him power.
Wake him in this final hour.
Demons come and demons go,
We must let our Master know,
Our strength is his, we side with him,

Now bring him forth, from Hell's rim
May his power surge and grow,
Letting his disciples know,
That time of control soon returned,
Approaches now to take its turn.
Summon him, let him pass,
For his Kinghood now shall last.
I send for you from deep below,
With embers that no longer glow
Lakes of dust and rivers of flame,
Burning brighter on this day!"

Then, the Nymer drove the blade into the podium, sending blue sparks flying and a green flame erupting around the base. "I now give you the blood of the four lands!" it screeched. "Water, Fire, Sky and Earth!"

Four creatures appeared. An otter, a Dragon hatchling, an eagle, and a dark brown wolf. They were all chained by something that was also invisible.

I only needed to see the wolf, and I knew it was Fallenoak. His aqua eyes shone with fear, but that only reassured me that he was still alive.

Goldensun saw him too. They locked gazes, and some brief hope flashed in Fallenoak's eyes as he came to understand we weren't just there to finish this, but to save him too.

The Nymer took my blade, my knife, turned magic with Dragon fire, and drove it into the otter's back. It squealed and quickly died. "I give you the blood of water!" The Nymer held the carcass over the podium, letting the scarlet blood drip onto it.

The beast repeated the act with the hatchling and the eagle. It turned to Fallenoak.

"And last, I give you the blood of earth! With the blood of the four elements, you may rise from the underworld and claim what is rightfully yours!"

Time seemed to slow down. The knife drove towards Fallenoak at a devastatingly sluggish rate, but in that time, I drew and notched my bow. Part of me knew that it was no use, but another part of my brain said that I had to try anyways. I let the arrow soar, and it passed through the barrier without a split second of hesitation. It flew into the Nymer's eye. A direct hit, killing it instantaneously.

I stared in shock. The knife, still in the beast's talons, clattered to the stone. Fallenoak was lying on his side, but was staring at me with absolute astonishment on his face.

Everything was silent. No demons came to avenge their fallen brother, and none came to finish the ceremony. I walked calmly over to Fallenoak, passing through the barrier just like my arrow, and I grabbed my knife. He flinched, as if I were going to cut him. Instead, I felt for the ties that held him and slashed them instead. They were invisible, but they weren't a problem for my magic knife.

Now freed, Fallenoak dashed happily towards Goldensun. The sky began to turn more blue than red, and I looked up joyously to see that the Red Moon had now begun its descent. The demonic shadows lurking at the edges of my vision were slowly creeping away.

But the joy was not to last.

Somehow, some of the blood from my own arm had splashed onto the dais, granting the ceremony with the last component needed; the blood of earth.

A grumble louder than anything I had ever heard creaked through the air, and the mountaintop shook with the force of it. A long, deep crack opened in the ground, to reveal a bright fiery light burning beneath. I dashed back to my friends, away from the gap, and into Niyol's arms, my knife held tight in my hands. As a group, we instinctively closed in tighter.

I looked desperately for Hinto, but I had to remind myself he was gone. I realized that he must have flown off in the heat of battle, leaving us with the burden. *I should have known*, I thought angrily, *why would he help us? He's a Dragon, and Dragons hate people. I was a fool for trusting him.*

Dark, thick smoke appeared from the crack, and from it rose a shadow that appeared in the form of a Dragon I had hoped to never encounter.

The Kena Dragon was the kind that children were told of to make them behave. "Eat your meat, or the Kena will come get you! Do your chores, or the Kena will take you away!" They were the very embodiment of nightmares, the scariest thing that was out there. Knights in shining armor were said to have thrown themselves off of bridges if they were to see a Kena, because they knew that it delivered the least merciful death. They were just a myth, a rumor started up by the ancients. And yet, I was standing here, looking at one.

In reality, it looked not too much different than a normal Dragon. It had the long, scaly neck, four legs, a long tail, and leathery wings. But its mouth practically glowed from its fire, just brewing inside, and it crouched on its hind legs only. It was very humanoid in posture and build, but at least four times larger than Hinto. The wings started at his shoulder blades were folded, but clearly large. The leathery part attached down at his hips. His wings were huge, even for this mammoth beast. They were tipped with massive claws, and I tried to ignore the razor-sharpness of the ones on his hands and feet. His tail swept the ground behind him – a motion I had become quite used to – and a little fan of fur sprouted from it. His eyes glowed white hot. Now I knew why so many people were afraid of this beast.

You thought you could stop me? he bellowed. I remained silent.

A laugh came from deep within his chest; so dark did it sound that it made we want to cry, for it made me believe that this is where I was going to perish.

You have made a fatal mistake, child. For as you can see, you did nothing stop me. The strength of the Red Moon has brought me back, and now I am stronger than ever! He paused, cocking his head slightly in an almost innocent gesture as he stared at me. **Ah, what a beautiful young girl. So full of** *potential!* He spat the last word as if it were poisonous. **Yet, you chose to throw your life away here, trying to do something that cannot be done.**

"Don't tell me what I can and can't do," I said defiantly, stepping closer. Somehow, bravery found me and dared me to do it. "They said I wouldn't survive on my own. They said I couldn't live with people. They said I would never make friends. And they all said that I couldn't make it here. But look at me now. I *did* survive all on my own. I *did* live with people," I gestured behind me, still glaring at the Kena, "I *do* have friends and I will *not let you stop me*."

Again, he laughed deeply. **Do not you know who I am? I am Tatsuo! I rule the creatures of the underworld, I lived when the Shadowland had a rightful place on the surface, I created the Dragons; I am the strongest of them all! I now walk amongst you and will take back what was rightfully mine, and I know that a determined little girl and her vagabond friends can't stop me!**

I glared up at him angrily, no longer afraid to look him in the eyes.

Goldensun's voice broke through. *Careful, Kohana. He is messing with your mind. He is playing with you like a predator plays with their prey once they know it's good and cornered.*

Tatsuo switched his white-hot gaze to Niyol for a fraction of a second, before returning to me. **Oh, and who is this?** He growled, crouching down on and snaking his neck around to look at him. **Is this one of your so-called friends?**

Niyol's crossed his arms to keep them from shaking, but his voice was steady as he said, "Kohana has been my friend from the first day I met her, and never once have I regretted that decision." I sent a grateful smile towards him, but he didn't see me.

Is that so? What about when you found out she was the Outcast? You regretted leaving High Point from the very beginning, did you not?

Niyol's eyes narrowed and he shook his head, but the sweat on his brow showed his concern. "No. I had nothing to go back to."

But an overwhelming surge of anger washed over me, and before I could help myself, I shouted, "So I'm just second choice? Would you have gone with me if your 'grandmother' wasn't a demon? Would you have even cared if I left without saying goodbye?" The venom in my voice made him flinch.

"Kohana, I never said you were second best! If I didn't want to go, *I wouldn't have*. But with that aside, did you ever think that I came for more than just the fun of it? Excuse me for being so bold, but I had just lost the only family I had, and I didn't exactly want to stick around to be reminded of it." He paused, looked away, and looked back to me. "I was worried about you, Kohana. I didn't even know you, but I cared. A lot. And we hadn't ever made up for that fight. Just try to imagine that. Someone you love being killed without ever getting the chance to make up for a stupid mistake, to say you're sorry and to tell them how you really feel."

Love. The word echoed in my head. He loved me even before he got to know me. I didn't mean to, but I growled, "I can't imagine how horrible that is."

Kohana... Goldensun growled. *You're not angry at Niyol, stop this! It's all in your head! Tatsuo is doing this to you!*

I hardly heard her words, but I angrily turned back to the Kena as he said, **I hate to interrupt this little drama, but I do have a time frame to keep.** The Dragon laid a firm hand on my shoulder. It was cold as ice. I squirmed out from under it, but the only place I could go was in Niyol's direction. My face burned as my pride melted inside me.

Kohana, he said with a toothy, sadistic grin, **You know just as well as I do that you cannot succeed. And if you try to fight me, and my army, for that matter...I do believe all of your little 'friends' will die alongside you. But it doesn't have to be that way.**

I glare openly at him. "Oh, it doesn't?" I ask sarcastically. Tatsuo shook his head.

Oh, why of course not! You can come with me, and leave them here. I promise not to lay a claw on them.

I rolled my eyes, scoffing. I don't know why I was suddenly brave enough to laugh in the face of a Dragon standing well over eighty feet tall, but somehow, I was. "No thanks," I said in mock politeness. "I think I'd sooner get torched by Dragon fire then come with you, if it's all the same."

Tatsuo shook his head. **What a shame. I'm afraid that's not in the books for you today. You're going to have to live and fight. And I have quite a feeling that you will die trying.** He laughed again, a rumble that I could feel deep in my ribcage. **Oh, and how is that wound?**

A blaze of pain shot up my arm and I looked down. The bleeding, by then, had slowed to a small trickle, but was now gushing out of my arm at an alarming rate. The pain was incredible, and I clutched the unscathed parts of my arm until the nails broke the surface.

I let go of my knife, and it clattered to the ground. Tatsuo picked it up and held it between two ridiculously long talons. **My, what a beautiful knife. I must keep it; it will go great with the rest of my collection.**

"No," I gasped, "It's mine."

The Kena Dragon bared his long, white fangs. **Is that so, girl? Then come fight me for it!**

Niyol took an angry step forward, but I held him back with my bleeding arm. "This is my fight," I said. The venom from earlier had left my voice, and I now spoke with only a clear determination. I thought about what he had said minutes ago. *Just try to imagine that. Someone you love being killed without ever getting the chance to make up for a stupid mistake, to say you're sorry and to tell them how you really feel.*

As I stepped up to meet my enemy, I thought about everything that had happened. About all our battles and our laughter and stories, of my friends and family, of Goldensun and her sister, and of Niyol and how I never got to tell him how I really felt.

"Give me my knife," I hissed. The Dragon tossed it across the ground, sending it skidding to a halt at my feet. With my good hand, I picked it up, ignoring the pain in my left arm. "Don't forget, Kena, that you need a weapon too. Don't think I'd face an unfairly armed opponent?"

Tatsuo smiled. **Don't worry, girl. I didn't forget.**

A long, copper sword materialized in his clawed hands. **You might want this,** he said, giving me a golden shield as well. I shook my head, my eyes never once leaving his face. "I work best with the lightest of weapons and the lightest of protection."

Tatsuo smiled wickedly. He then began to circle around me, teasing me with insults. I stayed firm, determined to make him make the first move. But he was persistent. Until finally, he hit the wrong nerve, but not with me.

You were never loved, never have been or will be. Who can love an Outcast?

Niyol exploded. He took his sword and, in blind rage, thrust it towards Tatsuo, who whipped around and parried. Silver, Falcon, Goldensun, the Phoenixes, Doli and Fallenoak all cried out in an attempt to stop him, but it was a trivial effort.

Niyol and Tatsuo stared each other in the face for mere moments, and then fought.

Silver quickly drew her bow and shot a stream of useless arrows at the Dragon. They bounced off his scales, doing nothing. She shot more at his wings, which procured the same effect. Mortal weapons had no use on him.

The clash of Tatsuo and Niyol's swords stunned me. I could only stand and watch as man and Dragon attacked one another. Clink after clash of metal-on-metal filled the air, and although the light was now blue from the moon, I knew the night was barely beginning.

Then, in the blink of an eye, Tatsuo had his sword at Niyol's throat. **You thought,** he hissed, with even more venom than I had previously used, **that you could defeat me? That you could beat me with a *mortal weapon*, none the less? What do you take me for, a fool?**

Something clicked in Niyol's mind; it was visible in his eyes. He knew this was the end. I wanted to run to him and save him, but I was impossibly far away. "Yes, I do take you for a fool. And I know that you'll kill me without hesitation, but that my friends will defeat you, because I know that they can." Niyol looked past Tatsuo, straight at me. "I know that they can do it."

Cute, hissed the Dragon. Then, he raised the sword to deliver the final blow. Niyol spared me one last glance, filled with so many emotions that it broke my heart, before he closed his eyes in acceptance.

Time slowed. I moved my legs, which felt heavier than lead, and ran to get Niyol out of the way.

My intent was not to get us both out of the way. I wanted solely to move him, so the Dragon could not take his life. I didn't even consider what would happen to me; I needed to save Niyol. I pushed him out of the way. For a moment, I was victorious; Niyol was safe and sound. But as I flew through the air, I saw a copper blade thrust through my midsection.

An excruciating pain filled me for a split second, but then the whole world disappeared, and I was left in darkness.

Chapter 16
Dawn

At first, there were only sounds. Dark, deep, mumbling sounds that made no sense to me at all. They jumbled together and sounded like liquid, as if I had been hearing things underwater.

I tried to open my eyes. Everything I could possibly see was blurred as well. I could make out dark shapes and a pinkish glow behind them, but that was all.

I felt a sharp pain in my arm, which brought some clarity. It jolted me awake, and I could now hear clearly, even if my vision still swam.

"I used the magic, but I don't know if it works! Niyol, I'm not a mage. I can't do anything more!"

"So why can't we take her to Fae? She should be able to do something about her! We can't just let her die; she gave up everything for us! The least we can do is try something else!"

"You don't understand, Niyol. It's a magic potion, yes. But I don't know if it works on the dead! Fae never told me the extent of what it can do, so I don't know!"

"Don't you want her alive?"

"Of course I do! But all I'm saying is-"

A new voice interrupted the first. "Guys, come here. She's moving."

Crunching footsteps came closer and the shapes bent over me. I could distinguish some more colors now; dark browns and sea green.

"Oh, Falcon she's alive!" The two voices from earlier cried out in joy. My mind felt like churned up mud, and I couldn't put any thoughts together.

As my vision cleared, so did my mind. I realized the creamy pinks and oranges were the dawn. All my friends were clustered around me. Falcon, Silver and Niyol. They were all alive.

I blinked several times. *Stand up*, I growled to myself.

A flood of memories hit me. *He'll kill you, you have to get up. Tatsuo is still here; you must get to him before he can get to you,* I thought, urging myself onward.

I struggled to sit up. With that came a rush of further clarity in vision, thoughts and sound. But no sooner had I sat up than I was nearly tackled by three different weights.

"Kohana, you're alive! I can't believe you're alive!" Niyol exclaimed. Still somewhat drowsy, I tried to stand up. His face rapidly turned from excitement to concern. "Kohana! Don't try to stand up yet...you got really hurt." Something flashed in his eyes that I couldn't place.

"What do you mean?" I mumbled. Tears were streaming down all of their faces. *I just got hit,* I wanted to say, *I've gotten hurt before. What's the big deal?*

But then everything else came rushing back in a tidal wave of emotions and thoughts and sensations. "Oh...I didn't just get hurt, did I?" I asked.

Silver shook her head first. Her cheeks were moist with tears. "Kohana, you sacrificed yourself for Niyol. Tatsuo thrust his sword right through you, but it never even touched Niyol. You saved him."

"But...but how...how did I survive?"

Everyone's face was grim. Again, Silver spoke first. "You didn't."

My head spun. *Dead. I was dead. I'm alive now...but I was dead. Just like in my vision.*

"How am I alive then?" The words spilled from my mouth; I didn't remember saying them of my own accord.

Falcon answered. "After the battle, Silver pulled out a potion. A tiny, little flask filled with this weird, blue, glowing stuff. And she poured some down your throat and some on your chest wound. And it healed, like, right away. We didn't know if it would heal your wounds or actually bring you back...but we had to try."

I was going to ask about the battle. But then, I realized something, or some*one*, was missing. If I was dead...a thought crossed into my mind, but I refused to let it stay.

"Where's Goldensun?"

Everyone became quiet. Niyol unwillingly glanced over to the edge of the mountaintop, where a golden mass was laying.

I scrambled to my feet and stumbled over to her. "No, no, no. Goldensun, please no…" I remembered our bond. If she died, I could live, but if I died, she would too. But if I got brought back…what about the other half of my soul? My pack-sister? The one being with whom I shared a closer bond too than anything else?

I looked up to my friends, my vision blurry with tears again. I saw Niyol shake his head sorrowfully, and I lifted my companion's body. Tears streamed openly down my face now; my best friend, my hunting partner, my pack-sister. The wolf who sacrificed herself countless times for me, the one who I would have done the same for. Her tail limply hung over my arm, her ears pulled back against her skull. Her teeth were still bared in the faintest of snarls. My friends came and stood at my back.

I looked half-heartedly at Silver. "Do you…?" The end of the question was evident. But she shook her head.

"Kohana, none of us realized that this would happen. We all attacked Tatsuo…and it was chaos. Nobody noticed until after…we were too late. She's gone."

"What…would Phoenix tears…?" Again, I couldn't finish my question.

Falcon mournfully shook his head 'no'. "They only work on flesh wounds, Kohana. They'll clean and heal and do anything you want them to on one of those…but that's it."

I refused to believe it. "Where's Fallenoak?"

Silver gestured to where we came from. "He left not long ago. Doli said he'd wait for us at the base of the mountain, but he wanted to get off this peak.

I pulled Goldensun up to me, burrowing my face in her scruff. I cried, soaking her golden fur. The fur I once thought held stars in it. I recalled how she once ran as fast as the wind, and when she did, she was a comet blazing across the forest floor.

I didn't say anything for the rest of the day. I sat there with Goldensun in my lap, stroking her pelt and relishing in three years worth of memories. From the beginning to the bitter end, and I cursed myself. Niyol's words rang true again; I never got to say goodbye. I never got to tell Goldensun just how I felt…or how sorry I was for all my stupid mistakes I made.

I didn't sleep, despite how much I knew I needed it. I stayed with Goldensun all night and into the next morning. A hand on my shoulder woke me from the memories.

"Kohana, it's time," Niyol said. A fresh wave of tears spilled down my face as I gently laid her down and stood up.

I pushed away from Niyol's open arms, so I was standing at Goldensun's feet. Then, I let loose a howl that only a pack-sister can have for the other. One that I filled with all my grief and anger at the world for taking her from me, and one I filled with the curse being laid upon me for letting me live while my sister died. I soon couldn't breathe, and I collapsed into a sobbing heap as reality hit.

She really was gone. There was no loophole, no twist, no surprise ending that would bring her back. She was gone for good. All my days with Goldensun, the wolf that had shown me who I was inside…they were over. Now and forever.

Niyol came over and wrapped me up in his arms. I knew how much this had to hurt him, too. How I said such terrible things, and then got myself killed, and now when I am back…I don't even pay him any attention. But the overwhelming sorrow I felt quickly overtook the guilt.

"Niyol," I whispered in between sobs.

He stopped stroking my hair. "Yes?"

"I'm sorry. I'm so sorry for the way I acted with Tatsuo, and I didn't mean any of that. I…I just got really mad at nothing, and I blew up."

He tilted my chin up so I would look at him.

"I know. And I'm not mad. I'm just so glad I have you back again that I don't think I can ever be mad at you."

I almost smiled. But the gut-wrenching loss was overwhelming, and I couldn't do anything but stare into his eyes and fall back into his embrace.

He sat with me, and I didn't realize it at the time but we were alone. Silver and Falcon were gone, and so were their companions. Then, Niyol filled the air with a song I hadn't had sung to me since I was little;

When the wind whispers
And the shadows fall
When the sun rises
And the robins call

I will be there
To hold your hand
I will be there
To help you stand.

When the wind dies
And the night returns
When the sun sets
And for songs we yearn

I will be there
To hold your hand
I will be there
To help you stand

No matter what
And through it all
I will catch you
If you fall"

I stared at Goldensun, lying on the rocky terrain. I was overcome with the idea to just leave her. "I don't want to bury her," I whispered. Niyol kept humming and just nodded.

"Look," he said, as he directed his gaze towards the east. "The sun's coming up."

I looked. He was right; the sky was pink and the gray above was fading.

"The night is always darkest just before the dawn..." I whispered.

A cool breeze wafted from somewhere. It almost sounded like a familiar wolf's howl. It beckoned my gaze away from the sunrise, so I turned west and saw something I'll never forget.

The sun coming up over the horizon, now behind me, lit up the world before me. I could see the mountains we had traversed in only a few days and far beyond that. I couldn't see anything from Desaria and barely a landmark in Aliyr. But as I gazed at the world turned the color of the sun, I realized that Goldensun was still with me.

She was still watching, and I knew she always would be.

Epilogue

All throughout our journey back home, I spoke very little. The first night I said anything was when we were clear out of the Outlands, on the plains, sitting around a campfire.

"Tell me how you guys did it," I said. My voice was hoarse from disuse.

Silver looked anxiously between the two of them, and she told me.

"Well, all demons are fallen angels. They are the very embodiment of hate and anger. So naturally, they are…weakened, so to speak, by love and compassion. You sacrificed yourself for Niyol, and you had no idea that you would come back. It was an act of compassion, an act of love for a friend. The very sight of anything so selfless caused Tatsuo to become visibly weaker. And I shot an arrow at him in the heat of the moment, and he cried out when it pierced his skin," she said. Falcon picked up after her.

"We all then realized that he could be injured with mortal weapons now. So we fought him. It was really an easy victory; none of us got hurt, but the birds did most of the work. They essentially just distracted him while we delivered the crucial blows."

I looked over at Niyol. He was strangely quiet, drawing in the dirt with a stick. Silver caught me looking at him and pulled Falcon aside, saying she needed to talk to him.

I scooted closer to Niyol, staring at the fire. "Why are you so quiet?" I asked.

For a little while, he said nothing. Then, "I can't get over it. I…I can't believe what you did. You sacrificed yourself without a second thought." He looked up at me, and for a moment I was paralyzed by his sea-green eyes. "You knew that you were going to die, and you did it anyways."

I felt myself blushing and tore my gaze away. He made me sound like a hero, when I knew I was anything but.

"I honestly didn't think I was going to die. I didn't think anything at all, other than I wasn't going to let you go. Plus, I got myself *and* Goldensun killed. And she can't come back." Her name sounded foreign on my tongue. I had tried to not even think about her, but it was impossible. Tears burned at the back of my eyelids. I forced them back.

I longed for a dream. I wanted her to come to me and assure me that she was okay, that she was happy, that she was with her true sister now and they were running through the skies.

I could feel Niyol staring at me, but I avoided his gaze. "But you saved me nonetheless. And you made it possible to fight Tatsuo. You saved the world, Kohana. Don't beat yourself up. I don't think I would have had the courage to do that."

I shook my head. "I wish I...I wish Goldensun were still here." I then began to cry, a wall of tears long held back pouring over my eyes and spilling on my cheeks. Niyol gave me a warm, reassuring hug.

"I do too."

From the east, from where we had come, I heard a howl. A lone wolf, calling for someone. It wasn't Goldensun, but as wolf songs always did, it made me smile.

The last day we were all together as a group, we stood on top of a hill to watch the sunrise. The sky was gray, but the streaks of gold and pink and red made it look like a fiery explosion. Like a Phoenix, the sky was reborn from the ashes of the night.

And I realized it on that morning. The message that had haunted me throughout the journey now rang clear.

The night is always darkest just before the dawn.

Glossary

Here, you will find pronunciations for names of places and people. Some characters' names have their meaning with them, and main characters' names include why they were named that way.

Names

- Achak – (uh-CHAAK) – Native American Algonquin name meaning "spirit"
- Ahote (uh-HOE-tay) – Native American Hopi name meaning "restless one".
- Aylen (ay-LIN) – Native American Mapuche name meaning "clear" or "happiness".
- Chayton (CHAY-tawn) – Native American Sioux name meaning "falcon". Named when a wild falcon landed in a tree just outside the castle wall, in front of the King just after he was born
- Chu`si (choo-SEE) – Native American Hopi name meaning "snake-flower".
- Darkshadow (DARK-shaad-oh)
- Doli (doh-LEE) – Native American Navajo name meaning "bluebird"
- Echosong (eh-COH-song)
- Fae – (FAY)
- Falcon (faal-CUN) – named for the bird of prey
- Fallenoak (FALL-en-ohck)
- Goldensun (goal-den-SON)
- Hinto (hin-TOE) – Native American Dakota name meaning "blue". Named for the color of his scales.
- Jaci (jay-SEE) – Native American Tupi name meaning "moon".
- Kitchi (keet-CHEE) – Native American Algonquin name meaning "brave".

- Kohana (koh-HAUN-uh) – Native American Sioux name meaning "swift." Named for the Swift River wolf pack, who ran by the King just after she was born
- Niyol (nye-ALL) – Native American Navajo name meaning "wind". Named for his eyes, the speculated color of wind
- Pheo – (fey-OH)
- Saph – (SAAF)
- Silver (SILL-vur) – named for the precious metal
- Stormchaser (STOARM-chaas-ur)
- Tobie (TOE-bee)
- Tokala (toe-KUH-luh) – Native American Dakota name meaning "fox".
- Tse (SAY) – Native American Navajo name meaning "rock".

Places

- Aliyr (aal-EER) – Kingdom in Calleo
- Calleo (caal-AY-oh) – landmass where Swift takes place
- Enin (EE-nin) – capital of Desaria
- Enyd Cliffs (END KLIFS)
- Desaria (des-AAR-ee-uh) – Kingdom in Calleo
- Galdur Fjall (GAL-dur fee-ALL) – Icelandic, meaning "magic mountain"
- Idess (eye-DESS) – Kingdom in Calleo
- Kryt (kurr-ITE) – city in Desaria
- Orazin (oar-AAH-zin) – capital of Aliyr
- Roali (roe-AAL-ee) – city in Desaria
- Tyrus (tye-RUSS) – city in Idess
- Voyr (voy-UR) – capital of Idess
- Zomer River (ZOH-mehr rih-VUR)

Acknowledgements

A big thank you and lots of hugs to everyone who helped me get this idea off the ground. It started as a fantasy, as a list of characters, as a few words on paper, and then somehow became a chapter, then two, and suddenly, seemingly out of nowhere, it was finished. I had written my first book, something I'd been trying to do for nearly 4 years.

And although I dedicated this book to my dad, there are several other wonderful people and groups that deserve to be mentioned and have my thanks.

To Hannah, my best friend, the one who has the strongest shoulders to cry on, and supported me even in spite of everything we've been through. You are beautiful.

To Lisa, the girl with the magic touch, the biggest, happiest heart, and who always knows exactly what to say. I owe you so much.

To Charis, the one who can go her own way without anyone's approval, who has the greatest laugh, and is crazy enough for all of our antics. You are my idol.

To Morgan, the one who helped me through all of my toughest writer's blocks and who proved to hold the most electric brainstorms. Your words deserve to be, and will be, heard.

To Nathan, the one who proved himself a fearless blue Dragon, an incredible friend, and probably one of the best listeners on the planet. You have made me a stronger person.

To Jacob, the one who is my endless source of comic relief, one of my first writing friends, and the proud owner of that fiery personality. You helped me become fearless.

To my family, the one who stood by me regardless of what I wanted, and who held endless surprises as I reached for my dreams. I would never be here without you.

To Mr. Loucks, Mr. Weldon, Ms. Porterfield, Ms. Clifton, and Ms. Forbes, for encouraging a love of reading, for supporting me on my writing journey, and giving me pointers to become a better writer. You all helped spark the passion that has gotten me so far.

To all of my friends – past and present – for putting up with my constant ramblings about my characters, my book, this scene and that scene, to a point where I'm sure the lot of you are sick of it by now. Your feedback encouraged me to keep writing.

To the people who came up to me, out of the blue, and asked me when they can read my novel, where they can buy one, when it will be out. You all reminded me that this wasn't just a small project, that this was something that you were waiting for.

To J.K. Rowling, Suzanne Collins, and Veronica Roth, for being excellent authors and creating beautiful stories and characters that were easy to fall in love with. You helped me strive to be great, like you.

To David Clement-Davies, for being the man whose stories inspired me to follow in his footsteps, and to become an author in the first place. You've given me the greatest gift of all.

Finally, to Kohana, the one and only, who showed me a braver side of myself, who courageously does everything I tell her to, and shows me the path when others cannot. With you, I will never be alone.

And of course, to you, for following my characters, for reading my words, and for all the support you give. I'm sure you've heard it from every musician, writer, artist, athlete, and idol that you have, but I will say it too. Because I mean it when I tell you that you are the best fans a girl could ask for, no matter how many there are. From the first to the last, my oldest to my youngest dedicated fans, I thank you from the bottom of my heart for picking up my book and reading it.

~Delaney

About the Author

Delaney Traynor wrote <u>Swift</u> at the age of 13, finishing and publishing it at the age of 15. She has been writing and drawing her entire life. Delaney lives in Colorado with her parents, younger brother, and two dogs. She is currently a sophomore in high school.

VALOR CHRISTIAN HIGH SCHOOL
3775 GRACE BLVD.
HIGHLANDS RANCH, CO
80126

DATE DUE

BRODART, CO.   Cat. No. 23-221

15236613R00133

Made in the USA
Charleston, SC
24 October 2012